A Casterglass Garden

A Casterglass Garden

A Keeping Up with the Penryns Romance

KATE HEWITT

TULE
PUBLISHING

Dedication

To Rachel and Sophie, for keeping me tethered to the Lake District. Thank you for your friendship!

Acknowledgements

Many thanks must go to the incredible team at Tule who help bring my books into being: Meghan, Cyndi, Nikki, and of course Jane, as well as Sinclair, Helena, and Beth, who have all worked on this series. Thank you also to the readers who have stuck with all my series set in Cumbria and are ready to read another. The Lake District really is a wonderful place to live, even with the rain!

Chapter One

THE CROCUSES WERE pushing their small, bright heads up through the earth in cheerful clusters that reminded Olivia Penryn of little bells as she walked through the walled garden of Casterglass Castle, the remnants of its beauty now hidden beneath a dense thicket of frost-tipped nettles and tangles of bindweed. She'd arrived back at her ancestral home a week ago, and she needed to get to work. The trouble, she thought ruefully, was knowing where—or how—to start.

Olivia crouched down to caress the silken head of a determined crocus, stubbornly insisting on flowering even amidst the choking weeds, the frozen ground. There had to be a metaphor in there somewhere, Olivia thought wryly, if she could summon the energy to find it. Something about rebirth, blossoming amidst the trials, strength through the suffering. *What doesn't kill you…*

Of course she didn't really have the right to think that way. If anything, she was the thing that almost killed you. Or at least one person in particular.

With a creak of her knees she stood up, brushing her hands along the sides of her jeans as her dispirited gaze roved over the acre of brambles and weeds that had once been a neatly tended kitchen garden, with beds of vegetables and herbs, trellises climbing with roses and grapes, thickets of raspberries and borders of lavender. She was meant to transform this into something people would pay a tenner to see how…?

Just over two months ago her older sister, Althea, had suggested that instead of selling Casterglass as their father had sadly deemed necessary, they transform it. Turn it from a dilapidated ancestral castle into a vibrant going concern, complete with glamping pods, an assault ropes course, a tea room, artisan shops, and a beautiful garden. Olivia, as the Penryn with the greenest thumb, had been put in charge of the garden. Althea was the overseer; Sam, when he returned from his latest charitable adventure, was going to do the glamping and assault course, and their sister, Persephone, who had been a happy surprise to their parents and was only twenty-two, was planning to run the artisanal workshops.

It all sounded amazing, Olivia thought, and she'd been quite excited to get stuck in—as well as escape the life she could no longer bear in York. The trouble was, all that fizzy, empty-headed optimism had started to go flat when she'd returned to the castle and realised what a, well, *wreck* it really was. A lovable wreck, but there could be no denying it, not when they'd had water pouring down the stairs on Christmas

Eve, and with the garden looking like something out of *Sleeping Beauty*, a hundred years on. She wanted it all to both challenge and inspire her, but instead, under a dreary, heavy-laden February sky, she just felt tired.

So very tired…of everything.

Heaving a sigh, Olivia started walking back towards the castle. It was a hive of industry these days, thanks to Althea. She'd turned a room off the kitchen that had been a housekeeper's parlour back in the Edwardian age into her own office, papered with surveyance maps of the property, estimates from a dozen different professionals, and metre-long to-do lists that were constantly being ticked off. Just going into that room made Olivia feel overwhelmed, and also like a schoolgirl being summoned—and scolded—by the headmistress.

She loved her older sister madly, but the renovation of Casterglass had turned Althea into something of a whirling dervish, and a bossy and demanding one at that. It reminded Olivia of when they'd been small and Althea had always organised them relentlessly, whether it was into armies for a game of soldiers, or the cast for one of their classics-mad mother's Greek tragedies, enacted in the ballroom with a bedsheet for a curtain.

Olivia had always gone along with it, because she'd more or less gone along with everything, although usually she would have been happier to find a secluded nook to curl up in with a book, a pad of paper, and a couple of coloured pencils, or even just a daydream. Too bad that wasn't possible now. She wanted to be distracted from her ever-circling thoughts, not search out the space to give them free rein.

"Olivia?" Her mother's voice wafted through the garden, a distracted, musical trill. "I think Althea said something about lunch…"

One of her sister's new initiatives was a weekly lunch around the big kitchen table, where they all shared their progress in their various departments and Althea sat at the head of the table like the unofficial CEO of Casterglass. This would be only Olivia's second such lunch, yet she already found herself half dreading it. She suspected the rest of her family felt similarly; last week her mother, sitting next to her, had murmured, "She's rather terrifying, isn't she? Where do you supposed she gets it from?"

Olivia hadn't replied, although she wondered if Althea had filled the void left by her parents' rather hands-off method of child-rearing. She had, she thought with a sigh, filled it admirably.

"Olivia," Althea called as she came into the kitchen where her parents were already waiting, looking slightly cowed, her father still smiling, her mother staring into space with a slight, puzzled frown. "You're just in time. Sam is joining us on a video call so we can have full updates from everyone."

"Fab," Olivia murmured as she washed her hands at the

deep stone sink. Her younger brother, Sam, was in New Zealand until next month, when he'd return to Casterglass and take up his part of the bargain. At least, she hoped he would. From the patchy Skypes they'd had she couldn't tell if Sam was actually enthused about this prospect or not, although perhaps Althea had enough enthusiasm for all of them.

"Right, then," her sister said as she took her place at the head of the table. Their father, smiling genially, took the other end, while Olivia and her mother sat on one side, and Persephone sloped in at the last minute to sit on the other. Olivia gave her younger sister a smile, but Seph just scowled. She knew better than to take it personally; that's just how Seph was. She'd spent most of her childhood alone, prowling through the castle and working for the neighbouring farm, run by John Braithwaite, who was now newly divorced Althea's significant other, or at least something close to it. Althea liked to say they were *good friends*, but their mother had murmured in her dreamy way, "If that isn't a euphemism, I don't know what is. As Catullus wrote, 'The sun may come up each day but when our star is out, our night, it shall last forever.'" She'd given a long, contented sigh. "*That's* being good friends."

Olivia had managed a laugh, but in truth she did not want to think about love or romance or any of it. She'd had a bellyful of it recently, and it had given her something of a stomach ache. Not heartbreak, she told herself. Never that.

Just…a deep-seated nausea and an aversion to making the same mistake twice.

"Right," Althea said in a voice like a loud clap as she began doling out the quiche and salad. "Let's have our updates. Daddy, how is the orchid room going?"

"Well…" Their father tugged at his collar as he gave an abashed smile. "I've been awfully busy…"

"*Daddy.* You love orchids." Althea gave him a not-so-mock-stern glance. "Why are you dragging your feet on this one?"

"One can hardly say I'm dragging my feet," Walter Penryn, twelfth baron of Casterglass, replied with some asperity. "I'm merely being *judicious.*"

Althea raised her eyebrows as she handed him a plate of quiche. "How judicious?"

"*Quite* judicious. It takes planning, Althea. You can't just bung a bunch of orchids in a room and call it good."

"Well, you could," Olivia interjected with a smile, "but it wouldn't be right."

Her father beamed at her. "Exactly, my dear. Exactly."

Olivia couldn't help but preen a bit under his praise; she felt so battle weary and heartsore that it was nice to have an easy compliment, a bit of camaraderie. She'd always got along with father, bonding over his collection of rare orchids when she'd been barely more than a slip of a girl. She'd watch him tend the fragile plants like a mother with her children, and she'd thought, *I want to love something that much.* Or someone.

"So what needs to be done to the orchid room to get it up and running?" Althea asked, and Olivia tuned out her father's lengthy explanation about fluorescent heat lamps and proper ventilation as she picked at her quiche. She knew Althea was likely to ask her next how the garden was going, and the truthful answer would be not at all. She'd had such big ideas, and she'd been raring to get started, or at least she thought she had, but somehow as the days had passed under a dreary February sky, she hadn't been able to summon either the enthusiasm or the vision.

"Olivia?" Althea's voice pierced her melancholy thoughts. "What about the garden?"

There was something shrewd and assessing in her sister's gaze, Olivia thought. She had to know as well as she did that she hadn't made a start on the garden, besides wandering along the old brick paths and plucking at a few weeds. She'd also made a few notes and sketches, but nothing she could talk up now, at least not much.

"Er," she said, and Althea banged her fist on the table.

"Why is no one taking this seriously? We're meant to be up and running for the May bank holiday weekend. That's less than three months away. We've *got* to have something to offer."

"But we will, darling," their mother said as she speared a lettuce leaf with her fork and waved it in the air. "We have the castle already."

"And it's falling down about our ears!" Althea exclaimed.

"I wouldn't say *falling*," their mother replied mildly. "The roof is being replaced, after all."

Althea let out a groan. "We can't charge visitors to see our new *roof*. What's the hold-up, Olivia? I thought you were buzzing with plans."

"I was," Olivia replied with the same touch of asperity her father had shown. "And I still am," she added hastily. "But I can't go digging things up just now. First of all, it's February and the ground is half-frozen. Plus I need to have a design in place, and that takes time. I'm still in the planning stages."

"All right." Althea sounded very slightly mollified. "How is the design going, then?"

"Er," Olivia said again, and Althea looked as if she wanted to explode.

"Olivia—"

"I'm working on it," Olivia said quickly. She thought of the couple of pages of chicken scratching that currently constituted her notes. "I will work on it, I promise."

Althea let out a groan. "Seriously, Olivia."

"Darling," their mother intervened, flinging out one hand. "You can't rush genius."

Olivia stifled a guffaw of slightly hysterical disbelief. Genius? She felt far from it. She always had. She was the invisible Penryn, the one who always slunk to the shadows, who was happiest when left alone. Although, actually, maybe that was Seph. She glanced at her younger sister, who was—predictably—scowling, and at nothing in particular.

"All right, can you give me a timeline, then?" Althea asked. "Of when you might have a completed design, and also when you can begin putting it into place?"

She sounded so exasperated that Olivia couldn't keep from wincing. "I won't need to start planting till mid-March at the earliest," she replied placatingly. "So that gives me several weeks to work on the design. But I'll need help with the labour—I can't do all the digging and shifting on my own."

"All right," Althea said grudgingly. "I am sure we can find someone suitable when the time comes." She looked down at her notes, riffling through the pages. "Now, Seph, what about the workshops? And then we'll try to get Sam on the laptop…"

Olivia let her mind wander again. Not that she wasn't interested in the workshops, of course, or the planned tea room and gift shop, or Sam's ropes courses and glamping yurts. It all sounded marvellous. She just couldn't quite get her head round any of it coming to pass. She felt stuck, so stuck that she couldn't imagine anyone managing to change, least of all her.

"Why the long face?" Althea asked in her blunt way once lunch was over, and they'd said goodbye to Sam on Skype. Their mother had drifted back to her study, and their father had gone to potter about his orchids. Seph had simply disappeared. Althea dumped a stack of plates into the deep stone sink with a clatter. "What's wrong?"

"Nothing's wrong," Olivia replied, just a little too quickly. Althea arched an eyebrow.

"I thought you were happy to come back to Casterglass."

"I am." But you didn't leave a life you'd built over ten years without a little sorrow and grief. Surely Althea understood that; she'd left twenty years of marriage and domesticity back in Surrey. She'd found happiness up here in the wilds of Cumbria, it was true, and she seemed better and stronger for it, but it hadn't always been that way. Two months ago she'd been a wreck, and Olivia had done her best to bolster her sister's sagging spirits and help her to get back on track.

She wished her sister could afford her the same latitude now, but Althea was always a go-getter, striding forward rather than looking back. Olivia was the plodder—quiet, dreamy, middling in everything.

How many teachers had said with a laugh, when she'd spoken or uncurled herself from the corner of classroom, "Goodness, Olivia, you gave me a fright! I hadn't realised you were there." How many girls had glanced over her, not in derision, but as if she were simply invisible? She hadn't actually minded; her school days had been a quiet utopia spent in nooks of libraries or the peaceful solitude of the school's gardens or greenhouse, busying herself with the friends who never let her down: books and plants. She hadn't wanted to be noticed. She hadn't even wanted to be *seen*.

That had changed, a little, at university; she'd found a small tribe of like-minded friends and while the rest of the world still skipped right over her, her friends saw her through and through. That had been rather wonderful, but thirteen years on they'd all drifted their own ways, married, had children…except Olivia.

Which, in a way, was what had led to the whole dispiriting destruction of her life in York.

"Well?" Althea asked as she turned on the taps and squirted nearly half a bottle of dish soap into the sink.

"Well what?"

"What's going on?" Althea asked, as if she'd asked it several times already. Perhaps she had, and Olivia simply hadn't been listening. She had a dreadful tendency to disappear into a daydream while someone was talking, and her sister's voice could be awfully easy to block out.

"Nothing's going on," Olivia said as she cleared a few glasses from the table and lined them up next to the sink. "It's just that I'm still recovering, Althea."

"Recovering?" Althea frowned. "You mean from that jerk who led you up the garden path? No pun intended of course, when it comes to gardens…"

Olivia tried to smile, but she had a feeling she'd flinched instead. Althea could afford to be a bit blasé when her own life had been so easily and neatly sorted, but Olivia felt as if she were still standing amidst the smoking wreckage of her own.

"Liv." Althea put a soapy hand on her arm, soaking her jumper. "He's not worth a second of your time. You know that, right?"

"Yes, I do, but it's not quite that simple, is it?" Olivia returned, a slightly waspish note to her voice. "You can't just press a delete button in your brain and never think about someone again." Not that she was pining over Matt—far from it. She was just constantly cringing over her part in that ill-fated non-romance.

"I know." Althea was quiet for a moment, no doubt thinking about her ex-husband, Jasper. She'd spent far more than a second thinking about him, even after it was all over. Olivia had talked her through a good deal of it, listened to her struggle and moan, and she'd been glad to, of course she had. *But no one can listen to me moan, because I don't want to admit to any of it.*

It was true she'd told Althea the basics of the sordid story…how she'd met Matt at the garden centre where she worked, how he'd chatted her up and taken her out. She'd hinted at how smitten she'd been, although she hadn't confessed to hoarding bridal magazines only a week after they'd met. There was only so much crazy you could admit, even to your sister. Despite all that, Olivia knew she hadn't told Althea all of it. And she never would.

"I'm sorry, I know I'm nagging," Althea said with a small, apologetic smile. "About a lot of things. It's just I want to see you move past this, and I think the garden—and you—have so much potential. I just want to help, Liv. Honestly."

"I know." Olivia gave her sister a quick, tight hug. "Sorry I'm being so mopey. I'll get over it soon, I promise."

"I think we need a night at the pub," Althea declared. "Drown your sorrows, maybe meet a new man."

"At the Casterglass pub?" Olivia asked, wrinkling her nose. "You snagged the last eligible bachelor in all of South Cumbria, Althea. Unless you want me falling for Edward Bransholme?" He was a local farmer, eighty years old and missing most of his teeth, but he'd always brought a huge burlap sack of vegetables to the castle every Christmas, like some sort of medieval tithe.

"Maybe he has sons…?" Althea suggested with a wicked glint in her eye.

"He's a known bachelor, and no, thank you." But Olivia was smiling, and she felt a little lighter than she had in some time—weeks, maybe even months, ever since Matt Westcott had walked through the garden centre doors and given her a boyish grin…

You couldn't help me, could you? I'm looking for a house-plant that can survive my lack of attention…

She'd been quick with the witty repartee, telling him he shouldn't buy a plant if he couldn't be bothered to water it, all the while flirting with her eyes, just as he had been, her heart racing with excitement at being noticed, chosen.

But I want some greenery in the house. Have mercy…

She'd directed him to a tray of succulents, and as he'd selected a cactus he'd asked her out. She'd been so thrilled. She'd been such a *sap*.

Olivia straightened, banishing the memory of Matt's aw-shucks attitude and her own cringingly giggly response. It was over. She would never, ever make that kind of mistake again. She'd make sure of it.

Chapter Two

THE CASTERGLASS ARMS was a half mile from the castle, in the centre of the tiny village that consisted of no more than a handful of houses, situated across from the small square of green. The pub was made of good grey Cumbrian stone and looked as if it presided over all it saw, little as it was.

Olivia had been in it plenty of times before—Althea had taken her out there for her first legal drink on her eighteenth birthday, and they'd often gone there on breaks from uni, over Christmas or Easter, or long, lazy summer nights with Pimm's in the pub garden, when the sun didn't set till after ten o'clock and the Cumbrian chill could be warded off with a thick jumper and an oft-necessary umbrella.

Still, she hadn't been inside in several years, and never with such a crowd. Althea had organised it all—her and John; Seph and her friend Doug, who had at first terrified Olivia with his dreadlocks and many piercings but was perfectly friendly and approachable; and Althea's son, Ben, home from university for his Feb break, bringing his friend

Penny, a slim, quiet brunette.

"We seem to have a great deal of *good friends*," Olivia's mother had intoned mysteriously, making her mouth twitch in a smile. Ben was being tight-lipped about Penny's status, but as far as Olivia could tell they seemed to be practically joined at the hip.

As a result, as they shouldered their way into the pub and settled onto a few battered sofas by the open fire, Olivia was feeling a bit of a third, or really a seventh, wheel, the only single among a cosy trio of couples.

"White or red?" Althea announced as she stood up to go to the bar, and John let out a disbelieving guffaw.

"Neither, woman. We'll be having lager."

"You might be, but I'm not," Althea returned. "Olivia?"

"White, please." She sank back against the worn sofa cushions as the good-natured banter flew around her. She was terrible in situations like this, utterly rubbish at making small talk and coming back with the witty replies. Her mind blanked and if asked a question directly she usually got a look on her face like Munch's *The Scream*. To Olivia there were no words more horrifying than "tell everyone that funny joke…"

Fortunately when it came to a crowd, she was used to being invisible, and no one paid her much attention at all as they joked and chatted about the castle, Althea's plans for it, the weather—fairly mild for February—as well as the local craic: Cumbrian for village gossip.

"It's a bottle between the two of us," Althea told her as she returned from the bar brandishing a bottle of white and two glasses. "Everyone else is having lager."

"More for us, I suppose," Olivia said as she held out her glass and her sister filled it up to the brim. It was easy enough to settle back in the sofa once more and sip her wine while everyone else continued to joke and chat with careless ease.

Olivia sipped her wine and remembered, reluctantly, the last time she'd been in a pub like this. The low wood beams, the glowing embers of the fire, the bottle of red they'd finished easily, and Matt had insisted they order a second…

She closed her eyes briefly, as if she could will the memory away, or maybe some contrary part of her still wanted to savour it. His fingers laced with hers, his sleepy smile of intent, the way her heart had fluttered even as a voice in her head, insistent and shrill, had told her not to do this; don't mess up your life so spectacularly…

Another glass of wine had silenced that voice, and another had made her return Matt's sleepy smile as he'd drawn her from the table…

"Olivia?" John's amused voice startled her out of her unhappy daydream. "You look like you're a million miles away."

"I am," Olivia agreed with an attempt at a laugh. "Sorry."

"How's the garden going?"

"Barely," Olivia confessed, feeling she could be honest with John in a way she was reluctant to with Althea, when she was at her most intimidating. He was affability itself, with a craggy, weathered face and a shock of brown hair going grey at the temples. "I've done a few sketches, but not much more," she told him. "I think Althea thinks a bit too highly of me. I worked at a garden centre, for heaven's sake. I'm not a landscape designer by any means." Something she hadn't dared to tell Althea when her sister was insisting she could oversee all of Casterglass's thirty acres of garden.

"You are now," John told her seriously. "Whether you like it or not. And for what it's worth, I think you'll be wonderful. Althea told me about your idea of making it like a secret garden, something half-forgotten that's been discovered. That sounds absolutely brilliant."

"Oh, well." Olivia blushed and ducked her head, flattered by his obvious sincerity. "Thank you."

"It also means less work," John continued with a grin. "A few fallen-down stones and a tangle of brambles are all part of the charm."

"Exactly," Olivia agreed, smiling back. Doug on John's left asked him something, and with a small grimace of apology he turned away. Left to her own devices once more, Olivia picked up her cocktail napkin and, after taking a stub of pencil from her pocket, she began sketching. She was barely aware of what she was doing; drawing had always been an outlet, an escape, and she hummed a little under her breath as her pencil flew across the paper napkin—tumbled rocks like John had said, artful brambles, climbing roses... She felt inspired by that little snippet of conversation, the realisation that maybe she *could* do this, simply because she had to.

She barely heard the commotion as someone else joined the table, or the scrape of a chair being drawn next to her. She was sketching a swing, the kind with thick rope handles and a flat board for a seat. There was an old oak at the bottom of the wood beyond the walled garden that had started rotting inside. They could hollow it out, make a little den, and save the tree in the process...

"Hi, I'm Will."

It took Olivia a few belated seconds to realise this greeting had been directed at her. She looked up from her napkin, blinking the world back into focus, and saw a man around her own age giving her a rueful smile as he stuck out a hand for her to shake. "Sorry, I can see you're busy, but as everyone else is engaged, I thought I should introduce myself."

Sure enough, Seph and Doug were chatting, as were Ben and Penny, and Althea and John, all cosy couples. And here she was, with...Will?

"Sorry, I'm Olivia. I didn't even realise you'd joined the table." She gave a grimace of apology that Will shrugged aside.

"You looked completely enthralled with whatever you're doing."

"Well…" She glanced down at the crumpled napkin, and what she realised were really no more than scribbles, and quickly scrunched it in her fist. "I'm easily amused, I suppose." She nodded around the busy group. "Who are you friends with here?"

"I know John from work. He invited me along." He gave a nod towards John, who had slung his arm around Althea, who was tilting her head back as she looked up at him. *Ah, young love.* Or rather, middle-aged love. It still seemed rather sweet to Olivia, and utterly beyond her right now.

"Are you a farmer, as well?" Her small talk was a bit stilted, but at least she could give it a go, thanks to the glass of wine she'd already bolted.

"No, not at all. I'm a landscaper. That's my fancy title, anyway. General gardening handyman is more appropriate."

"Really? I'm working on redesigning the gardens at Casterglass Castle." She blushed because it sounded so ridiculously arrogant, especially in light of the scribbles on a cocktail napkin that were pretty much the sum total of her redesign.

"John mentioned the castle's getting a makeover," Will returned with a smile. "The gardens, too, then?"

"Yes, although I haven't even started yet."

"Well, it is February."

"True." She smiled at him, liking the way he looked— pleasant, unthreatening, the tiniest bit homely. His hair was a nondescript sandy brown, his eyes a few shades darker, and his face was round and weather-beaten. His body, beneath a flannel shirt and faded jeans, looked fit and muscular, no doubt from all that landscaping, but not in a buff way. Olivia jerked her gaze up as she realised she had, for a few seconds, been unabashedly checking him out. Hopefully he hadn't noticed.

"Are those some of your designs?" he asked, gesturing to the crumpled napkin, and she gave an uneven laugh.

"Yes, as a matter of fact, they are. You can see I'm quite the professional."

"Hey, when inspiration strikes…" He gave a little shrug as he took a sip of his lager. "Can I have a look?"

"Oh…" Surprise and embarrassment caused her to blush. Again.

"Sorry, that's a bit presumptuous of me, isn't it? I'm just curious. I've never seen the castle gardens, but I imagine they're quite something."

"They are," Olivia agreed, "or at least they would be— *will* be," she amended. "Right now they're little more than a mass of nettles, I'm afraid." Abruptly, feeling both daring and foolish, she thrust the napkin at him. "Here. Take a look if you want."

Smiling bemusedly, he took the napkin and studied it as if it were a complicated diagram or a long list of figures rather than a few dashed lines. Olivia reached for her wine, her heart rate starting to gallop. It was ridiculous to feel nervous about a stranger's opinion of her scribbles, and yet she did.

Finally, after what seemed an age, he glanced up, his eyes crinkling at the corners as he smiled. "It's got a bit of a *Secret Garden* vibe, doesn't it?"

"Yes, something like that—"

"I like it."

"You do?" Why was she so *pleased*?

"Lots of hidey-holes and secret dens, perfect for children to muck about and discover things."

"I was thinking about making a sort of grotto—here, let me show you—" She reached for the napkin and started sketching a few lines. "There's a big rock overhanging by the river," she said as she drew. "There's a crevice in it, and you could carve it out a bit more to make a proper cave. At least I think you could. With ferns hanging down like a curtain—" She drew another line, only to have her pen rip through the napkin and the whole thing fall apart in her hands. "Oh." She let out a wobbly, embarrassed laugh. "Sorry. I'm most likely boring you to tears."

"Not at all," Will replied easily. "I'm fascinated, to tell you the truth. I'm more of a pushing wheelbarrows and shifting piles of dirt type of bloke, but the design aspect is fascinating. I wish I was able to do more of it."

Olivia tucked a few tendrils of hair behind her ear as she grimaced self-consciously. "I wish I'd done more of it, because this is the first time I've designed so much as a flower bed," she confessed in a rush. "I worked in a garden centre before. I always wanted to do this kind of thing, but I never managed to find the opportunity."

"Well," Will replied, holding her gaze, "it seems like a golden opportunity has fallen into your lap."

"Yes." For some bizarre reason Olivia found she couldn't quite look away from his warm brown eyes. They reminded her of the chocolate buttons she'd loved as a child. Finally, with far too much effort, she pulled her gaze from his and picked up her wine glass the way you might heft a shield. "I just hope I don't scupper it completely."

"I don't think you will." He nodded towards her glass, which was now empty. "Can I get you another one?"

"Oh…" Olivia glanced at the bottle of white Althea had bought, and saw to her surprise it was empty, as well. "All right," she said shyly, handing him her glass. "Thank you." Not that she needed another drink, she acknowledged as Will made his way to the bar. Her head was spinning already.

She glanced down at the crumpled, ruined napkin with a small smile. Having John and then Will both approve of her ideas had given her a much-needed confidence boost. Her fingers were practically itching to curl around a pencil, to start sketching properly—plans for the walled kitchen garden, a labyrinth made of different herbs, a hidden wood, a secret grotto, a wild flower meadow…

"Here you are." Ducking in his head almost bashfully, Will handed her a glass of white.

Olivia took it with murmured thanks, and when he sat down with his own pint of lager she realised she was completely tongue-tied. When she wasn't talking about garden plans, she had no idea what to say.

"Do you come here often?" she asked, and then cringed visibly. What a cheesy line.

"No, not too often. I live over near Eskdale, so it's a bit of a drive."

"You grew up here?" Olivia guessed, because most people in this forgotten corner of Cumbria had been born and bred there.

"Nope." Will shook his head with a grin. "I'm from Norfolk originally. Didn't even know where Cumbria was until I looked it up on a map."

"So what made you move all the way up north?"

A slight hesitation, and then he shrugged. "Property, mainly. Wanted to buy a decent house, and you can't do that down in Norfolk on my salary. And opportunity. I started my own business." He paused as if he were going to say something else, and then he just smiled and shrugged again. "What about you? A Casterglass lass through and through?"

"Not precisely. I left for boarding school when I was eleven, over in North Yorkshire. And then uni in York, and I stayed there afterwards, for work. So I suppose I've lived more of my life on that side of the country than this, but…" Now she was the one shrugging, unable, or perhaps just unwilling, to explain how she'd come back to Casterglass.

Will, understandably, asked. "So what brought you back to the family pile?"

"Opportunity, same as you." She spoke a bit quickly, as if she could convince herself as well as Will that her sudden move back home had nothing to do with her life in York becoming unbearable. She would not think of Matt. She *wouldn't.* "My sister Althea suggested I redesign the gardens, and I couldn't resist the challenge." Even if the prospect still terrified her.

"I don't think I'd be able to resist it, either."

The smile he gave her was warm, approving. It made her tingle—or perhaps it was just the wine—but suddenly Olivia found herself blurting, "You could come and see them, if you like? The gardens? I haven't done anything yet—it's all in my head. But if you were interested…and I'd love to hear someone else's ideas…" She trailed off, blushing, flailing. She barely knew this guy. What on earth was he going to think? As she reached for her wine she couldn't keep from glancing at him and seeing how startled he looked. Great.

"I'd love to," Will said, after what felt like an endless, excruciating pause. "Thanks."

"You don't…" Olivia mumbled, trailing off yet again, her nose buried in her glass.

"No, I would." He sounded more certain now, more enthused. "I really would. I don't have too many jobs on Monday. Would around one suit?"

"One o'clock on Monday?" As if she had to check, as if

she actually had any pencilled-in plans. "Yes, I think that would work."

"Great." His smile widened as his gaze lingered on hers, and Olivia found she couldn't look away. What on earth was happening here? Why did she feel so…fizzy? Will was just a stranger, a man she barely knew, a very ordinary-looking man with a round face and friendly eyes and slightly crooked teeth. Why did she have to keep herself from grinning like a loon?

"Oy," Seph called over, jerking Olivia out of her ridiculous, moony stare. "It's your round, Olivia."

"Is it?" Olivia lurched up from the table. Her head was spinning more than ever and she certainly didn't need anything more to drink, but she'd buy everyone else a round if they wanted. "What are the orders?" she asked, fumbling for her purse.

Everyone spoke at once, and Olivia didn't take in any of it, until Althea cut across the din, stating firmly. "A bottle of red and five lagers." She glanced at Will, her eyebrows raised, her look turning speculative in a way that made Olivia prickle. She did not need an inquisition from her sister about a man she'd just met.

"None for me, I'm afraid," Will said. "I've got to get back."

"Get back? It's barely past nine!"

He shrugged, looking slightly uncomfortable, and thankfully Althea let it go. As Olivia made her way to the bar, Will followed her out.

"I look forward to Monday," he said, and she smiled and nodded.

"Yes, me too—" She stopped abruptly as she clocked the hand he'd held up in a wave, but Will didn't notice because he was already turning and heading out of the pub.

But Olivia had noticed. She'd very much noticed what he wore on the fourth finger of his left hand—a wedding ring.

Chapter Three

"J AKE, *NOW*."

Will tried to keep the exasperation from his voice as his eight-year-old son dragged his feet along the kitchen floor, giving him a tragic look.

"I can't find them, Dad."

"You should have looked for them last night." Today was Monday, PE day, and as usual, Jake couldn't find his trainers. Will glanced at the clock above the cantankerous Rayburn with a barely stifled groan. They had three minutes to get to school on time, and it was a four-minute drive. "They're not in the boot room?"

Jake, his fringe sliding into his eyes—he badly needed a haircut—shook his head mournfully. "No."

"Your bedroom?"

"No, I looked."

"Da-*ddy*." Lally's plaintive voice came from the bathroom off the hall. "I've got toothpaste on my cardy."

"Oh, Lall—" How had Rachel done it? Will wondered, for about the six hundredth time in the last eighteen months, as he hurried to his five-year-old and did his best to sponge the toothpaste stain off her school cardigan. How had Rachel managed their two children and a job, as well? How had she kept the house clean, the laundry done, meals on the table, and all with a smile on her face? Well, mostly.

He knew he had a tendency to idealise his wife now that she was no longer in his life, but he certainly admired the way she'd made it all seem effortless. For the last eighteen months he'd felt as if he were mountain-climbing, juggling, and tap-dancing all at the same time. While feeling as if he could barely drag himself out of bed.

"Dad, I found them!" The sound of Jake's ebullient voice had Will smiling wearily.

"That's brilliant, bud. Where were they?"

"In the bathroom."

"Excellent. Let's get going." School had started two minutes ago, but never mind. Mrs Tabbard, the head teacher, had been generous in cutting him some slack, although Will suspected the understanding bonhomie was starting to wear thin. He'd discovered that you could only play the grief card for so long before people found it boring, although they would never say so.

Whistling to Piper, the black Lab puppy they'd bought when they'd moved to Cumbria two years ago, full of optimism and plans, Will locked the house up, hunching his shoulders against a cold, needling rain. Lally and Jake had already scrambled into the back seat of the battered pickup truck he used for work, and Piper gamely leapt up into the truck's flatbed.

Will swung himself into the driver's seat and off they went, trundling and bumping down the two-mile dirt road that hadn't seemed quite so long when he and Rachel had been looking at the house with the real estate agent, thinking how lovely the views of the fells were. Now the views of Whin Rigg and Red Pike, Scafell peeking over them in the distance, were obscured by a thick, grey mist as the rain continued to drizzle down—mizzling, they called it, as if that somehow negated the wetness of it. Cumbria, Will had discovered after they'd moved there, had two hundred and twenty rainy days a year, at the least. That was, he'd soon come to realise, a *lot* of rain.

The rain, somewhat surprisingly, did not bother the children. They'd learned, quite gamely, to play outside when it was drizzling, or even in a downpour. Rachel had bought them all full sets of waterproofs—jackets, trousers, wellies, the works—so they were kitted out for walks in all weathers. Will had always thought he was a fairly hardy guy, but some part of him had resisted taking a three-mile hike in a freezing downpour.

"You can't wait for a perfectly sunny day to get out and about," Rachel had told him, wagging her finger teasingly, and he'd felt as if she were making a pronouncement about life—or at least his life. He did prefer conditions to be a *bit* more optimistic than she had before making that flying leap into the unknown.

And hadn't he been right? Look how their move to Cumbria had turned out.

"Daddy, you drove past the school." Jake's voice was sorrowfully reproachful as Will jerked himself out of the unnecessary reverie. He *had* driven past the school—a tiny primary with less than ten pupils in any year group, housed in a Victorian building of grim, grey stone and huddled against a hillside with nothing else in sight. Biting his lip to keep from muttering something he'd regret, Will yanked the wheel to turn around in a lay-by and then headed back down the single-track road to the school.

Five minutes later he'd managed to double park the truck in front of the school, and bundle Jake and Lally out of the car and towards the building's imposing black door. Mrs Tabbard opened it for them, ushering them in with a smile before she gave Will a rather stern glance.

"Drop-off is at eight fifty, Mr Turner," she said, impressively pitching her voice somewhere between scolding and sympathetic.

"Sorry, we were running late," Will said, unnecessarily. Rain dripped down his neck and he gave the woman an apologetic grimace before getting back in the car. He needed to do better. He knew that. He'd been telling himself that for the last eighteen months, since he'd held Jake and Lally by their little hands as they'd said their final goodbye to Rachel.

Bye-bye, Mummy, Lally had said in a singsong voice as Rachel's casket had been lowered into the ground. The memory still held the power to make Will's eyes sting. Lally's innocence, Jake's stoic silence at all of seven years old, his own grief and terror. He was a single dad now, he'd realised, in a place where he knew hardly anyone, struggling to set up his own business, having left almost all the housekeeping and parenting decisions to his wife. It had not been a good place to be. It still wasn't. But he hoped it was getting at least a little better.

A prospect that made him think, improbably, of Olivia Penryn. He was due at Casterglass Castle at one o'clock today, and it was a meeting he was looking forward to, perhaps more than he should. He hadn't so much as blinked at another woman since Rachel had died, not even close, and he still wasn't ready to, but when he'd chatted with Olivia he thought he *might* be, one day. Maybe.

It had been a heartening thought, even as he'd struggled not to feel guilty. How could he think of moving on, when Rachel wasn't able to? And yet he knew he had to, for his sake, for his children's sake. They were just kids, and he was only thirty-seven. They all had a lot of life still to live, even if he hadn't always wanted to live it, since Rachel had died.

The sun broke from beneath a bank of grey cloud, which suited Will's mood. He wanted to feel upbeat, if only a little. He liked having something to look forward to, for once. But first he had to reinforce a retaining wall at a Londoner's second home in Windermere. It was the type of job that had become his bread and butter since setting up his own business here—dull but decent-paying.

It wasn't quite what they'd dreamed of when they'd decided to up sticks and move to Cumbria from Norfolk—Will had imagined landscaping gardens, rewilding National Trust properties, the kind of intricate, creative work Olivia Penryn was currently involved in. Her sketches, even on the back of a cocktail napkin, had been both interesting and impressive. Will had felt admiring and envious.

As for Rachel—she'd imagined their sprawling farmhouse, a huge vegetable garden, camping on the fells, trips to market towns to poke in antiques stalls. None of it had ever really come to pass. The garden was now nothing but weeds, and the house—a seventeenth-century cottage that they'd been going to do up slowly, with a big addition to the kitchen and living area that Will would oversee himself—remained in the same state as when they'd bought it. To call it shabby chic would be far too kind. Even to call it just shabby would be generous.

But enough of that. Will spent so much time lamenting the past that he could hardly summon the energy to think of the future. But he wanted to think of the future now—this afternoon as well as the distant day when he would finally relearn how to be happy.

The job in Windermere took several hours of repointing stone while standing in a lashing rain with Piper faithfully by his side, but by the time he was driving towards Casterglass his hair had started to dry, sticking up in wild tufts, and the sun had come out for the fourth time that day. Hopefully it wouldn't retreat just as quickly.

Will was curious to see Casterglass—he'd heard about the place after doing a bit of work for John Braithwaite—and he'd been admiring if slightly sceptical about the local aristocracy's plan to renovate the largest private estate in all of South Cumbria. This forgotten corner of the world was just a little too far from the tourist hot spots of Windermere and Ambleside to make it an easy sell, but he admired the Penryn family for trying. He hoped, for their sakes, they succeeded.

He almost missed the sweeping drive to the castle because the rhododendron bushes on either side of the rusted gates were so overgrown they nearly obscured the narrow lane. They had to be forty feet tall at a minimum. Olivia had her work cut out for her when it came to pruning, Will thought, quite literally.

He turned up the lane and drove slowly past sweeping, overgrown lawns and dense wood, the muted glimmer of a pond in the distance that looked like it seriously needed dredging. The castle was in a gorgeous spot—a mile from the sea, which Will suspected he would be able to glimpse if he craned his neck, grey and white-ruffled—and rolling hills to the fells beyond. When he came round the final turn and saw the castle itself, he couldn't keep from letting out a low whistle. It was made of dark grey stone, squat and square in the style of a Norman fortress. As he pulled around to the back as Olivia had instructed, he saw a hodgepodge of additions—impressive rectangular Georgian rooms with large, sashed windows, Victorian nooks and crannies, and a turret Will suspected was an eighteenth-century folly. Looking at the castle was like seeing history played out through wood and stone. Already he was fascinated.

He'd only just opened the door of his truck when Olivia came out of the castle's kitchen door. She was wearing a woolly jumper and jeans, along with mud-splattered wellies. Her hair was plaited and tossed over one shoulder and the smile she gave him was tentative, shy. She reminded Will of a violet, or perhaps a trillium, something fragile yet beautiful, hesitant yet strong. Or was he being uncharacteristically and really rather ridiculously fanciful? Probably. It was unlike him, and he was glad no one was party to his thoughts but himself.

"You made it," she said, stopping a few feet in front of him. Despite her smile, her voice sounded a little cool. Or perhaps now he was being *really* fanciful. Either that or paranoid. He hadn't a lot of socialising in the last eighteen months, thanks to being a single dad and not knowing many people in the area. The result was he sometimes had no idea if he was behaving normally or not, which a little disconcerting.

Still, something in her tone made Will give a more reserved greeting in return than he'd anticipated. "So I did," he replied with a brisk, businesslike nod, like he was coming here for a job. "Almost missed the drive, actually, but I'm here."

They stared at each other for a few seconds before Olivia's gaze flitted away. Why did this feel awkward? It hadn't at the pub, and he didn't think that had been down simply to the social lubricant of alcohol, although on second thought, maybe it had. He cleared his throat, then wished he hadn't, because the sound was so loud it made Olivia jump a little. Unless she was just jumpy? He had no idea. "So, shall we?" he asked.

"All right." She flipped her plait over her shoulder and Will went around to the back of the truck to release Piper.

"Is it all right if I bring my dog?" he asked. Kind of a bit late to check, he realised, but Piper went with him everywhere.

"Yes, of course." As Piper came bounding down with slobbering excitement and great joy, a smile softened Olivia's face and she bent to fondle the dog's ears, which he loved, his tail beating against the ground in a heartfelt staccato. "He's lovely," she said, and the warmth in her voice made Will realise she *had* been acting cool with him. Maybe it was just nerves? Although why either of them should be nervous he didn't know—but he did know that he was. Maybe Olivia was, as well, for whatever reason.

Telling himself to relax—something that never actually

helped him relax—he followed Olivia down the drive to a wrought-iron gate set in a high stone wall. She lifted the latch, stepped through, and then held the gate open so he could follow, Piper darting in after him. As he walked past her, he breathed in the old-fashioned smell of lavender water, and somehow he thought it suited her.

Then he looked past her to the garden stretching out in front of them to the far stone wall—he could barely make out the paths and beds that would have once been neatly tended beneath the thickets of weeds and nettles. Piper was bounding about, sniffing madly, tail wagging.

"Wow," he said, and she let out an uncertain laugh.

"Yeah, it's a mess, isn't it? You must think I'm mad."

"No…" He walked slowly towards the start of a narrow path that wound through the tangles, barely visible beneath the brush, feeling as if he were on the start of the Yellow Brick Road. Rain-drenched nettles brushed his jeans with a shower of tiny droplets.

"Careful," Olivia murmured from behind him. "It's easy to get stung."

"There's a lot here," Will remarked as he started down the path. He nudged some nettles aside to see the vestiges of what he suspected was henbane beneath the weeds; it would develop yellow flowers in the next month or two. A little farther along, he thought he saw the remnants of what would have once been a patch of spiky-leafed wormwood. "Do you know the history?"

"A bit. This was the kitchen garden—the walls are from Victorian times, but my father thinks there was a garden here since the early years of the castle—1400s, maybe?"

Will nodded towards the henbane. "I was wondering. These herbs look like they might have once been part of a physic garden. You know, herbs for medicine, back in medieval times?"

"Ah, yes." Olivia nodded as she crouched down to examine the wormwood. "That makes sense. My mother used to give us the most curious remedies when we were little. All sorts of herbs and foul-smelling poultices from the garden." She glanced up at him, her navy eyes sparkling, their faces close as they were both crouched down. "We're a bit of an odd family."

"I think all families are odd, in their own way."

"Yes, that's probably true. What did Tolstoy say? 'Happy families are all alike, but unhappy families are unhappy in their own way'? Not," she continued quickly, blushing a little, "that we were or are unhappy. Just different." She straightened, moving past what would have been the physic garden to another section; Will could just about make out the symmetric lines of flower beds underneath the brambles.

"I think this was for soft fruit. I remember picking raspberries along here, when I was little." She gestured to the brambles; Will could see the stark branches of raspberry canes amidst the thorns. It wouldn't take much to coax them back to life; raspberries were hardy.

"When did the garden go to weed?" he asked, and she shrugged.

"I don't actually remember. Ten years ago, maybe? When we moved away—well, all of us but Seph—and my parents got a bit older. It doesn't take long." She let out a sigh as she surveyed the acre of walled garden, her shoulders slumping a little. "And this is just one small bit of the whole project—there's the wild flower meadow, the ha-ha, the rhododendrons that are out of control, the river…"

"You won't be able to do it all by yourself," Will pointed out in what he hoped was a reasonable tone. As they continued to stroll through the garden, he felt a quickening inside him, an excitement, a hope that he could somehow be involved in this. It would be a phenomenal project. "The digging and weeding and lifting, I mean. The design—"

"I'm not sure I can do the design all myself."

"I liked what I saw."

"On a cocktail napkin?" Her gaze met his before flitting away again, as if she didn't want to look at him. Nerves or natural reserve or something else? He still wasn't sure.

"So?" he challenged good-naturedly. "Picasso used to leave sketches on napkins to pay for his bill. Great minds, you know…"

"Right." A shaky laugh and then she moved on, quickly, as if she wanted to distance herself from him. Or was he really just being paranoid? Part of him was desperate to get involved in this project—to be the one to help her with all the stuff he'd just mentioned. He also would love to help with the design, not that he would suggest such a thing, and in any case he couldn't keep from feeling that she was being skittish for some reason. She wasn't giving off I'd-love-to-work-with-you vibes, alas.

"Let me show you beyond the garden," she said, walking quickly towards a gate in the far wall. Will followed her, whistling for Piper before he stepped through another gate of curlicued wrought iron, his gaze sweeping over the land-scape, tumbled and wild—a ribbon of river down a gorge, rushing towards the sea, huge moss-covered boulders that looked like a set of giant, lumpen marbles. Willow trees drooped their bare branches toward the ground, and he could imagine it in spring, when their fronds touched the grass, creating secret dens, perfect hideaways.

"It looks like a child's playground, before you've even started," he said, and she turned to him with a sudden rush of enthusiasm.

"Yes, that's exactly what I was thinking! You barely need to do anything, in a way, just let them have at it—" She stopped abruptly, her smile dropping as she took a few steps away from him. "Of course, it needs some landscaping," she said in a more subdued tone. She folded her arms, her shoulders hunching inside her coat. "Is there anything else you wanted to see?"

Will was startled; he'd planned to spend the whole after-noon exploring the Casterglass gardens, and she seemed ready to send him on his way after fifteen minutes.

He hesitated, and then said frankly, "I'd love to see it all. I've got till three. But if you have things to do, I'd understand."

"Oh…" She glanced at him, uncertain, a bit flummoxed, and Will decided to grasp the nettle. He'd always been too blunt for his own good. Rachel had always said so, anyway.

"Is there some reason why you don't want me to be here?" he asked baldly. "I'd understand if you feel it's your project, and you don't want someone sticking their nose in, but…I don't know." He shrugged, tried to smile, although the truth was while he didn't mind being blunt, he hated being vulnerable. "I can't tell if you're glad I accepted your invitation to visit or you wish I'd stuck with a polite refusal."

"Oh." Olivia's face was turning fiery as she flashed him a guilty look. His instinct *had* been right. Something was up.

"So," he asked, keeping his voice pleasant, "which is it? Should I stay or should I go?"

Chapter Four

OLIVIA WAS MORTIFIED. The last thing she'd expected was for Will to ask as bluntly as that. He was supposed to take the hint and see himself off, complete with polite excuses, rather than give her that direct, smiling stare that she had trouble meeting.

Yes, she might have been blowing a bit hot and cold, because she *liked* him and she valued his opinion but that wedding ring kept glinting every time he moved his hand, and she couldn't escape the horrible, terrifying feeling that she was walking right into a trap of her own making. She'd been feeling a slightly flirty vibe from him at the pub, although now she was wondering if that was just in her own head, just as the fizzy sensation she had when she looked at him was in her own body, and not his.

He was probably just being friendly. Professional. And meanwhile she was acting as if she were insane.

"Well?" he asked lightly and she had no idea what to say.

I've been acting cool because you're married and I don't want to flirt with you even though I'm tempted was not the answer that sprung to her lips, even if it was the truth. "I'm sorry," she managed haltingly. "I don't mean to come across as rude. I'm not very good with social situations, to be perfectly honest." Which was true, along with the other stuff. "First-class awkward introvert right here," she added in what she hoped passed for a wry tone.

Will frowned, his eyebrows knitting together as his speculative gaze scanned her face. "Are you sure that's all it is?"

"Yes, honestly," Olivia said as firmly as she could, because there was no question of telling him the truth.

"Okay," he said after a moment. "So I can see the rest? Would that be okay?"

Olivia hesitated, then realised there was no way she could refuse. Besides, she realised despondently, she didn't even want to. Married or not, Will was pleasant company.

"Okay," she said as Piper frisked about their heels. "But it might be a bit muddy."

"I'm well used to that." He lifted one mud-splattered work boot. "I came prepared."

"So you did." She managed a smile even though she felt a confused welter of feelings inside, predominant among them unhappiness. *He's married, he's married* kept running through her mind like a ticker tape. She knew this was a problem of her own paranoia and neurosis; a married man could walk through a garden with her discussing landscaping without it being a scandal. *Obviously.* She was the one who felt as skittish as a colt, jumping or startling practically every few minutes. She seriously needed to get a grip and behave like a normal, reasonable person.

"Right, then," she said, slapping her hands against her thighs. "We can walk along the river towards the sea, and then back through the forest and then the meadows to the front of the house."

"Sounds good."

She managed a smile, even though it felt stiff, and started towards the narrow gorge that led to the river, Piper scrambling down ahead of her. She'd walked down it hundreds of times in the course of her childhood; they'd used to swim in a pool near the mouth of the river, and she had a favourite solitary spot on a flat rock jutting over it, near the sea, but today the steep side was muddy and slick and she was already feeling jumpy and nervous, so it really was no surprise that she lost her footing and started sliding towards the bottom, windmilling her arms inelegantly, as a little yelp escaped her.

"Whoa." Will's voice was low and warm as he steadied her with his hand on her waist, anchoring her in place, his own feet planted solidly on the steep, muddy side, as if he were rooted like a tree. Olivia felt herself blush, felt the heat of his hands on her waist for an instant before he dropped them, giving her a quick, apologetic smile.

"Sorry, I didn't want you to land in the river."

"No, it's okay, it's fine, thank you—" She stopped abruptly, because she sounded as if she were babbling. She managed to edge down towards the bottom of the gorge without any more mishaps, although her face still felt fiery. "There's an overhang of rock near here," she said as they walked alongside the river, towards the sea. "I thought it could be made into a secret den, a sort of cave..." She gestured to the rock nearby, and Will nodded in agreement.

"Children would love that. Any connection to pirates or smuggling here, do you think?"

She laughed uncertainly. "Not that I know of, but I'm sure my father knows all the local legends."

"And what about the river? Any plans for it?" Piper was splashing in the shallows, sniffing out all manner of interesting things, judging by his wagging tail.

"It empties into a pool a few hundred metres from here—there's a little waterfall, but I thought something more could be done, to make it a bit more dramatic. More of a lookout point."

"There are ways to do that," Will told her easily. "You can edge the sides of the river with stones to channel the water, and build up the gradient so it's a steeper drop-off and increased flow."

"Yes, that was along the lines of what I was thinking," Olivia replied, although she wouldn't have been able to put it into such confident-sounding words. "Not that I have any real experience. I designed a water feature in the garden centre where I worked, but it was tiny compared to this."

"Still, the principles are the same, whether you're talking a tiny stream or a raging river." He smiled at her—an open, easy smile that made her heart flutter as she mentally gave herself a hard slap. *Do not engage. I repeat, do not engage.*

"True," she said, turning away to walk a bit faster. "It just feels a bit more intimidating, when I'm out in the wild."

They'd reached the waterfall, a burbling, crystalline drop of about two metres into a large, still pool that glimmered darkly under the rain-heavy sky before another, smaller waterfall cascaded into a smaller stream that emptied out into the sea.

"Wow." Will stuck his thumbs through his belt loops as he rocked back on his heels. "What a spot."

"We used to go swimming here, as children. It's quite deep. I was always a little afraid to dive down to the bottom, but my brother, Sam, did all the time. He was looking for treasure."

"Did he find any?"

"He found some old bits and bobs, junk really, but fascinating to children." She smiled faintly, recalling those halcyon days of her youth, when she, Althea, and Sam would spend hours in the woods and river, exploring, swimming, picnicking, living out *Swallows and Amazons* as best they could. It had been glorious, if, in retrospect, slightly terrifying. They'd certainly got into a few scrapes—at least Sam had. He'd been fearless, along with Althea, while Olivia had been content to splash in the shallows, stay on the sidelines.

Will crouched down by the edge of the river, examining its bed. "If we built a channel here, to narrow the stream, it would create more of a water feature," he told her. Olivia did not miss the *we* and felt a stupid little thrill. He didn't mean literally, of course. "I think this would be a brilliant place for a bridge," he added as he straightened, brushing off his muddy hands on his already mud-splattered jeans. "Something natural, made of wood, but not too twee, overlooking the waterfall? And you could create a footpath from the walled garden to the bridge—maybe even with a treasure map for kids, things to look out for?" He ducked his head as he grimaced apologetically. "Sorry, I'm letting my imagination run away with me. It's just such an amazing space."

"It is," Olivia agreed. "And your idea sounds brilliant, thank you." She wanted to say something more about how she appreciated his help, how she'd like more of it, but the words bottled in her chest. He was here just for curiosity's sake, she reminded herself.

"Shall we keep going?" Will asked, and nodding, she led him down past the waterfall and pond towards the sea.

The Irish Sea always took Olivia's breath away, stretching on in a flat, blue-grey sheet to the horizon. If she squinted, she could see the Isle of Man, no more than a violet smudge. As they came out onto the flat stretch of damp sand of the tidal beach, Piper racing towards the water, they both stopped and gazed out over the sea.

"Somehow I forget how close we are to the sea," Will remarked musingly as Piper frolicked in the shallows, barking joyfully. "When I'm among the fells. Of course, we're a bit farther over, near Boot."

Again Olivia clocked the *we*, knowing it had a different meaning this time, and she tried to find some way to broach it; she felt the need, if only in herself, to establish that he was married, that she knew it, and that was fine. "Does your wife work in landscaping, as well?" she asked in a voice that sounded far too jolly and struck a jarring note, if the sudden, stricken look on Will's face was anything to go by.

"She handled the accounts and advertising of the business," he said after a moment, and he sounded a bit guarded. "But I'm afraid she died a year and a half ago."

"Oh." The syllable escaped Olivia in something between a yelp and a gasp as she gazed at him in both horror and sympathy. Talk about putting her foot right in it. "I'm so sorry. I didn't know."

Will nodded jerkily. "Thanks."

He turned and started walking down the beach, his boots squelching in the sand. Olivia followed him, wondering if that was all they were going to say on the subject. Asking how she died or how he was coping seemed either nosy or inappropriate; what did you say to someone in this situation?

"Sorry, perhaps I should have mentioned it earlier," he said after a moment, his gaze trained on the stretch of sand in front of him. "It can feel a bit like the elephant in the room if I don't say anything, but then when I do it feels even worse, like no one knows how to talk to me or be normal." He gave himself a shake as he turned to her with a rueful, apologetic smile. "Sorry."

"You don't need to be sorry." She dug her hands into the pockets of her coat. "I'm sorry I don't know what to say."

"There isn't anything to say, really." He shrugged. "It happened, I'm dealing with it, or trying to. It's not easy." He paused. "I've got two kids—a girl and a boy. The single dad thing is really quite tough, I'm finding." He let out a slightly uneven laugh, and Olivia's heart gave a painful twist in response.

"I can imagine," she said, even while she yearned to offer more comfort, more support. *You barely know this man*, she reminded herself sternly. *Don't go thinking you could fall in love with him just because he's a widower with two children.* "How old are they?"

"Five and eight."

Oh, help. "That must be…challenging." She sounded so *lame*, like she was reading from a manual provided by the NHS. *How to support the bereaved.* Good grief. "Do you have any help?"

"Not really. My family's all in Norfolk—at least they were." He shook his head, a look of impatience flitting across his face. "Look, this is all sounding a bit too much of a sob story for me. Enough about my life. I'd love to keep learning about the estate. Does this beach belong to Casterglass?"

"About two hundred yards of it, I think, towards the head over there." She nodded towards a heather-covered promontory. "It's tidal, so there's never any dry sand, and the seabed is quite rocky—not great for swimming. Do you think we could make anything of it?" Now she was the one using *we*.

"I don't know." Will squinted as he gazed out at the sea. "It's a lovely spot, wild and lonely, and yet only about fifteen or twenty minutes from the castle itself. It would be a shame not to utilise it somehow, but I suppose you'd have to do a risk assessment."

Olivia grimaced. "I haven't even thought of risk assessments."

"A few 'visitors at their own risk' type signs should do the trick, as long as you have the paperwork completed." He nodded towards the narrow path that led up a rocky incline, towards a stand of oak trees. "Is that the way back?"

"Yes, we can go through there and then across the meadows, if you don't mind getting a bit wet."

"Not at all."

They walked in silence through the copse and then the meadows that ran between the sea and the castle, the grass knee-deep and soaking wet from the rain, Piper leaping joyfully through the golden-green waves of grass.

"Does he ever get tired?" she asked with a laugh.

"Yes, at about eleven o'clock in the evening. We got him as a puppy when we first moved here. It seemed like a good idea at the time."

What happened? Olivia wondered, but knew she wouldn't ask. Had his wife had an accident? Got sick? She kept silent.

"Truthfully, though, I'm glad I have him." Will nodded to the black Lab. "He's good company. Goes with me everywhere. Do you have a dog here at Casterglass? It seems like the kind of place that should have a brace of lurchers lounging by an enormous fireplace."

Olivia gave a laugh. "Yes, I'm sure it did at one time, but we've never had a dog during our tenure, I'm afraid. My parents were a bit too absent-minded, I think, to care for a dog along with four children."

"They sound like real characters."

"That," she told him with a smile, "is an understatement." She adored her parents, even as she recognised their foibles. Althea, she sometimes suspected, had something of an axe to grind with what she termed parental neglect, and perhaps she'd felt the weight of their insouciantly abdicated responsibility a bit more keenly, as the eldest. As someone who could be a bit absent-minded herself, Olivia hadn't really been bothered by it.

She'd relished a childhood where she could spend an entire week devouring the complete *oeuvre* of Enid Blyton without anyone caring—or really, even noticing. She'd appreciated dreamy afternoons with her father, pottering in the greenhouse with his precious orchids, lost in a world of delicate blossoms and crumbly soil. Admittedly, her education contained a few noticeable gaps—she hadn't actually learned to tell time until she went to boarding school, which had been something of an embarrassment, and even as an adult she was a bit shaky on her multiplication tables, but really, what was that compared to the experiences she'd been able to have? Even if many of their childhood adventures she'd merely observed from a safe distance.

They'd walked round to the front of the property, the castle looming greyly in the distance, under a sky that now looked swollen with rainclouds.

"I think we might get caught in a downpour," Olivia observed, and Will shrugged.

"I'm used to it after two years up here."

"Even so, it's not particularly pleasant. I can give you the generalities—the rhododendrons need cutting back, as you've already seen, and the pond needs dredging. It's currently more of a swamp. The front gardens were once terraced, but it's all slumped a bit now—I'd love to get some of that formal grandeur back, compared to the wildness of the back. Something really impressive people can look at as they come up the drive—the box hedging trimmed, the fountain working again, although I don't think it has in about two hundred years."

"I think that all sounds grand."

"Do you?" She had a sudden longing to ask him to help, to be part of this. She didn't think she could do it on her own, and more significantly, she didn't want to. But she barely knew this bloke and he really might have come here just for curiosity's sake. She could hardly ask him to commit to being part of such a huge project, especially when she didn't even know if there was a budget for it. Althea was very much in charge of the purse strings, and she held on to them tightly.

"I think it will all be amazing when it's done," Will told her, which both heartened and disappointed her. It sounded as if he had no intention of being a part of it, and why should he? Once again, she was being ridiculous, building castles in the air.

Olivia opened her mouth to make some reply, but before she could the heavens opened instead and just as she'd predicted, it began to pour, so they were soaked in a matter of seconds, the raindrops pelting down like bullets. "Oh," she said helplessly, and then, with a grin, Will grabbed her hand and started to sprint towards Casterglass.

Chapter Five

IT WAS LIKE something out of one of those soppy rom-coms Rachel used to make him watch—the pouring rain, the soaked clothing, as hand in hand they ran for shelter. Will wasn't sure what had made him grab Olivia's hand; it wasn't the sort of thing he'd normally do, not with a woman he barely knew anyway, and yet he'd done it, and he wasn't sorry. She managed to keep up with his long-legged strides, her plait flying out behind her, as they made for the castle. The rain was coming down in punishing streaks, stinging his skin and soaking him utterly.

"Around the back," Olivia panted breathlessly. "The front door doesn't open anymore, not from the outside."

"Right," Will said, and swerved, nearly tripping over Piper, who had been excitedly running alongside them, barking joyfully. They ran in tandem towards the back of the castle, matching stride for stride, practically falling through the kitchen door, both of them laughing.

"Goodness," Olivia managed as she wiped the rainwater from her face. "That was a proper soaking." She'd dropped his hand and moved away from him, and Will was disconcerted to find he missed it, the sensation of togetherness, of touching. That was new. He turned away to hide the expression on his face, which he didn't trust. He had no idea how he felt about feeling all that, after so long.

"I'm sorry you got so wet—" Olivia began, only to have Piper decide to give a good shake over the pair of them.

"I'm sorry *you* got so wet," Will returned wryly, and she laughed, the sound as clear as a bell, ringing right through him. Why was he thinking like this? Why was he noticing the raindrops that glittered on her lashes, turning them spiky, and the way her eyes had turned to the colour of violets? He hadn't thought about a woman like this in eighteen months. And he hadn't thought about a woman like this who wasn't Rachel in over twelve years. He wasn't sure he was ready to think this way now, even if this morning he had been thinking that he might be one day. Not *today*.

"Will?" Olivia's voice sounded uncertain, and he realised she must have been asking him something.

"Sorry, I was miles away there for a second."

"And I'm usually the one caught out spacing. I was asking if you'd like to warm up with a cup of tea."

Which, for one blazing second, made him think of *other* ways he could warm up. Good *grief*. He really needed to get a hold on his thoughts, as well as a few other things. "Um, yeah, sure, that would be great." He checked his watch, and saw he had an hour before he needed to pick up Lally and

Jake.

"Great," Olivia murmured, and went to the big stone sink to fill up the kettle. Will glanced around the room, which despite practically being the size of a tennis court, was surprisingly cosy. A huge table took up one end, along with several Welsh dressers crammed with china, and an Aga that was three times the size of the poky and temperamental Rayburn back at his cottage. A large, squashy sofa took up the other end of the kitchen, and was piled with both cushions and papers.

"Sorry if it looks like a bit of a mess," Olivia called over her shoulder, "but I should warn you, this is actually quite tidy."

"It's tidier than my house," Will said, which was quite true. He sat down at the table, Piper sprawled at his feet.

Olivia brought their mugs over, along with a pretty pottery jug of milk. Her hair had fallen out of its plait and a few damp tendrils curled about her face. Will tried to act as if he hadn't noticed, as if he wasn't thinking how lovely she was.

"So the garden and grounds," she said, her slender hands cradled around her mug. "You think it's doable?"

"Definitely." He hesitated. "But like I said, you'll need help. I imagine you'll have to hire a digger for some of the wilder stuff, and it will be a lot of weeding and reinforcing the raised beds in the walled garden, to start, plus the bigger jobs—dredging the pond, getting the fountain working, trimming those massive rhododendrons... Are you planning on hiring some specialists?"

"Well, I'm not thinking I can do it all on my own." She lowered her gaze as she glanced down at her tea. "I just wondered…and of course it's perfectly okay if you're not…if you don't…but I was wondering if you wanted to be involved?" She glanced up at him, biting her lip, clearly uncertain.

Will felt as if his heart were expanding in his chest. He took a sip of tea to hide what he feared would be a megawatt grin. "Involved how?" he asked as neutrally as he could, when part of him wanted to jump up and down and say *yes, please!* This was exactly the kind of project he'd dreamed of when they'd moved up to Cumbria, the kind of promise Rachel had coaxed him up here with. *It's different up north, Will. Fewer constraints. More freedom to do your own thing, get involved in a big project…*

He hadn't found much freedom in pruning people's trees or shoring up their retaining walls. But this…a castle garden…acres of grounds…some creative control…

And yet he knew he couldn't afford to heedlessly follow his emotions; he had bills to pay, little mouths to feed, and he had no idea if Olivia was asking for some free labour or a proper stake in Casterglass's renovation.

"Well, I suppose it depends how available you are. And I need to consult my sister Althea about the budget, because she controls the purse strings. I did tell her I'd need help, and she said there was money for it, but…" Olivia shrugged and looked down again. "I don't know how much. And obviously it would need to be a proper job, one that's worth your while. Are you very busy right now?"

"There's always odd jobs that can be done," Will replied cautiously. He could fill up his days with the dull and dreary jobs that kept food on the table, but he'd much rather be doing something like this. "But I'd like to be involved in a big project like this, if it's possible." It always felt grubby to talk about money, although running his own business he'd become used to asking for payment up front when it seemed necessary, and not always trusting that the cheque was in the mail. He'd also learned how to know who he could trust to pay when they said they would.

"That's great." Olivia's smile broke across her face like a ray of sunshine. "Maybe you could work up something, a proposal of sorts? Hours, costs...?" She gave a little shrug. "I don't actually know how these things work. I'm definitely someone who comes down on the creative side of things, rather than the practical. But if you are interested in helping out..."

"Sure, I'll do a proposal. That is, if you could let me know how much help you're looking for...?"

"I don't even know." She let out a little, embarrassed laugh. "I sound hopeless, don't I? I just...want a partner, really. A partner in work, I mean," she added hurriedly, flushing. "In crime, as it were. Someone to tackle it all with me, because I know I don't have the confidence to do it on my own." She blushed, as if she'd admitted too much, but Will was thrilled. It sounded as if she really wanted his involvement, both practically and creatively.

Before he could respond to any of that, however, a young woman with pink dreadlocks and a sullen expression, wearing dungarees and a tie-dyed T-shirt with unlaced work boots, slouched into the kitchen.

"Hey, Seph," Olivia said brightly. "This is Will—goodness, I don't even know your last name!"

"Turner."

"Will Turner, who is going to work on the garden with me. Will, this is my younger sister, Persephone, but we call her Seph."

Seph gave him the surly semblance of a nod before turning to the kettle.

"It's boiled," Olivia said helpfully, and Seph grunted in reply. "Sorry," she whispered when Seph had slouched out again with her mug of tea. "She's not very sociable."

That was an understatement. Seph couldn't be more than twenty-two or three but Will had been intimidated by her. Olivia had been right when she'd said her family was odd.

As if to prove the point, another woman, this one closer to forty, sailed into the kitchen and then stopped theatrically when she caught sight of Will.

"Hell-*oo!*" she said, the greeting a musical question, her eyebrows rising expectantly.

Olivia made the introductions again. "Althea, you re-member Will from the other night at the pub?"

"Ooooh...yes," Althea said, her tone so knowing Will felt like blushing although he wasn't sure why. He hadn't done anything remotely untoward at the pub.

"Will's a landscape designer. We were just talking about him helping with the garden."

Landscape designer was overegging the pudding a bit, but in any case Althea didn't seem all that impressed. "Oh?" she said, her eyebrows arching even higher, her tone reserved to the point of cool. She switched on the kettle.

"It's already boiled," Olivia said again. "And yes, he's got loads of ideas about the garden—"

"I thought *you* had loads of ideas about the garden," Al-thea remarked as she made herself a cup of tea.

"Well, I do, but I'm going to need help, obviously."

"It's an amazing place," Will cut in, feeling the need to keep that particular line of conversation from continuing. It was clear there was a family power dynamic at play, and he definitely didn't want to be a part of it. "Olivia gave me the grand tour."

Althea's gaze had turned speculative. "I see."

Will decided it was time to go. He'd been hoping to chat more with Olivia, get to know her properly, but clearly that wasn't going to happen right now. "I should get back," he said as he rose from the table, taking his mug to the sink, Piper trotting behind him. "Thank you for the tour, Olivia, as well as the tea."

"I'll walk you out," she said quickly, shooting her sister a rather quelling look before she followed Will outside. The rain had downgraded to a misting drizzle, although it hardly mattered since he was still soaked from before. "Sorry, Althea can be a bit officious," Olivia said in a low voice. "She's always been that way. She's lovely, but…"

"No worries. If it works out, great. I'd love to be a part of this. If it doesn't, then, well, I had a lovely afternoon." He'd be gutted, though, not that he'd admit it to Olivia.

"Thank you," Olivia said, "for wanting to be part of it. It…it makes me feel so much better, to think I don't have to do this all alone."

"You could, you know." He glanced down at her, seeing how anxious she looked, the way she was nibbling her lip. He didn't know why she was having such a crisis of confidence, because the ideas of hers that he'd seen were great, but he sensed she needed an injection of encouragement. "You could do this all on your own, if you wanted to. You just need to believe you can."

"That's the tricky bit, isn't it?" she replied wryly, and he had an urge to touch her—squeeze her shoulder, or even give her a hug—which of course he didn't act on.

"Yes, I suppose it is."

A silence stretched between them as they stood by the car, their heads close together as the rain misted down, Piper sat between them, panting expectantly. It felt awkward, but there was something lovely about it, too, a brimming of unspoken possibility that made Will's heart skip a beat before he suddenly found himself mentally rearing back in alarm.

"I should go," he said abruptly. "Bye." And then he climbed in the truck without waiting for her to reply, Piper leaping into the back.

"WELL," ALTHEA SAID as Olivia came back into the kitchen.

"Well what?" Olivia went to the sink to wash up their mugs. "You know, you could have been a bit more welcoming."

"What!" Althea looked amused rather than annoyed. "I don't even know the bloke, Liv."

"You'll get to know him, if he's working here every day with me."

"Every day? This is progressing rather quickly."

"Or every other day. Whatever. You could have been a bit warmer to the idea." Her sister's obvious reserve had made Will uncomfortable, Olivia sensed, and that had annoyed her.

"Warmer to what idea?" Althea was sounding cool again.

"Warmer to the idea of Will helping me with the garden renovation. He's really keen, and like I said, he's got great ideas—"

"And like I said, *you've* got great ideas. Why do you need

someone else?"

"Because it's a huge project." Olivia strove to sound reasonable when she felt like stamping her foot. Why did Althea have to be so bossy? And why was she the one making all the decisions, just because it had been her idea to renovate Casterglass?

"There are a lot of huge projects, Liv," Althea told her in an oh-so-reasonable tone. "And there are lot of us—"

"Althea, the gardens and grounds run to over thirty acres. I can't handle that by myself, or even with Seph offering to mow the lawn, or whatever. Most estates would have a team of gardeners. Some of the jobs that need doing are really big—like dredging the pond, for example, or pruning those massive rhododendrons by the gate. I can't do that on my own, and that's just upkeep, never mind turning this place into an actual attraction." She ran out of breath, shaking her head when she saw how unmoved her sister seemed.

"That may be," Althea allowed, "but we're on a shoestring here, as you very well know. Besides, most of the thirty acres is forest or meadow that doesn't need to be managed—"

"*Everything* needs to be managed," Olivia cut across her, her irritation building. She hated confrontation, and the last thing she wanted was an argument with her sister, but Althea's overbearing manner was getting right up her nose, especially because Will had been so lovely. "You can't just leave a meadow or wood to its own devices and expect it to be something people want to spend time and money looking at."

"Well, surely you *could*—"

"Look," Olivia cut across her, anger firing her words, "the bigger question is, why do I need your permission to manage the garden, which was my job spec? Who put you in charge—besides you, I mean?"

Althea's mouth dropped open and then she snapped it shut. "*Someone* needs to be in charge," she said in a tone that managed to be both bristling and martyred—although perhaps Olivia was being unfair. She *felt* like being unfair. "And someone needs to stick to a budget," Althea continued, her voice rising. "This place has been slowly but surely going down the tube for the better part of five hundred years. Saying yes to everything is *not* the way to get it up and running in a sustainable fashion."

"I'm not," Olivia informed her tersely, "asking you to say yes to everything."

Althea rolled her eyes. "You know what I mean."

"No, I don't, actually." She put her hands on her hips. "What exactly are you suggesting? That I do all the gardening and landscaping by myself? Because you hinted, at least, a while ago that I should be able to get some help."

"Some," Althea allowed, "but I was thinking of maybe getting Ben to do some weeding or digging…"

"Ben? Your son, Ben? Who will be back for three weeks at Easter and probably doesn't want to spend the whole time mucking about in the garden? *That's* what you were thinking?"

"Be reasonable, Olivia."

"You're asking *me* to be reasonable?" Olivia felt near tears, which is what always happened when she got angry, which only made her angrier and more tearful. She wanted to be strong, but she wasn't. She never had been. "Althea, you're the one being unreasonable!" she exclaimed, her voice rising on a squeak, and then, because she didn't want to burst into tears in front of her sister, she whirled around and stalked out of the room.

She was *not* the one being unreasonable, she fumed, blinking back tears, as she stormed into her room and flung herself on her bed like a stroppy teenager. Goodness, what was she doing? Fighting with her sister and living in her childhood bedroom, complete with candy-striped wallpaper and frilly white pillows, when she was *thirty-six*. It was so very pathetic.

Olivia rolled onto her back and stared up at the ceiling, with its spiderweb of cracks. She wished she could have spoken more calmly to Althea, explained in an oh-so-reasonable way how she needed Will's help, but she hadn't, because she'd been so frustrated and upset. For a little while, when talking to Will, she'd seen how it could all work, and she felt as if she could be the one to make it happen. But then Althea had come and made her feel like a six-year-old even as she seemed to think Olivia could manage it all on her own. The irony was yet another irritant.

And what about Will? Just the thought of him made her stomach flutter, even though she knew it shouldn't. Not yet, anyway. She barely knew him. And yet what she knew... Still, it had been awkward and rather embarrassing, to have him watch Althea behaving so high and mighty. And if Althea refused to budget for someone to help her... Olivia groaned. There was a reason people advised you not to go into business with your family. A reason why it was important to make everything legitimate and legal, instead of scrawling designs on the back of napkin and a budget in your sister's notebook that you never got to see.

Will had made her see the myriad possibilities of the garden, but Althea had thrown up all the obstacles—and Olivia didn't know if she was strong enough to overcome them.

Chapter Six

"DADDY, I CAN'T sleep."

Will looked up from the spreadsheet he'd been making on his laptop, bleary-eyed with tallying numbers, which was definitely not his strong point. Rachel had always handled the business side of things. He barely knew his way around Excel, and usually ended up deleting a whole bunch of columns or rows without meaning to, and struggling to find a way to get them back.

"Why can't you sleep, Lall?" he asked as his five-year-old daughter stood in the doorway of the kitchen, dressed in her polka-dot pyjamas, her hair a tousled mess, expression tragic.

"It's so windy."

"Ah." Over the last two years Will had managed to tune out the sound of the wind coming off the fells and battering the house as if they were in a gale in the mid-Atlantic. The wind had been one of the less-than-pleasant surprises about moving to Cumbria; he'd been expecting rain, but wind? Wind screeching down the hills at seventy miles an hour, slanting the rain sideways and making a summer day feel like mid-December? It was definitely more than he'd bargained for, and he'd fought against it for the first few months, while Rachel, typically, had seen only the bright side.

"We won't need a tumble dryer," she'd assured him with a kiss. "The clothes will dry in five minutes in this wind, and I can get them down before it rains again!"

She'd been so cheerful, and he'd been so grumpy and grim. He was sorry about it now, of course he was, but hindsight, he'd discovered, was pretty pointless.

"Come here, then," he told Lally, and with a sly little grin—she had always known how to work a room, or at least him—she clambered up onto his lap.

Will put one arm around her as she nestled closer, her cheek against his chest, her hair tickling his nose. At his feet Piper let out a sleepy, satisfied groan and stretched his legs before flopping back down again. The Rayburn gave a comforting clank—comforting or ominous; it had broken down four times since they'd moved here, but Will couldn't afford to have it replaced. Still, it warmed the room, which was something.

"Whatcha working on, Daddy?" Lally asked as she elbowed him in the stomach in her attempt to get more comfortable. Will let out a soft *oof.*

"A new job. At least, I hope it's a new job."

"What kind of job?"

"Helping to fix up the gardens of a castle."

"A castle!" Lally's eyes rounded. "Does it have a princess?"

A smile tugged at Will's mouth as he pictured Olivia—her dark blue eyes, her hair coming out of its plait, the way she bit her lip. "Well, sort of."

"Will you take me there?"

"I don't even know if I'm going to get the job, Lall. Anyway, you're my princess." He kissed her head and with a hum of satisfaction she snuggled closer. Will glanced at the numbers he'd been working up—two and a half days a week, at one hundred and fifty pounds a day, for two months. The steady work would be most welcome, but was it too much to ask? He was stumbling around in the dark when it came to what Olivia wanted—or what her sister would approve.

That had been a bit of a strange dynamic, he mused. Althea clearly was in charge, but why, when Olivia was a grown woman with gardening experience? Well, it wasn't his business. He knew how complicated families could be—his parents were still hurt he'd moved up to Cumbria, even though they'd been the ones to move to Portugal. As for Rachel's family…the less thought about them, the better.

"Come on, princess," he said, closing his laptop and scooping Lally up in one armful. "Back to bed. I'll put on a story to drown out the wind."

"*The Magic Faraway Tree?*" Lally asked hopefully, and Will nodded, a lump forming in his throat. Before she'd become too ill, Rachel had recorded all of Enid Blyton's *Magic Faraway Tree* series for Lally and Jake, because they'd been her favourite books growing up. Listening to her read them, hearing her light, laughing voice, knowing she'd already been given a terminal diagnosis when she read the words so playfully, caused an ache deep inside him, and probably always would.

He ducked his head under the low, smoke-darkened beams as he carried Lally upstairs to bed. He could hear the wind howling outside, battering the little house on the hillside like a ravenous beast. Gently he laid Lally on her bed, drawing her pink duvet up to her chin while she blinked at him earnestly.

"And the story, Daddy?"

"I'm getting it." He fumbled for Rachel's old iPhone, now used as a speaker for the voice memos she'd recorded on it. Sometimes he swiped to see the photos, his thumb flicking across the screen as he looked for those snapshots from before she'd complained of stomach pain, laughing how she needed to wee all the time, claiming her bladder had never been the same after giving birth to Lally, who had weighed in at nine and a half pounds. *Oh, Rachel...*

"Daddy?"

"Here we are." He pressed play on the voice memo, and a second later Rachel's voice, warm and rich, filled the room with the book's opening lines. Lally snuggled under the covers, content.

Will turned the volume down a bit lower, bent to kiss Lally's forehead, and then tiptoed out of the room.

Downstairs he prowled around the kitchen, feeling restless; it was nine o'clock in the evening and normally he was so knackered by then he'd just fall into bed, wanting to block the world out for a solid ten hours, just as he had been doing since Rachel had died. Now he glanced out the window at the darkened landscape, the fell in the distance barely visible in the rain and gloom. Rain lashed the windowpane, along with the wind, typical weather for the end of February. Typical weather for July, as it happened, or any time of year. Why had he moved to Cumbria again?

Because your wife wanted to. Only she wasn't here anymore to remind him of all the good points of living up here—the fresh air and the cheap cost of living and how friendly everyone was, even if he couldn't understand their accents. With a sigh Will reached for the whisky bottle he kept in the back of the cupboard, and then with another sigh he put it back again. He'd bought it the day after Rachel's funeral, and there were about two inches left in the bottle. That wasn't too bad considering it had been a year and a half, but Will had only turned to the bottle when he'd been feeling particularly low. He was a single dad with no support; he couldn't afford to get trolleyed just because he was feeling sorry for himself.

But on nights like this, when the wind was howling and the evening stretched ahead of him and the only sound was the creak of timbers shifting and the faint lilt of his wife's voice reading out that damned story, Will felt as if he could expire from loneliness. He *wished* he could, but he never did. He just went on and on, aching and alone.

He glanced again at his laptop, now shut. He *needed* this job at Casterglass, he realised. Not just because he wanted it, which he did, but because if he didn't get it, he might plunge right off the cliffside he'd been balancing on for the last year and a half, into total depression and despair. He really hoped Olivia had meant what she'd said…and that her sister Althea could be reasonable.

"DADDY, ARE YOU busy?"

Olivia hovered in the doorway of her father's study, while her father looked up from the book he'd been reading, blinking owlishly. "Not at all, my dear. Come in."

Carefully Olivia edged across the threshold, unable to keep from feeling just a tiny bit traitorous. Althea didn't know she was here.

"What's bothering you, Olivia?" her father asked.

"How can you tell something is bothering me?"

"Because whenever you're anxious, you bite your lip, and right now it looks as if you might do yourself some serious damage." He closed the book and sat back, his elbows braced on the armrests of the large leather chair that had been behind this desk as long as Olivia could remember. Nothing in the room had changed since she was a child, or perhaps even since her father was a child—dusty curtains of dark green velvet framed the windows, and leather-bound books lined the walls. A huge, ancient globe perched on the edge of her father's desk, made at least two hundred years ago, if its map of the world was anything to go by.

Olivia rested her fingertips on top of the globe and gave it a spin. "It's about the garden," she said after a moment. "Although not just about the garden. I'd like some help with things—the digging and the landscaping and the design—and Althea is reluctant to spare the money." Another pang of guilt assailed her. She felt childish, going to her father like this, but had her sister really given her a choice? She had refused to discuss matters, snapping when Olivia had tried again that somebody needed to be in charge. And that somebody was, of course, going to be her.

"You've spoken to her about it, I presume?"

"Yes, that's how I know she's reluctant. It's not just that, though," Olivia burst out. "It's everything. Renovating this place is meant to be a family project, but it feels like it's just Althea's. She's in charge of *everything*. She won't give so much as an inch—I haven't even seen what she's budgeted for the garden! And shouldn't I decide the budget for the garden, anyway?" Olivia lapsed into silence, embarrassed by her outburst. And yet all of it had been true.

Her father's bushy eyebrows were knitted, his fingers steepled together. "Have you mentioned these concerns to Althea?"

"Sort of. We argued."

"Ah."

Olivia sighed. "I'm sorry for complaining so much, but it's been really difficult to talk to Althea about any of it. What do you think I should do?"

Her father matched her sigh as he shook his head. "As much as I have enjoyed the idea of us all working together, the particulars of it remain challenging, and always will. That's the nature of families, I'm afraid."

"I know that," Olivia replied with a small smile. "And I don't mind it being challenging, but I just want to be able to have a discussion. I'm trying to work it out with Althea—"

"Oh, really?" Her sister's ringing voice from the doorway had her stilling, and then slowly turning as her heart dropped down to her toes. "Because it doesn't look like that from here," Althea fumed. Her face was flushed, her eyes sparkling with what Olivia feared were tears.

"Althea—"

"You could have just said, you know," she cut across her. "You didn't have to run to Daddy!"

"I was just looking for some *advice*."

"Girls. Ladies, I should say." Their father held up his hand. "If we're going to argue, let us at least do it reasonably, and with refreshment." He rose from his chair while Althea and Olivia both watched him, silent.

"Where are you going, Daddy?" Olivia asked as her father walked out of the study.

"To the kitchen. There are only so many heated words

that can be exchanged over a decent Welsh rarebit."

Olivia exchanged a look with Althea, who smiled reluctantly even though she still looked angry. Welsh rarebit—a grilled and sauced version of cheese on toast—was the only thing that their father made in the kitchen, but it *was* delicious.

"Come, girls," their father barked, and obediently Olivia and Althea followed him to the kitchen.

"The secret to Welsh rarebit," he intoned as he retrieved an enormous block of cheddar from the fridge, along with some milk and butter, "is—"

"The mustard," Althea finished. "A teaspoon of wholegrain, but Dijon will do if you don't have it."

Their father beamed at her. "Exactly, my dear. I have taught you well, haven't I?"

"Daddy." Althea rolled her eyes, but their father was unperturbed. They both watched as he grated the cheese and made the sauce, adding the allotted teaspoon of mustard, as well as a handful of chives.

"My little secret," he told them with a wink.

He toasted the bread, poured the sauce over, and plonked it all under the grill. Olivia's mouth was already starting to water.

Soon enough they were all sat down at the table, a slice of Welsh rarebit each in front of them.

"Now," their father said as he cut off a square and popped it into his mouth. "Let's talk."

Olivia had to admit her ire had deflated somewhat now that they were seated and eating. Althea, too, seemed more sheepish than anything, although when she spoke she still sounded a bit prickly.

"I'm not trying to be difficult, but someone has got to be in charge."

"I'm not asking you not to be in charge," Olivia returned levelly. "Just to let me be in charge of the garden."

Althea sighed. "You *are* in charge of the garden, Liv. You can do what you like with it."

"But I need a budget. A proper one."

"There's no budget for anything!" Althea exclaimed, her voice rising. "The roof is costing nearly twice what we thought, and the rest of my payout from Jasper is going on the renovations for the tea room and shops, as well as promotion and publicity. I'm trying to do everything on the absolute cheap as it is. I'm not trying to be stingy, you know, but this isn't just about you." She shook her head in exasperation while Olivia frowned. She knew Althea was using most of her alimony from Jasper—a whopping three-quarters of a million pounds—for Casterglass, but surely she hadn't spent all of it?

"I thought we'd sold a few things," Olivia said uncertainly, for she knew her father had sold a select few of the castle's many antiques. "Isn't there enough money now?"

"We can always sell a few more," their father interjected calmly. "I daresay a few more paintings or knick-knacks won't go amiss."

"Oh, it's not that," Althea burst out irritably, pushing her half-eaten rarebit away. "It's not just about the money."

Olivia glanced at her father, who smiled faintly in return. Did he know what was going on? His kindly, slightly perplexed air was his usual MO, so she had no idea if he felt as confused as she did.

"What is it about, then?" Olivia asked, because it had certainly seemed as if it were about the money. Althea gave a huff.

"Everything," she said and rose from the table. "Now, if you'll excuse me, I have work to do." She strode off to her little office, while Olivia watched her go, fighting a mixture of frustration and regret. Perhaps she shouldn't have forced the issue, but her sister needed to be more open. If it wasn't about the money, what was it about? And what about her budget for the garden?

"Well," her father said mildly as he began to clear their plates, "I think that was a success, don't you?"

"What!" Olivia stared at him in disbelief. Even for her dotty father, that was putting quite a ridiculous amount of spin on what had been basically an argument that had solved nothing. "How do you reckon?"

"Oh, you know, first shot across the bow and all that," he replied, smiling. "You'll see. Althea will come round. They'll be money for your garden, I'm quite sure of it."

Privately Olivia doubted that, but she kissed her father's

cheek before she headed out into the garden. Over the last few days, while she'd been waiting for Althea to "come round" and for Will to send her his business proposal, she'd decided she might as well plough ahead, quite literally. She'd started on the walled garden, weeding the flower beds and repointing the brick paths as best as she could. She'd watched a few videos on YouTube and she'd found several barrows full of old bricks in one of the sheds, which had helped. Perhaps Althea was right, and they didn't need much of a budget. But she still wanted Will here to help.

She headed to the bed that had once been chock full of medicinal herbs, the physic garden of old, as Will had said. Yanking on a pair of battered work gloves, she reached for her trowel and started digging out the weeds. It was amazingly therapeutic—the physicality of it, her arms aching, sweat beading her forehead despite the chilly air. And then to see the weeds come out—was there anything as hopeful as freshly turned earth? Olivia's heart lightened just to look at it, to run it through her fingers…

"Olivia."

She turned, wiping her forehead with the back of her wrist as she saw Althea standing on the path. Glowering.

"Yes?"

"I'm sorry." She didn't sound sorry; she sounded grumpy. But Olivia appreciated that those two words could be hard to say.

She dropped the trowel and leaned back on her heels.

"I'm sorry, too. I didn't mean to go behind your back."

"Didn't you?" Althea asked with a huff of laughter.

"Well, yes, I suppose I did, but not maliciously. It's just…you wouldn't *talk* to me, Althea, at least not like an adult to an adult. I felt like a six-year-old to your responsible grown-up."

"I have that habit, I know." Wearily Althea sat right there on the ground, her elbows braced on her knees. "I suppose I am a little possessive of this project," she confessed quietly.

"Because it was your idea?"

"And because I've put a lot of money into it, along with my heart and soul. But I know it's not just mine, and neither is it fair on you—"

"I can understand why you feel that way." Olivia realised she had never stopped to properly consider how much Althea had invested, both financially and emotionally, into Caster-glass. Considering she'd only been home for a few weeks herself, and had barely made a start on anything, she could appreciate Althea's hands-off approach a little more. But she still needed money.

Althea heaved a sigh from the depths of her being. "How much do you need?" she asked. "For this Will person to come and help you?"

Olivia's heart leapt a little at that. *This Will person.* Yes, indeed. "I'm not sure," she hedged. "He's sending me a business proposal, but a good landscape designer or just plain old gardener costs between one and two hundred pounds a day." Althea winced. "And I need him here for two or three days a week for at least twelve weeks, until the opening," Olivia continued more firmly. She could negotiate down from that if she had to, but she might as well start with a dream.

"So, that's what…" Althea did the maths in her head, her eyes cast to the pale blue sky. "Between three and five thousand pounds?"

"Yes, plus I'll need money for the actual landscaping," Olivia returned quickly. "Seeds, cuttings, fencing, brick—"

Althea waved a hand in dismissal. "We'll keep that separate."

"Plus some specialist work," Olivia inserted quickly. "Will can do most of it, I'm sure, but we might need a tree surgeon or something—"

"We'll keep that separate, too, although I am hoping this Will can really do most of it," she said rather severely. "That's why you want him, isn't it?" Olivia blushed, and then wished she hadn't. Althea's gaze narrowed. "This isn't just you crushing, is it?"

"I'm not crushing, for heaven's sake!" Olivia practically snapped. "I just need some help."

"Fine, fine." Althea held up her hands in mock surrender. "You can have your Will. No more than three days a week, for twelve weeks, and hopefully less." She glanced at Olivia with a tired smile. "Happy?"

"Yes," Olivia told her sincerely. She found she was grinning. *Your Will.* She rather liked the sound of that.

Chapter Seven

"SO WHERE DO we start?"

Will gave her a frank look over the kitchen table. It was his first day of work, two weeks after Olivia had first made the suggestion. When she'd messaged him to say he could be hired for three days a week for twelve weeks, Will could hardly believe it. A proper job, something more than digging ditches or fixing walls. A lot more, for a good amount of time. Something to get properly stuck into. He'd been elated, and the feeling excitement and anticipation had seemed almost foreign, barely memorable. He'd been in such a slump for so long, this really felt like a lifeline.

Now they were having a coffee, the kitchen surprisingly quiet, Piper at their feet. It was early March and it felt it— cold and blowy, but with that fragile hint of spring in the air. The Aga rumbled comfortably and the wind battered the windowpanes, making the kitchen, huge as it was, feel especially cosy.

"I thought we should tackle the longer term projects first," Olivia suggested hesitantly. "So we have time to fix them. And also focus on the walled garden, because that's the first thing most people will see, and I do think it's a highlight."

"Good idea."

"I've been weeding the beds and repointing the paths, but it's slow going. A lot of things need pruning or cutting back."

"I'm sure. And the longer term projects?"

"Well, as you probably noticed on your tour, the pond needs dredging and the rhododendrons cutting back. The ha-ha could use some fortifying, and I'd like to make a clear footpath to the beach and around the meadows, the same way we went, but signposted for visitors. I also really liked your idea of the bridge," she finished shyly, "as part of that path, a few attractions along the way, like you suggested—the cave we could make out of the rock overhang, a wild flower meadow, a secret glade…"

"We should make a list," Will said, and Olivia nodded.

"I've got my laptop, or we could use good old-fashioned paper."

"Let's do it on paper."

It was sweetly companionable to sit side by side at the table, a notepad in front of them, and Olivia writing down their to-do list in her gently sloping scrawl. Will's heart beat a little harder, a little stronger. He liked working on the creative element of the garden, but more importantly he liked being part of a team. He'd been lonely for the last year and a half, really lonely. Having this back and forth, the sharing of ideas, the bouncing off one or another, was a balm to his soul.

"Right, that seems to be enough to be getting on with," Olivia said with a laugh when they'd filled up three pages. "You can see why I've been overwhelmed."

"If we take it one at a time, we should be all right." He smiled at her, and she smiled back, shyly, like she wasn't used to it. He wasn't, either. He got a sense from Olivia, he realised, as if she'd been hurt, wounded—not the same grief he had, but something painful. He wondered if she would ever tell him about it.

"Which should we tackle first?" she asked, giving the pad of paper before them a frowning glance.

"I think, actually, the first thing we need is an office." It hadn't taken him long to figure out that Olivia wasn't the most organised person around, sketching on the back of napkins and making lists on scraps of A4. He wasn't a paragon of that particular virtue, either, but Rachel had taught him a filing system, at least. She'd been organised— briskly so, the quartermaster of their family. He wanted to bring some of that to this enterprise.

Olivia's frown deepened as she looked at him question-ingly. "An office?"

"This is going to be a big project." He felt the need to speak gently, although he wasn't sure why. Maybe that sense of woundedness. "We'll need to keep track of orders, suppliers, specialists…" At her perplexed look, he continued, "We'll have to be in touch with a lot of different people—tree surgeons, seed suppliers, reclamation yards that sell the brick or stone we need…" He trailed off again as he saw her dawning look of unease. "What is it?"

"Althea budgeted for your help," she said, blushing a little. "And not much else. Not yet, anyway. I did tell her we'd need some of those things, but…" She shrugged. "I have a feeling each one is going to be a battle."

"Okay." Clearly there was a family dynamic as he'd suspected, but he supposed the castle itself had only a certain amount of resources. "Well, let's start with an office, at least. In a place this size, surely we can find a little corner somewhere? It doesn't have to cost anything."

"Yes, I'm sure we can." Olivia squared her shoulders and did her best to smile, before she shook her head wryly. "You must think I'm completely hopeless, not to have even got this far by myself."

"No, I don't," Will replied honestly. "But I do think you need some organisation." Along with a shot of self-confidence. Something had knocked it, he thought, but what? "Where do you think we can set up an office?"

She nibbled her lip, while Will found himself looking away, embarrassed and disconcerted by the sudden flash of desire he'd felt at that simple little gesture. It had been such a long time, but he didn't need to go feeling things like that, or making things between them awkward. "There's a load of little rooms along the kitchen—why don't we have a look?"

He followed her down a dim, flagstone corridor lined with doors, Piper trotting behind him. "This is the old housekeeper's room," Olivia said, lightly tapping a closed door. "It's Althea office now."

If Althea had an office, Will wondered, why didn't Olivia? There was something strange about the Penryn family dynamic, but he couldn't put his finger on what it was. Perhaps just sibling roles cemented into place after decades of the same old, same old. He'd felt a bit like that in his own family; he was the responsible one, Kerry was the adventurer. When he'd told his parents he and Rachel were moving to Cumbria, they'd looked both surprised and hurt. *But that's something Kerry would do, not you.* They hadn't said it, but they hadn't needed to.

"And this is the drying room…" Olivia paused on the threshold of a room with a wooden drying rack hanging suspended from the ceiling; it was covered in drying clothes, including several lacy bras and knickers. Olivia blushed and closed the door quickly. "It's already in use, obviously."

They went through several other rooms—a boot room, a room to polish silver, another room piled with old furniture, and another with what looked like a lot of old garden toys—a dusty croquet set, a set of wooden skittles, a couple of hula hoops. All the rooms were small and dark, with flagstone floors and one poky window each. Even if they'd cleaned them out, none of them would have been suitable for an office for two people, and they'd hardly be inspiring places in which to dream up a garden.

"I suppose we could look upstairs," Olivia offered hesitantly. "Clear out one of the bedrooms, perhaps…"

"Are there any rooms in the garden?" Will had a vague memory of spying a summerhouse in the walled garden, but he couldn't be sure.

"Yes, there's a little summerhouse… My grandfather built it as an art studio." She brightened. "It has electricity, I think—shall we have a look?"

Will felt his heart expand when, a few minutes later, they stepped into the walled garden, Piper running off to investigate some interesting smell or other. The sky was a fragile, robin's-egg blue with wisps of cloud scudding across it, and the air, although chilly and slightly damp, held the promise of future warmth.

"You've been working," he said, impressed, and Olivia gave him another one of her shy smiles.

"Just a little."

"The paths looks much better… Where did you get the brick?"

"In one of the barns. We probably should make an inventory of everything we already have. There were piles of brick and flagstones, and quite a bit of timber, plus loads of pots—some plastic, others quite a nice terracotta."

"That sounds like a good idea." Maybe they wouldn't have to budget that much for supplies, after all. They could probably rustle up quite a bit, just poking around in forgotten corners.

He followed Olivia to the north-east corner of the garden, where a little rectangular summerhouse had been built against the brick wall, its south-facing side taken up by long dusty windows that would let in loads of lovely light once they were cleaned.

"I don't think anyone has been in here for ages," Olivia said as she tried the handle. The door didn't budge. She put her shoulder against it and gave a somewhat half-hearted shove, and it moved maybe an inch. Will stayed quiet, not wanting to take over; it had always annoyed Rachel if he'd tried to muscle in.

"I *can* open this jar," she would tell him with an exasperated look. "Even if you can do it quicker. You don't need to flex your biceps for me. We're already married."

Olivia tried again, and then she gave Will a wry look. "Sorry, it seems to be stuck."

"Give it another shove," he advised, smiling. "This time like you mean it."

She let out a little laugh and then, with a bit more oomph, she pushed her shoulder against the door. It creaked in protest, and then with another shove and a louder creak, it finally opened.

"There." She rubbed her shoulder, smiling, and then stepped inside. "I did it." She sounded surprised, and a little bit proud. "It will certainly need a bit of a clean," she remarked, looking around. It wasn't an enormous space, but it was big enough for two desks, a couple of chairs, a filing cabinet and maybe a table to hold a kettle and a few mugs. Will could practically see it all, and again he felt that leap of excitement. This was really happening. The Casterglass Estate office. Or something.

Olivia rested her hand on an old, rotting easel. "My grandfather was the most atrocious painter. Honestly, his watercolours look like someone has wept all over the paper, and his oils are even worse—like they've been painted by an overenthusiastic four-year-old, with fingerpaints." She smiled faintly. "But he loved it so much, or so my father says—he died before I was born—and my grandmother always supported him. She insisted on hanging one of his paintings in a gallery in the castle. It's next to a portrait by one of Rembrandt's students."

"Wow."

"Daddy always said he didn't understand why a Rembrandt would be worth millions, but something by his students is barely a tenner. They both look the same." She sighed and then shook her head. "But why am I wittering on? Should we get clearing? I think this can all be for the bonfire." She nodded toward the easel and a little three-legged stool by it, the only furniture in the studio.

"All right," Will agreed, rolling up his sleeves. "Let's get cracking."

WHY WAS IT fun to dust and sweep? Olivia wondered. She'd tied her hair back with a scarf as she'd attacked the dusty, cobwebby studio with a broom as well as a feather duster, while Will tackled the windows with a full roll of paper towel and a bottle of Windex. They'd both coughed from the dust that flew in the air and down their throats, and Olivia's eyes stung from the grit that had flown up, but she was still having fun. She liked Will's cheerful, jokey personality, and she appreciated it all the more knowing how he'd been bereaved. How could he be so upbeat, when he'd so recently lost his wife? It was a lesson to her, she supposed, not to marinate in her own feelings of guilt and regret. Life moved on.

At one o'clock they stopped for lunch; Will had brought his own, and Olivia made a sandwich in the kitchen and joined him outside, enjoying the fragile sunlight that was filtering through the shreds of cloud as they sat in the courtyard off the kitchen, Piper sprawled beside them.

"It almost feels like spring," she told Will, and he nodded, and then, to her shock, reached out and brushed his fingertips across her cheek.

For a second she was speechless; it felt as if he had trailed little sparks along her jawbone, and it was only after another second or two that he ducked his head and explained, "You had a bit of dirt on your face."

"Oh." She held her hand up to her cheek, mortified by how she'd reacted, and hoping desperately that Will hadn't been able to tell. Quickly, almost frantically, she wiped at the spot, and he shook his head, smiling wryly.

"It's gone now."

"Right. Well." She let an altogether too shaky laugh. "I must look a fright."

"You don't," Will said, and then looked away, rather quickly.

Olivia's stomach gave a little fizz. This was getting just slightly weird, but in an exciting way, which wasn't good, considering she had to work with Will for three months at least—and he was bereaved and she was a virtual home-wrecker. Not *exactly* an optimal pairing. Besides, she'd told herself she was going to swear off romance for at least six months, to focus on the garden and give her heart a chance to heal. And, she knew, also as some sort of punishment for having got together with Matt in the first place. It had seemed a relatively easy proposition in Casterglass—but she hadn't counted on meeting and working with Will.

They ate the rest of their lunch in a mostly companiona-ble silence, although Olivia felt a little echo of the awkwardness of that mini-encounter; really, it was ridicu-lous, to have felt anything at all, considering all Will had done was touch her cheek. Yet she'd felt it, along with the ensuing awkwardness, and she had no idea if Will felt it, as well. Probably not, she decided, as—having finished his sandwich—he'd tilted his face to the sun. She was the neurotic one, after all, making way too much of such little moments.

They spent the afternoon hauling in furniture to their new office; Olivia had located a couple of old desks in one of the barns that was piled with furniture no longer used in the castle, antiques slung in there along with IKEA.

"There might be some really interesting pieces here," Will said as he ran his hand over the carved leg of an antique end table made of cherry. "You should have them valued."

"We've had everything in the castle valued," Olivia told him. "But I don't know if they bothered with this old barn. I think it's mostly junk—old junk, but junk nonetheless."

"And junk we can use in our office."

He smiled, and she smiled back. They'd been doing a lot of that today, Olivia noted. Sharing smiles, almost as if they knew a secret. Or maybe, just maybe, she was overreacting. Again. But it was exciting, to be making this happen, and she really didn't think she was imagining that. Will felt it, too.

By three o'clock, amazingly, their newfound office was starting to look shipshape. There were two desks, two chairs, an old, dented filing cabinet, and a funny little teak cabinet that Will said would be perfect for holding a kettle and mugs.

"We've got to have our tea breaks," he told her, wagging a playful finger. "Very important part of this whole business."

"Absolutely," Olivia agreed. She liked the cosy image of her and Will kicking back in their chairs with mugs of tea after a morning digging out flower beds or fortifying the riverbed or doing goodness knew what else.

Olivia had also managed to find a couple of lamps and a dodgy old printer that Will had tinkered with and had, amazingly, got to work. They could bring their laptops out, and Will said he'd bring a big calendar to tack on the wall so they could pencil in their projects.

"But we haven't done a thing in the garden," Olivia couldn't help but lament as they walked back to the castle.

"There's always tomorrow," Will replied easily. He glanced at his watch, his eyes widening in alarm. "I'm going to be late for pickup again. I've got to shoot off, I'm afraid. The school is starting to get very annoyed with my lack of punctuality."

"All right. See you tomorrow, then."

Olivia stood by the garden gate as Will hurried to his truck, Piper at his heels, and she waved him off. It had been a good day, and she was already looking forward to tomorrow.

"Well," Althea said with far too much emphasis, eyebrows raised expectantly, when Olivia came into the kitchen a few minutes later to make herself a cup of tea. "You and Will seem to be getting along *rather* well."

Olivia felt herself go annoyingly pink. "He's a nice chap," she said as noncommittally as she could. "And it's good to have someone to work with. He'll keep me organised and on task, I think." She switched on the kettle, hoping its burbling noise might drown Althea out, but no such luck.

"Are you sure that's all it is?"

"Althea, I barely know him. We've spent all of one day together."

"And the other afternoon, and the night at the pub," Althea replied, ticking off her fingers.

Olivia rolled her eyes. "Exactly. Hardly any time at all."

"Still, there definitely seemed to be a vibe between you."

"A vibe?" She tried to scoff, but she feared there was a betraying note of eagerness in her voice. If Althea thought there was some kind of energy or attraction between them…but, no. That was just Althea, being nosy and seeing hearts and butterflies everywhere because she'd had a few of her own with John Braithwaite. "There's no vibe," Olivia declared as the kettle switched off and she poured water into her mug, over the teabag. "And please don't make things awkward by insisting there is."

"Awkward? Me?" Althea assumed an air of innocence. "I would never do that."

"Do what?" Poppy asked as she came in from school, throwing her bag down and diving for the biscuit tin. Twelve-year-old Tobias followed, and they tussled over a pack of custard creams while Althea watched with mingled exasperation and affection.

Tobias was finally victorious, raising the packet of biscuits high while Poppy broke apart the one she'd managed to snag, licking the cream inside in a way Olivia found revolting but could remembering doing herself as a child. "Do what?" Poppy asked again.

"Never mind," Olivia said, giving her sister a severe look. The last thing she needed was Althea bringing her kids in on the whole vibe conversation. "It doesn't matter."

Althea pursed her lips, and Olivia knew she was tempted to make mischief. But then she shrugged and grabbed the packet from Tobias. "Don't eat them all—tea's in an hour," she said, scoffing to herself.

"Do *what?*" Poppy asked again, insistent now, and Olivia decided to beat a retreat. She headed back outside, her heart lightening as she caught sight of the summerhouse in the corner of the garden. She slipped inside, amazed at how a little elbow grease and cleaning spray had made such a difference. What had been a dusty, dingy, dismal space was now filled with hope and possibility.

Slowly she turned in a circle as she imagined a calendar on the wall filled with pencilled-in projects, a kettle on the cabinet, muddy wellies by the door. Will and her sitting and chatting, discussing ideas on how best to save the ailing wisteria by the pergola…

It was all finally happening, and she was so very excited.

Chapter Eight

THE GARDEN WAS starting to look good. No, Will decided, it was starting to look *great*. He and Olivia had been hard at work for the last two weeks, mainly focusing on getting the walled garden into shape. They'd weeded, dug, pruned, trimmed, and tied back. It had filled Will with joy to see the henbane starting to bud, and the wisteria that had looked near-dead show the first stirrings of life. Although the garden was still mostly a sea of brown as they approached the end of March, it was a neatly tended sea, with marked-out beds of freshly turned soil and flowers and herbs beginning to grow. It was coming back to life, and even though he knew it sounded twee, so was he. At least a little.

As much as he'd enjoyed nurturing the walled garden, uncovering its secrets and beauty beneath the nettles and weeds, he'd enjoyed his time with Olivia even more. Working side by side. Chatting in their summerhouse-turned-office, with mugs of tea and a packet of biscuits—he'd brought a kettle on the second day, and made her a celebratory cup of tea, handing it to her with a silly flourish that had made her cheeks turn pink.

They'd devoured the packet of biscuits between them as they'd discussed how to tackle the garden—Olivia wanted to work on the flower beds, while he decided to deal with the wisteria and other climbing vines. Once the walled garden was under control, they would look to some of the other projects—dredging the pond, cutting back the rhododendrons.

"We'll need a very tall ladder for those," he'd said, and Olivia had frowned thoughtfully.

"Or a drone, with a pair of shears?"

For a second he'd thought she'd been serious, and then she'd burst out laughing. He'd liked hearing her laugh, properly, from her belly. He liked the thought that this garden was helping her, just as it was helping him.

Their chats had always been about work, but they had felt companionable in a way Will hadn't felt in a long time. He had a friend, a true friend, as well as a colleague and helpmeet.

Every afternoon, when he left to pick up Lally and Jake, he felt a little dip in his spirits, a sense of loneliness settling in. He'd missed chatting with someone, exchanging ideas, even just having a bit of a laugh and a joke. He had hoped that having someone to talk to would have made his empty evenings a little more bearable, but they'd only made them worse, the hours stretching on after he'd put Lally and Jake to bed, endless and empty, without anyone to chat to or simply sit with. He felt the absence of that person—of Olivia—all the more.

He'd done his best to catch up on work during those lonely hours, do the admin and filing that he found so tedious, and sometimes even sketch out a few ideas for Casterglass, but none of it was enough. He still went to bed with an ache in his chest, and an even deeper and more pervading sense of loneliness than he'd had before. All because of Olivia.

He did his best not to notice the way her eyes darkened to violet when she was thinking, or how she nibbled her lip when she was about to make a suggestion. He tried not to think about how lovely she looked in the middle of a flower bed, elbow-deep in topsoil with mud on her nose and a fierce expression on her face as she battled bindweed. He didn't want to be aware of her as a woman, because he knew he wasn't ready to face that, and yet he was. His body was reminding him, rather insistently, of the fact—his gaze drawn to the way her fleece pulled against her breasts when she reached for something, or how gently her hips swayed as she walked down a path. The kind of stuff he hadn't noticed about any woman since Rachel's death, and he really wasn't sure how he felt about feeling it now.

As for how Olivia felt…he really couldn't tell. She was naturally quiet, maybe even shy, and sometimes she seemed guarded, as if she were hiding that woundedness he still sensed. He'd asked her once if she missed her friends in York and she'd looked at him with sudden suspicion, making him feel like a jerk for crossing some invisible line. He hadn't asked again. She seemed to be a very private person, and he supposed he was, as well, and so they kept their conversation about the garden, and he let that be enough. Hell, it was a lot more interaction and interest than he'd had since Rachel had died.

Now they were on the brink of April and the day looked to be dry, for once. He had high hopes of finally dealing with the riverbed; he'd been stockpiling stones to narrow the channel and he'd found a huge plastic tarp to line the bed in one of the castle's bottomless barns. With the walled garden mainly in hand, the pond dredged, and the rhododendrons on next week's to-do list, today, he hoped, was the day to tackle the river and the hoped-for waterfall.

"Dad, my stomach hurts."

Will looked up from the lunch he'd been packing to see Jake standing in the doorway of the kitchen, clutching his stomach as he groaned theatrically.

"Again?" He tried to sound light but his own stomach was sinking. This was the third stomach ache this week, and he didn't think it was appendicitis. Jake had been prone to stomach aches since Rachel's death—stomach ache, head-aches, and other more nebulous aches and pains throughout his body. He'd gone from being a quiet but grounded kid to one who saw death lurking around every corner, and some deadly ailment in every faint twinge or cramp.

Will understood; after Rachel's diagnosis, he'd become obsessive about checking himself out, looking up every symptom on WebMD, from a tickle in the back of his throat to knees that cracked when he bent, just to make sure he wasn't on death's door. For the sake of his children, he had to stay healthy. It wasn't until Rachel had died that he realised how utterly run-down he'd become; he'd come home after the funeral and felt as if he could have slept for a week, but of course he hadn't had that luxury. Single parents just had to soldier on—and on and on. Fortunately, he'd shed that somewhat irrational fear of getting ill at the drop of a hat, whereas it seemed only to have increased with Jake.

He planted his hands on his hips as he surveyed his son—they had to leave for school in ten minutes but he still hadn't put his uniform on, which meant he was *really* filibustering. "Tell me the symptoms."

"It really hurts." For good measure, Jake pressed one hand gingerly to his stomach and winced.

"You think you need to go to A&E?" Will asked, eyes narrowed, and Jake blinked up at him guilelessly.

"Maybe."

He was really giving this all he had, Will thought with a reluctant flicker of admiration. He had no doubt that Jake did have a stomach ache—of sorts. But one that would keep him off school? What was really going on here?

The trouble was, he had no idea. Rachel would have known—she would have somehow expertly sussed whether

Jake needed a cuddle and a push, or to be bundled back to bed with a kiss and some cinnamon toast. She would have figured out if he was faking or truly ill or worried about something. Even after eighteen months of solo parenting, Will wasn't sure how to begin that sort of expert assessment.

"Is something going on at school?" he asked as mildly as he could, turning back to spread jam on a slice of bread for Lally's sandwich. Back in January the reception teacher had sent home a note requesting parents pack healthy lunches for their children, with no fizzy drinks, sweets, crisps, "or other inappropriate foods". Will was pretty sure that last bit had been meant for him—a jam and butter sandwich was not exactly packed with nutrition, but it was the only thing Lally would eat at school ("the ham gets so slimy, Daddy") and he knew he needed to pick his battles. A healthy sandwich was not one of them.

"Nothing's going on at school," Jake said, and Will couldn't tell if he sounded guarded or just confused at the seeming non sequitur. "My stomach just *hurts.* Maybe I have intestinal ischemia." He spoke with something like relish.

"Intestinal what?"

"Ischemia." Now he sounded knowledgeable. "It's where the blood flow decreases to your intestines and can cause abdominal pain and, if not treated, even death."

Clearly Jake was spending too much on the NHS website, looking up different diseases and diagnoses. It was a macabre hobby of his that Will tried to discourage, but Jake sneaked it anyway, every time he got a hold of the iPad.

"And what are the symptoms?" Will asked, determined to be patient.

"Chronic, severe abdominal pain."

"That's it?"

Jake shrugged. Will reached for his phone. In a few seconds, with some help from autocorrect, he'd found the webpage for intestinal ischemia. "Symptoms include frequent, forceful bowel movements," he read out loud. He glanced up from his phone, his eyebrows raised. "Have you had some of those, bud?" Because he thought he would have noticed if he had. This house had only one toilet, after all.

"My stomach *hurts.*"

"Right." He finished making Lally's sandwich and called to her; she'd slunk off to the sitting room and turned on CBeebies without him noticing, even though he tried to have a semi-strict no-TV rule before school. "Does your stomach hurt too much to come to work with me today?"

Jake immediately brightened. "No."

Somehow he wasn't surprised. "All right, get dressed. We'll talk in the truck. Lally!" He went to the door of the sitting room and saw her lying on the sofa on her stomach, utterly absorbed in an episode of *Octonauts.* "It's time to go," he told her, trying not to sound as impatient as he felt. They were going to be late. Again.

OLIVIA WAS SPRAWLED in her chair, feet propped up on her desk as she studied a seed catalogue when she heard Will open the door to the summerhouse.

"I think we should order some veg," she said, her eyes still on the catalogue. "I was thinking we could have a pick-your-own…" She looked up, blinking in surprise when she saw that Will had a little boy in tow. He gave her a sheepish look.

"Sorry, I should have texted you to check it was okay, but…Jake's off school today. Just a bit of a stomach ache, nothing serious."

"It *could* be serious, if it's intestinal ischemia," Jake interjected in an aggrieved tone. Will gave Olivia a look of wry exasperation, and she smiled back. Jake looked adorable—about eight or so, with a mop of dark hair, a fringe that nearly covered his eyes, and freckles across his nose. And, it seemed, a stomach ache.

"Stomach ache, eh?" She gave him a serious look as she took her legs off the desk and sat up. "I had a lot of those when I was a child. You know what helped?"

Looking guarded, Jake shook his head.

"Hot water bottle. And lemon drops. Failsafe, guaranteed."

"Lemon drops?" Clearly he liked the sound of those.

"Yep, they're very settling, apparently. That's what my mum always said, anyway." Although Olivia wasn't sure she should be swearing by her mother's admittedly offbeat remedies. She certainly wouldn't recommend snail syrup for a cough, which her mother still swore by, but being curled up with a hot water bottle, sucking a lemon drop, was a poignant childhood memory. "Shall I set you up with both?" she asked, and a small smile bloomed across Jake's face like a flower.

"Okay." He hunched one shoulder, immediately trying to play it cool. "I mean, if you want."

It made her heart hurt to think he'd learned to feign indifference at such a young age. Was that because of his mother's death, or was that just how childhood was these days? Too cool for school by Year Three.

"I'll be right back," she promised him, and then glanced at Will. "If that's okay?"

The smile he gave was megawatt heartfelt, and it made Olivia's stomach flip. "It's more than okay. Thank you so much."

It was easy enough to fill a hot water bottle, and only a little trickier to find the promised lemon drops. Her mother kept them in a tin in the kitchen, and while Olivia had no idea of their sell-by date, when she popped one in her mouth it tasted just the same. Lemon drops didn't go out of date, did they?

"Hot water bottle?" Althea asked as she bustled in from her office for her second coffee morning. "Are you ill?"

"No, Will's son has a bit of a tummy ache and I thought I'd give him a hot water bottle."

Predictably, Althea's eyebrows rose practically to her hairline. "Will's *son?*"

"He has two children," Olivia explained, her voice stiffening in reaction to Althea's bug-eyed expression. "He's widowed. He brought Jake today because he was a bit poorly."

"I see," Althea said, and Olivia knew what she thought she saw—way too much. She really didn't need her sister's speculation and innuendo ruining a perfectly good friendship. Because, she'd come to realise, no matter how Will's smile made her stomach fizz, what she really needed was a friend.

The kettle clicked off and she filled the hot water bottle. "Now if you'll excuse me," she said, with unfortunate pomposity, as Althea flung a hand out, looking irritatingly amused.

"By all means."

Why did siblings, especially older ones, have the amazing and laser-focused ability to irritate you? Olivia wondered as she headed back to the summerhouse. She shouldn't have risen to Althea's questioning; she'd wanted to seem laid-back and relaxed, and instead she'd seemed anything but. It was so frustrating.

"Everything okay?" Will asked, his forehead crinkling in concern, as Olivia slipped into the summerhouse.

She must still be scowling. "Yes, fine," she replied, doing her best to clear her expression. "Here you go, Jake." She settled him with his hot water bottle and a bag of lemon drops, and was pleased to see he looked as happy as Larry. As she returned to her desk, he took out a massive *Encyclopaedia of Gross Stuff*, which made her smile. Sam had had a similar book when he'd been about that age.

"Thank you," Will said quietly. "You're a life-saver."

"I don't know if lemon drops and a hot water bottle are actually life-saving," she replied with a smile, "but they help a bit."

"You are," he insisted, giving her a look that made her stomach flip. Again.

"Well." She looked away, willing herself not to blush. Friend, remember? *Friend.* Parts of her body were refusing to acknowledge that memo, it seemed. "Anyway." She cleared her throat. "You wanted to start the riverbed today?"

Will glanced at Jake. "I suppose I should stay a bit more local, so I can keep an eye on him."

"I don't mind. I was hoping to dig out some raised beds for that veg patch we're planning. You can deal with the riverbed and I can keep an eye on Jake?" She knew Will had been itching to get started on the waterfall project.

"Are you sure?" He looked both torn and hopeful. "I don't want to put you out..."

"Not at all. As long as Jake is okay with it?" They both glanced at Jake, who looked up from his encyclopaedia and nodded shyly. "That's that, then," Olivia said briskly. "We'll meet up in a couple of hours for lunch. Hopefully you'll have made a good start by then."

"Definitely," Will replied. "And thank you." He reached over to ruffle his son's hair. "How does that sound, bud?"

"Good," Jake mumbled, his nose buried in his book, and a few minutes later Will was heading down to the river.

Olivia took a few minutes to catch up on emails, and keep an eye on Jake. She didn't want to abandon him the second he arrived, and in truth she felt a funny sort of sympathy for him—he looked quiet and shy, a little too skinny, his hair a little too long. He reminded her, in an odd way, of how she'd been as a child—dreamy, uncertain, glad to be invisible but also hurt by the inevitability of it. Or was she just projecting...? She actually knew next to nothing about this kid.

And so, after spending an hour on the raised beds, she decided to reach out to him, and went back to the summer-house to check on him as well as make herself a cup of tea. Jake, she could see, had started to get bored with his ency-clopaedia and was kicking his feet against the bottom of his chair.

"So, stomach ache," Olivia said with cheerful matter-of-factness as she dunked a teabag in her mug of hot water. "Do you get those often?"

"Sometimes." His voice was a mumble, his eyes barely visible under his fringe.

"I used to get them a lot."

"You did?"

She nodded. "Yup. A kind of cramp. I never felt sick, like I might actually throw up, which is what my mum always asked."

"That's what my dad does!"

Olivia nodded sagely. "No, it isn't like that, is it? But it still hurts. A lot."

"Yes." Jake nodded in heartfelt agreement. "It really does."

Olivia knew now her stomach aches had been caused by anxiety, and she wondered if this little boy's were, as well. How to find out, though? "Would you like a drink?" she asked him. "Some squash?"

Jake ducked his head. "Yes, please."

"Why don't you come into the kitchen? There's no reason you have to stay out here the whole day."

Looking eager for the first time that day, Jake tossed his book aside and followed her happily into the castle.

"Wow," he breathed as they came into the kitchen. "This place is huge."

"It is rather enormous," Olivia agreed wryly. "Which is not always a good thing. It tends to be freezing in winter."

"Our house is really small," Jake told her matter-of-factly. "And...I don't know...dark."

"Dark?" It occurred to Olivia that she get all sorts of interesting information about Will and his life from Jake, but she did her best to resist that temptation.

"Yeah, the wood is really dark, and there's beams on the

ceiling and stuff. My mum wanted a really old house." He clammed up suddenly, pressing his lips together, and Olivia had the sense he did not want to talk—or her to ask—about his mum. Was this the source of his anxiety? It made sense— life had to seem awfully uncertain to an eight-year-old whose mum had died.

"So, squash." She peered in the cupboard. Before Althea had arrived at Casterglass, the sell-by date of anything in the kitchen cupboards would have been highly questionable, and bottles of squash were likely to be twenty years old or more. But now, thankfully, Olivia trusted that the cupboard offerings were all recently bought—and ruthlessly organised, thanks to Althea. She did appreciate her sister for that, and other things, as well, she thought as she selected two bottles. "Lemon or blackcurrant?"

"Blackcurrant," Jake said definitively.

"I like someone who knows their own mind." She determined to keep things light, chatting about the garden and sharing some miscellany about the castle—the guard room had over two hundred shields—rather than digging for information, either about the source of his stomach aches or his father. That could come later.

Yet as she sat opposite him and watched him drink up his squash, Olivia couldn't keep a wave of longing from sweeping through her, painful in its intensity. She loved children. She still desperately wanted one of her own. And watching this little motherless boy look at her with such shy eagerness was both wonderful and heartbreaking, filling her with both longing and hope. She couldn't be Jake's mother, of course, not even close. But if she could help him…help the whole family…

And that, Olivia knew, was how things got dangerous.

Chapter Nine

T HE RINGING FROM Olivia's laptop surprised her. It was after ten o'clock at night, and she was just getting ready for bed. She clicked the mouse and her brother's photo flashed up on the screen, requesting a Skype call. Olivia couldn't remember the last time Sam had called her personally. She'd chatted with him during their family Skypes, but she tended to be in the background and in truth Althea did most of the talking.

"Liv?" After a second's blank screen, her brother's pixelated face came into view. He looked tanned, his blue eyes bright in his browned face, his sandy hair touched with blond sun streaks.

"You look like a surfer dude," Olivia said with a laugh. She sat cross-legged on her bed, her computer on her lap. "How's New Zealand?"

"It's good."

"You've been out there for ages."

"Only three months." Sam sounded a bit defensive.

"Still…isn't your charitable thing done?" Olivia couldn't

keep track of all her brother's charitable causes. He was forever doing something that was both ridiculous and noble—hiking up Kilimanjaro with a fridge on his back, or surfing for twenty hours straight in New Zealand, all for the latest charitable cause. He raised thousands of pounds, but Olivia couldn't help but be a little sceptical about the whole thing. How was doing something dangerous and absurd actually helpful to, well, anything?

"It ended in February," Sam said a bit grudgingly. "But I decided to stay in Auckland for a while. I can work from anywhere."

"Yes, I know, lucky." Sam worked for a start-up tech company, doing something with data that she didn't really understand, but he seemed to make a lot of money and could take months off to pursue his charitable adventures. "So what's up?" she asked lightly. There had to be a reason why Sam was calling her and not the whole family—unless he'd misdialled?

"I just wondered how you were doing," he said, and now he sounded evasive. "How long have you been back?"

"About a month."

"And how is it?"

"It's really good," Olivia said slowly. Since she and Will had started working on the garden in earnest, the days had been flying by. Truth be told, she could barely wait to get up in the morning and meet him in the summerhouse for their morning cup of tea while they went over their daily plans.

The garden was coming to life, too, especially now spring was well and truly on the wing. Every day there was something new to thrill her—the red-breasted robin hopping about on the bird table; bright purple crocuses coming up in colourful clusters; the tight pink buds on the cherry blossom trees, getting ready to unfurl and bloom in giant Dr Seuss–like puffballs. She loved it all, and she especially loved sharing each springtime discovery with Will. He seemed as thrilled by the wonders of the season as she was.

"You like being there?" Sam asked dubiously. "I mean…it's so remote."

"You're the one in New Zealand," Olivia returned lightly. "That's pretty remote, if you ask me."

"Yes, but the people…" Sam sighed. "There's not much going on in Casterglass, is there?"

"I suppose it depends what you mean. We're a hive of activity at the moment, but if you're looking for nightlife…" She hesitated. "I thought you were coming back in a couple of weeks?" This was meant with silence. "Are you having second thoughts, Sam?"

"I'm not sure I even had first ones. Althea just sort of dumped it all on me—must save the castle, can't do it without you, and so on."

"Well, we *could* do it without you," Olivia told him, "but we'd rather not. It's a family affair, and you have your part to play, if you want to. I thought you were keen on the glamping and stuff?" She tried to remember what Sam had actually said during their calls, but she couldn't recall any specifics, more just mumbled acquiescence to Althea's ever-growing to-do list.

"I mean, yes, I am, in *theory*," Sam said, shifting where he was sprawled on what looked like a leather futon, a glimpse of blue sky behind him. New Zealand was eleven hours ahead of England, Olivia knew, so it had to be morning there. "But I feel like I never got a chance to say yes or no. It was just full steam ahead from the word *go*."

"Well, you know how Althea is." Olivia eyed her brother as closely as she could, considering they were viewing each other through a computer screen, and the castle's lamentable internet meant she could practically count the pixels. "What's really going on, Sam? Do you not want to come home?"

"It's not that," he said, irritably enough that Olivia thought it probably was that.

"What, then?"

"I don't know." He sighed. "Do you really think it's going to work? The whole tourist attraction thing?"

"We won't know until the opening," she replied, "but we've got to try, haven't we?" It gave her a funny little jolt of both terror and excitement to think that they would be opening in just over two months, hopefully on the May bank holiday weekend. How on earth were they going to make that happen, when Sam hadn't even returned yet? But she supposed it wouldn't take too long to throw up a few yurts or whatever it was he had planned.

Although, from the sounds of it, he hadn't planned anything yet.

As for the rest of the estate…

"What changes have you made?" Sam asked. "Because the place was practically falling down."

"The roof is nearly completely replaced," Olivia told him. She'd got used to the constant hammering, and the scaffolding that covered the castle like a metal shroud. "And Althea has organised all the rooms in the original part of the castle, with Mum and Dad's help—it didn't take much, you know, besides a good dusting and a few plaques put up, with all the history. Dad's written those. Poppy's been designing a visitor's brochure, and Seph is clearing out the barns for workshops…so far we've got her woodcarving, a candlemaker from Brough, and someone who blows glass all setting up their shops." That had been the craic from last Monday's lunch, anyway. "They'll be paying rent to us, so that should help with the finances. And then we're planning a gift shop and tea room, but I think they'll take a little longer, with the planning permissions and things. Althea's in charge of those, along with Poppy."

They'd cleaned out the old dairy, and there had been workmen coming and going, but Olivia had been too busy to look into it. "I'm hoping we can have an adventure playground, but the finances aren't quite there yet." When she'd shown the brochure of rustic wooden playscapes to

Althea, her sister had nearly hit the roof, which was saying something considering they lived in a four-storey castle.

"Eighty *thousand* pounds for a bit of wood and rubber? Are you serious, Olivia?"

"They're good quality, and a playground, a proper one, would be such a draw for families. They could make a day of it. It could go in the meadow on the other side of the river—"

Althea had just shaken her head, but Olivia wasn't ready to give up on the idea quite yet. She'd try again when her sister was in a better mood.

"It sounds like you've all been working hard," Sam said, startling her out of her thoughts. He sounded both impressed and surprised.

"We have." It had all been happening so gradually, that Olivia hadn't realised until she'd said it out loud just how much work they'd all done. It still felt like early stages, but it was actually coming together—the café, the workshops, even the website. Seph had been in charge of that; somewhat to Olivia's surprise, her younger sister was a dab hand with tech. "And the garden is coming along, too. We've dredged the pond and trimmed the hedges out front and completely weeded the walled garden—repointed the paths, and repaired the trellises…and Will is making a waterfall in the river, to flow into the pool where we used to swim—do you remember?"

"Who's Will?"

"Oh, just a local landscaper we've hired," Olivia said

quickly, and then, for some reason, felt guilty for the "just". She'd come to know Will pretty well these last few weeks, especially after that day, a week ago now, when he'd brought Jake to work. She hadn't managed to get to the bottom of Jake's stomach troubles, but she felt she'd gained the boy's affection and maybe even his trust, and that had made her glad.

"Well, it does sound…interesting."

"You almost sound as if you don't want it to be." Olivia did her best to inject a teasing note into her voice. Clearly something was going on with her brother, but she wasn't sure what it was.

"No, that's not it at all," Sam said quickly. "It's just…it's a big commitment, isn't it? To come back to Casterglass and make a proper go of it?"

"Well, it doesn't have to be. You could commit to the summer, and then if you decide it's really not for you, we'll get someone else to run the glamping and outdoor activity things. You don't have to be frogmarched into it, Sam." She paused. "No one wants you here under duress. Have you spoken to Althea about how you're feeling? Or better yet, Mum and Dad?"

"Mum and Dad?" Sam snorted. "You know it's impossible to have a straightforward conversation with either of them."

"It isn't." Olivia felt fiercely loyal to both her parents— yes, they were scatty, disorganised, and eccentric, but they were lovely, they meant well, and she had absolutely no doubt that they loved all four of their children to absolute bits. Still, she appreciated that their vague ways could be aggravating to someone as goal-oriented as Sam. "Have you booked your flight?" she asked, and a second's silence was all the answer she needed.

"I haven't yet," Sam hedged. "But I'm going to. It's just…things are a bit complicated here right now."

A few minutes later, they'd ended the call with her having no clearer idea as to what Sam was really thinking or feeling. How could things be complicated in New Zealand?

"I HAVE A good feeling about this."

"I know you do," Olivia told Will with a laugh. They were getting into his truck, Piper in the back as usual, to drive across from Casterglass to Cartmel, to visit a reclamation yard. Will had seen on the yard's website that they had some paving stones of golden York stone that would be perfect for a path down to the river, and he'd wanted to see them in person before making the substantial purchase. Amazingly, Olivia had said there was a budget for the stones, although Will wasn't sure where it had come from. He still didn't get the family dynamic around money, and he didn't feel it was his place to ask…even if he felt as if he were getting to know Olivia better, and getting closer to her, every day.

"A good feeling about what?" Olivia asked teasingly. "The paving stones, or the fact that you're getting a day off hauling rocks?"

He grinned, grateful for the camaraderie that had sprung up between them over the last few weeks. "Both, actually." He'd spent the last few days hauling rocks from around the estate to the river, in order to build up the bed, and his back was aching from the effort. But the result, he hoped, would be fantastic—a proper waterfall spilling into a perfectly pristine pool, and then flowing out to the sea.

"It is nice to have a day off," Olivia agreed as she glanced out the window. They were bumping down Casterglass's drive before heading out to the A road and across to Cartmel. It was a beautiful day, with hazy blue skies, fleecy white clouds, and the promise of the spring in the air. The promise of possibility, although of what Will didn't exactly know or want to think too deeply about.

All he knew was that he was enjoying driving along a sunny road on a spring day, with a pretty woman sitting beside him and his dog in the back. Simple pleasures. Good ones. That was enough.

"Is there anything else you want to look at, besides the stones?" he asked as they drove along. They had decided to make a day of it—the reclamation yard had a café as well as an antiques sale room and a yard full of garden items—benches, bird tables, troughs, urns, and much else besides.

"I don't know. I'll see what takes my fancy. I can't remember the last time I went shopping. A day out in Cartmel feels quite exciting."

"You know the paving stones are a bit pricey?" he asked hesitantly, because he always hated talking about money. "A hundred quid each, I think."

"Yes, I know." She gave him another glinting smile. "My father sold a painting in the upper gallery—an oil by a student of Rembrandt. Too bad it wasn't by Rembrandt himself, but it turned out to be a couple thousand pounds, and not just a tenner, after all. He gave me the money for the garden."

"Tit for tat," Will surmised. He was still wondering why there wasn't a proper budget for a major part of the estate's renovation.

"Something like that. Althea's counting every penny at the moment. Everything's more expensive than you think it is, isn't it?"

Will thought of his own house, bought as a fixer-upper two years ago and still very much of one. "Yes, I'd say so," he agreed.

"She'd also had to allocate money for the glamping site—we can't find a few yurts up in the attics, unfortunately, the way we've been able to find all sorts in the barns."

"I wouldn't be surprised if there were a few yurts up there," Will only half joked. He'd been amazed at the treasure trove the nooks and crannies of the estate had offered up—timber stacked neatly in an old barn, perfect for the bridge they were going to build, and bricks and stones to build up beds and borders. Just yesterday Olivia had found some lovely slates she was hoping to use as hand-painted signs to the various parts of the garden.

"Well, we've looked," Olivia told him, "and sadly there aren't. My mother actually thought her father might have brought one back from one of his digs in the Middle East, back in the 1950s, but alas—no luck."

"Your grandfather was an archaeologist?"

"Apparently, although I never met him. But my mother had a most unusual upbringing, which might account for at least some of her eccentricity. Her mother died when she was young and her father took her all over the world."

Will had come across Violet Penryn a few times in the last few weeks, and had been bemused at how pleasantly vague she'd been, wandering through the gardens as if she'd never seen them before and conversationally murmuring things like "Hemlock...very good for aching joints, or if you wanted to kill someone."

Will had stammered his agreement, caught between laughter and horror. Violet had given him a wide-eyed look of perfect innocence. "And tansy is quite useful as well, in that regard. It comes from the Greek, 'athanasia', which means immortality, but in fact it's quite, quite deadly. *Do* be careful."

"You do have an interesting family," he told Olivia. He'd taken quite a liking to her father, Walter, who had come out to observe their progress in the garden with twinkly-eyed benevolence, but he was still intimidated by twenty-two-year-old Seph, who had not lost her scowl, whenever she'd emerged from one of the barns she was turning into artisanal workshops with the help of her mate Doug, who was just as intimidating-looking, with his piercings and dreadlocks. Olivia, he'd thought more than once, seemed the most normal of the bunch.

THEY ARRIVED AT the reclamation yard a little after eleven, and spent a good hour browsing through the yard full of garden items. Olivia was quite taken with a Victorian bird table, until she saw the price tag of three thousand pounds and blanched.

"These are sweet, though," she said, nodding to several small sculptures of woodland creatures, in wrought iron. "A thousand pounds apiece, though! It gives me an idea..." She turned to him, her heart-shaped face alight. "What if we had Seph carve animals like these? You know she does carvings? We could hide them around the garden...a sort of mystery trail...with a treasure map to follow. You'd mentioned a treasure trail before—"

"Yes, although I didn't think of woodland animals," Will returned, smiling. "That sounds brilliant. You could draw the map yourself, even."

"Oh, I couldn't," Olivia protested, which was always her

instinctive reply.

"I think you could. Your sketches are amazing. Put them in watercolour, on proper paper, and you're away."

She nibbled her lip, her blue eyes wide, her lashes sweeping her cheeks, looking so lovely that Will had to stifle a groan. He looked away, as discomfited as ever by this very inconvenient attraction he felt at the most awkward times. Desire would suddenly swamp him, and it was a difficult job to keep it at bay, and his mind on the matter at hand. *Focus, Will. Focus.*

"Do you really think I could?" she asked, and he nodded, his gaze still averted, just in case.

"Yes, definitely. Shall we load the paving stones into the truck before having lunch?"

They'd just put the last stones into the back of the truck, and Will was looking forward to tucking into a large piece of steak and ale pie, when his mobile rang, and his stomach dropped when he saw it was the school's number.

Probably nothing, he told himself as he murmured an apology to Olivia and took the call. Probably just a reminder that tomorrow was a dress-down day or maybe that Jake had forgotten his PE kit yet again…

Except Will knew that the school didn't call about things like that. They sent an email, or a notification by text, or a handwritten note in one of the children's schoolbags. And sure enough, when the school secretary answered, it wasn't about anything as innocuous as that, just as he'd known it wouldn't be, because eighteen months on from Rachel's death he still knew, deep down, to expect the worst. To wait for it.

"I'm afraid Lally has had an accident," the secretary told him, her manner managing to be both brisk and sympathetic. "She lost consciousness for several seconds, and although she seems fairly well in herself now, Mrs Tabbard thinks she should go to A&E, just to be on the safe side. Can you collect her from school as soon as possible?"

"Yes—yes, of course." Will practically had to gasp out the words. His heart was racing. "Yes, I'll come right away."

Chapter Ten

"WILL." OLIVIA TOOK an instinctive step toward him, one hand stretched out. "Will, what is it?" Since answering his phone, his face had turned ashen, and sweat had broken out on his forehead. Now, as he ended the call, he looked at her blankly, as if he had forgotten how to string two words together. "What's happened?" she asked gently. "Is it one of the kids?"

"It's Lally." He gave his head a quick shake, as if to clear it. "She's had an accident at school—she's hit her head." He drew a breath that was decidedly unsteady. "She blacked out for a few seconds, and they want me to take her to A&E..." His voice cracked then, and Olivia put her hand on his arm, although what she really longed to do was give him a hug.

"Oh, Will. I'm so sorry."

"Sorry, I know I'm overreacting." He scrubbed his hands over his face. "It's probably fine. It *is* fine. It's just...memories, you know? It's like a Pavlovian reaction. I start to panic."

She felt a rush of compassion for him; although he was

trying to get hold of himself, she could see how shaken he still looked, and really, it was no wonder. "Do you need to collect her now?"

"Yes…right away. I'm sorry, I won't have time to take you back to Casterglass…" He looked blank again, as if he didn't know what to do next.

"Of course you won't," Olivia agreed. "If you need to go to the A&E, I suppose you'll go to Barrow?"

He nodded jerkily. "Yes, that's where…that's where…"

Where Rachel had had her treatment, Olivia supposed. Perhaps even where she had died. "That's a good hour away," she said, surprised at how calm she sounded. She, who could be so cautious and timid, almost sounded as if she were in control. "You won't want to take Jake along with you. Why don't I pick him up from school and take him back to yours?"

Will looked at her with a sort of yearning incredulity, as if he couldn't believe she would offer such a thing. "You'd…you'd do that?"

"Of course," Olivia said, as if it were obvious, which to her, it was. "Jake already knows me. Do you think he'll mind?"

"No—that is…no." Will shook his head. "I'm sure he'll be glad not to be dragged along. But are you sure? You know how A&Es can get. We might be hours."

"All the more reason for me to stay, then," Olivia replied. "Of course I'm sure."

"Thank you," he said, sounding heartfelt, a little hoarse. "Thank you—"

"Honestly, it's no problem. Now we'd best get going."

They didn't talk much as they drove back towards Boot, near where Lally and Jake's school was. As they wound their way along the single-track lanes, Olivia was struck afresh at how remote this area was, even more remote than Casterglass, if that could be believed. The barren fells swept endlessly in every direction, punctuated only, very occasionally, by a lone house of grey Lakeland stone that huddled against the hillside, looking windswept and forlorn.

"You chose to do the whole rural thing in spades," she joked, and Will grimaced in response.

"Yeah, that was a bit more Rachel's dream than mine. She had this whole thing about sustainable living that obviously didn't work out."

He fell silent and so did she, because what could you say to that?

The primary school was as remote and isolated as everything else, a single Victorian building built against a hillside, with nothing else in sight. It made Casterglass village, with its little primary, seem like a booming metropolis in comparison.

Olivia waited in the car while Will went in to fetch Lally and Jake. A few minutes later he came out holding a tiny elfin girl by the hand; she had a head of dark curls and eyes like chocolate buttons. She was, Olivia thought, with a rush of affection, adorable. Jake sloped behind them, looking scruffy and a little sullen, although his suspicious look brightened into something almost like cheerfulness when he saw Olivia.

"Dad didn't say you were here," he said as he opened the rear door and flung his backpack in with vigour.

"Didn't he?"

"Sorry, no time," Will told her. He opened the other door and helped Lally into her car seat. She gave Olivia a bright-eyed look of curiosity that made her think her injury couldn't be too bad.

"I hurt my head," she announced somewhat triumphantly. "Right here." She pointed to her temple; Olivia saw a purplish bruise blooming there.

"That must have been pretty scary."

"It was *very* scary," Lally replied solemnly, and then sat back, sticking her thumb in her mouth as she regarded Olivia with wide-eyed speculation.

"Lalls, your thumb," Will said, half-heartedly, for now was surely not the time to have that battle. He climbed wearily into the driver's seat. "Right, I'll drop you guys off at home, and then I'll take Lally to hospital. Do you mind having Piper, as well?"

"No, of course not." Olivia glanced back at the black Lab who was standing in the truck bed, a faithful sentry. "It's fine."

A few minutes later they bumped down a long dirt track

winding through empty meadows before pulling up to a small, stone cottage, its sloping roof nearly touching the ground, its back against a muddy hill. The view was both beautiful and bleak, without another dwelling or soul in sight.

"Sorry, I haven't tidied up," Will muttered as he helped Lally out of the car and then went to unlock the front door.

"Daddy never tidies up," Lally confided, and Olivia smiled at that before stepping into a dim, cluttered hallway; a heap of welly boots were piled in the hall, and several coats were flung over the banister of the narrow staircase that ran along one wall.

"Right, Lally, we should get going," Will said with a jangle of his keys. He sounded both exhausted and anxious, and Olivia's heart went out to him. She was starting to get a glimpse of how demanding the life of a single parent had to be.

"We'll be fine here," she assured him, as she glanced around for Jake, and saw him disappear into what looked like a similarly cluttered kitchen. "Don't worry about us."

"Thanks," Will said, meeting her gaze with one of those intent looks that made Olivia's heart flip-flop in her chest. She had to stop reacting like that, but now was not the time to worry about it. She just wanted to be helpful.

"Will you be here when I get back?" Lally asked, taking her thumb from her mouth.

"I should think so."

"Good," she said, and stuck her thumb back in. Olivia was glad she'd so seemingly easily won the little girl's approval.

"Thank you again," Will said and Olivia shooed him off with a smile.

"Go."

Once he had, she picked her way through the clutter to the kitchen, which was, as she'd suspected, just as messy. The breakfast dishes were still on the table, including half a pint of milk that had probably gone off by now. Jake, standing by the fridge, looked unfazed by the mess. Piper had flung himself down on a ratty old blanket in front of a clanking Rayburn.

"Can I have a snack?"

"Yes, of course. Have you had your lunch at school?" It was only a little after one, and Olivia's stomach rumbled. She realised they'd missed out on their scrummy lunch at the café in Cartmel.

"Yes, we ate a while ago, but I'm still hungry."

"All right, then. How about some cheese and crackers?" Jake made a face. "Fruit?"

"Nutella toast?" Jake asked hopefully, and Olivia hesitated before deciding with his sister heading to A&E it might be a Nutella toast sort of day. She found half a loaf of bread in the bread bin and put three slices in the toaster—two for Jake and one for her, because she *was* hungry, and Nutella toast did sound rather tasty.

While she waited for the toast to pop she started tidying the kitchen, throwing out the milk and putting the dishes in the dishwasher; she'd just finished loading it up when Jake helpfully informed her it was broken.

"Dad keeps saying he'll fix it but he hasn't yet."

"Ah, I see," Olivia answered, and then started taking the dishes out again, before the toast sprang up and she slathered the slices thickly with Nutella, much to Jake's appreciation.

She took a seat opposite him as they ate their toast, Jake munching happily enough for a few minutes, or so Olivia thought, until he suddenly asked, "Is Lally going to die?"

"What?" Olivia practically spat out her toast. In fact, she did spray a few crumbs. "No, Jake, of course—" She stopped, started again. "She just hit her head," she said more gently. "And needs to get it checked out. But she's going to be fine." As she said the words, she prayed they were true; what if poor little Lally had some kind of concussion that manifested itself later on? But, no. She couldn't think like that. Although she could, she realised, understand why Jake was.

"She'll be fine," she said again, more firmly.

Jake shrugged, as if it didn't matter much to him either way, although Olivia knew it did. "I was just wondering."

"Well, you don't need to wonder about that," Olivia stated. "Your dad's taking her to hospital to get her checked out, just to be safe."

Jake nodded slowly and started on his second piece of

toast. After a few more minutes, he asked hopefully, "Can I watch CBBC?"

Olivia decided half an hour of telly wouldn't go amiss and she set Jake up in the small sitting room off the kitchen, which would have been cosy if it hadn't been such a mess. Papers everywhere, and a ratty old carpet covered in dog hair that desperately needed hoovering. Yet the room itself was sweet—one whole wall was taken up with a fireplace, and the matching leather sofas looked just the right amount of squashy.

This little cottage could be a lovely home, Olivia reflected as she washed the dishes by hand and then hunted through cupboards, trying to discover where they were put away. With a little tidy and yes, a bit of renovation, it could be a cosy spot, indeed. Right now, however, the whole place seemed to echo with the absence of a mother's love and care—from the pile of dirty washing left by the machine, and looked to have been there for some time, to the grease stains spattering the stove and the mud on the floor.

Olivia ached to give everything a good clean, but she was also conscious she didn't want to overstep. Would it be presumptuous, or seem censorious, to tidy everything up while he was away? And yet it seemed lazy and thoughtless not to do anything.

In the end, while Jake was watching *Horrible Histories*, she decided she could at least clean the kitchen. It wasn't as if she'd been poking through private things if she did that. And there was something innately, immensely satisfying about cleaning—scrubbing the mud off the floor, the grease from the stove, tidying away the packets of cereal and pasta that had been left on the counter…

That led to putting the wash in—because how could she not—which somehow led to organising the welly boots and returning the coats to the hall cupboard. Then she saw there was a load of washing hanging on the rack above the stove in the kitchen, and she supposed it was no great trouble to take it down and fold it.

"Do you want to help me put the washing away?" she asked Jake when he ventured into the kitchen after *Horrible Histories*, hoping for another snack.

"Do I have to?"

"Well, I don't know where anything goes."

"I don't, either."

She smiled, her hands planted on her hips. "I bet you know more than me."

Jake looked dubious, but then he shrugged and nodded. "Okay."

All right, she *was* curious, Olivia had to admit to herself as she followed Jake up the stairs to the bedrooms—a master and two small singles, and a further double bedroom that had clearly become a repository for junk. Now she was just being nosy, she knew as Jake pointed out Lally's room—a bed decked with pink netting and fairy lights and toys and clothes all over the floor. Olivia found the requisite drawers and put the clothes away before moving on to Jake's room, which was just as messy, and then Will's.

She paused in the doorway, conscious at just how invasive she was being, knowing she wouldn't hunt through his drawers the way she had with the children's. That, surely, was a step too far. She left his clothes neatly piled on top of the rumpled duvet, intending to leave again quickly but she couldn't keep herself from a quick scan around the room, her gaze snagging on the wedding photo on his bedside table. His wife was like a grown-up version of Lally—wild dark hair, laughing eyes, a generous figure and an even more generous smile. She looked like someone who was fun and full of life, and yet she was dead.

Olivia stepped closer to the photo. His wife had tilted her head to look up at him, and Will was smiling down, looking wry and a little self-deprecating. They looked, she thought with a pang, deeply in love.

I want that, she thought with a ferocity that felt painful. *I wanted that with Matt. I could let myself want it with Will. I just want it with somebody.*

"Olivia?"

She jumped; Jake was standing in the doorway, looking at her uncertainly.

"Sorry, I was just putting the clothes away. Shall we go back downstairs? I thought I saw a backgammon board in the sitting room—shall we play?"

"I don't know how to play."

"You don't?" Olivia raised her eyebrows. "Why don't I teach you?"

Jake looked surprised, then suspicious, then pleased. Olivia recognised the emotions flashing across his face because she'd felt them herself at his age; the progression of responses from a naturally shy child.

"Okay," he said, somewhat doubtfully, and with another encouraging smile, Olivia headed downstairs with Jake in tow.

Soon enough they were ensconced in the sitting room at the backgammon board. Olivia had played with Sam plenty—and usually won; backgammon was her secret weapon—and she enjoyed teaching Jake, who absorbed the rules with a rather adorable concentration.

As the sky grew grey, a chill entered the room and so Olivia made a fire in the fireplace, finding kindling and paper piled haphazardly by it, and logs outside. It was cheery, sitting in the room, rolling dice and moving their markers as the fire crackled and blazed.

I want this, Olivia couldn't keep from thinking again, with an even deeper longing. *I want this every day.* All her life she'd longed for a family of her own—she'd been obsessive about her baby dolls; she'd turned the crayons in her pencil case into a little family. Black and white had been the parents, blue and green the siblings, pink the baby. She'd even done it with the seedlings she'd nurtured while working at the garden centre, talking to them as if they were, embarrassingly, her children. Occasionally she'd been overheard; it had become something of a joke among her colleagues. But now she felt it deep inside, that old yearning coming alive again.

She'd done her best to squelch it after the disaster of Matt; it had been a sort of punishment, not to let herself think about children of her own, or dreaming of having a family one day. And it had been torture, because she was thirty-six and not getting any younger. If she wanted to have children, it was going to have to be soon.

Yet here she was, curled up on a sofa, pondering her next move in backgammon while an adorable eight-year-old studied the board and a fire blazed merrily. What more could she want?

Well, the man, obviously...

But she wasn't going to let herself think about that. Him.

She trounced Jake once, let him win once, and beat him just by a hair on the last—a technique her father had used on occasion, to build resilience and offer encouragement—and then, as it was after four and she hadn't heard from Will, she decided she might as well make dinner.

"Do you cook?" Jake asked baldly as she prowled around the kitchen, taking stock of the pantry contents.

"As a matter of fact, I do," Olivia replied. "Do you eat?"

"Yes." He sounded fervent.

"What do you like?"

"Spaghetti bolognaise is my favourite." A pause, and then

more quietly, "My mum used to make it."

She didn't want to venture into that territory, Olivia realised, at least not quite yet. "What about macaroni and cheese?" she asked. There was a block of cheddar in the fridge that didn't look too old, and plenty of dried pasta. "And sausages—I saw some in the freezer."

"Okay." Jake had adopted that nonplussed tone Olivia suspected hid a depth of feeling he was afraid to show.

She chatted to him as she set about making dinner—chopping an onion, grating cheese, making the white sauce and boiling the pasta.

"That smells *good*," Jake declared with a longing look at the Le Creuset pot with its bubbling, golden-crusted macaroni, or rather, fusilli, because there hadn't actually been any macaroni.

"Twenty minutes in the oven," Olivia told him cheerfully. "Hopefully your dad and sister will be back then." It was now nearly half five, and she still hadn't had a text, but the mobile reception clearly wasn't reliable, so she wasn't *too* worried. Yet. "Shall we lay the table for four?"

Jake nodded, and Olivia got out the colourful, mismatched pottery plates as well as knives and forks. She was just laying the last place when she heard the sound of a car, and then the front door opening and closing. For some silly reason her heart leapt up into her throat as she heard Will's familiar, rumbly voice.

"We're home!"

Chapter Eleven

A S WILL OPENED the front door, the smell assailed him—the comforting scents of woodsmoke and sausages, overlaid with the piney tang of laundry detergent. The smell of home, or rather *a* home, the kind of home he remembered. He stood in the doorway for a moment, breathing it in, and a single word coalesced in his mind, took over his heart. *Rachel.*

Lally must have been feeling something of what he felt, even if she couldn't have articulated it, for she raced from the hall into the kitchen without even taking off her coat. Will followed, dumbly, and it wasn't until he reached the kitchen doorway that he realised some elemental part of him had been expecting to see Rachel there at the Rayburn, exasperatedly nudging Piper aside, her laughing eyes meeting his across the room.

He must have looked stricken, or something close to it, for as Olivia turned from the stove her eyes widened and the smile slid from her face.

"Is Lally okay?"

"I'm *fine!*" Lally exclaimed, running past him while Will simply stared. "I don't have a con—con—"

"Concussion?" Olivia filled in with a smile. "I'm so glad." She glanced again at Will, everything about her uncertain. He needed to stop standing there like a complete lemon. "I made supper… I hope that was okay."

"Um, yeah." He found he had to clear his throat. "Thank you so much."

Lally had, perhaps in response to that comforting smell and the memory it had awakened within her, run straight at Olivia and thrown her arms around her waist. "I got a lollipop," she announced and Olivia smiled and hugged her back.

"Wow, aren't you lucky."

Slowly Will shed his coat. He was still adjusting to seeing Olivia there, moving around his kitchen, taking a pot of something bubbling and golden out of the Rayburn. Piper lumbered up to sniff hopefully.

"I learned backgammon," Jake told him. "And I won, too."

"Only once," Olivia reminded him with a little laugh. "Right now I'm the reigning backgammon champion, remember."

"Let's play again after dinner," Jake said quickly, and Olivia's questioning gaze slid to Will and then back again.

"That sounds fun," she said, and put the casserole dish on the table.

They continued to banter good-naturedly about back-gammon as she went to the fridge to get the milk, flipping her plait over one shoulder. She'd got the measure of Jake, Will realised; she wasn't coddling him, but taking him seriously. It was what he needed—stern but good-humoured. He was grateful she seemed to understand without even trying.

"Shall we eat?" Olivia asked, and Will was startled out of his brief reverie. Lally and Jake had already sat down, and Olivia was sitting at one end of the table, where Rachel used to sit.

"Um," Will said.

"That's where Mummy used to sit," Lally said matter-of-factly, and Olivia looked stricken.

"Oh! I'm so sorry! I'll…" She glanced around wildly for a second before she started to move her plate and cutlery to the seat next to Lally.

"It's all right," Will said, knowing he should have spoken more quickly. "Of course it's all right. Stay there."

"No, it's fine," she murmured, blushing, and she quickly moved over, giving Lally the approximation of a bright smile. "I wanted to sit next to you, anyway."

Lally beamed. Will felt a welter of emotions—exasperation at himself, for making it so awkward; gratitude to Olivia, for making it easier; and grief, because he missed Rachel now more than ever, and yet he didn't want Olivia to go, far from it.

Yet it was painful, he realised, to have Olivia dish out the macaroni while he did the sausages; it hurt to watch her cut up Lally's sausage for her, smiling at her as she did it. She listened with seeming interest to Jake list the top ten most contagious diseases and didn't even blink when he confided that infectious diarrhoea killed more people than malaria.

"Really, I had no idea," she said, wide-eyed, and Will gave Jake a quelling look. Really, they had to get into poo facts before they'd even finished their dinner?

"Infectious diarrhoea is caused by either bacteria or parasites," Jake continued, undeterred by Will's stern look. "And some of the parasites are *really* gross. Like with a tapeworm, it can grow to—"

"Jake." Will laid his hand over his son's. "Let's not talk about that kind of thing while we're eating, eh?"

Jake gave him a wounded look. "Olivia thought it was interesting."

"Maybe later, okay?" Olivia said quickly. "I'm not sure I can handle hearing about parasites while I'm eating pasta that looks like a lot of worms." She gave him a conspiratorial smile and Jake grinned back, delighted.

The rest of the meal passed without any further disgusting discussions, but Will couldn't shake the weird, wrong-footed sensation he had, like he'd walked into someone else's life, and he didn't know how to feel about it. Jake and Lally both cleared their plates without asking, something they didn't usually do, and Olivia went to the sink without saying anything and began to fill it up with hot water.

"Jake told me the dishwasher was broken," she told him with a laughing look, "after I'd filled it up."

"Oh…" Belatedly, *way* too belatedly, he realised how clean the house was. She must have been sweeping and scrubbing all afternoon. "Thank you for tidying up. You didn't…"

"She even mopped the floor," Jake volunteered. "The water was *so* dirty."

"I thought you were watching *Horrible Histories*," Olivia told him, and he shrugged.

"I noticed."

Lally tugged on the hem of Olivia's jumper. "Will you give me my bath?" she asked.

"Lally," Will protested, embarrassed at how needy and pathetic they must all seem, so unbearably eager for her to fill the yawning place in their lives, but Olivia just smiled.

"I'd be happy to, unless your daddy wants to do it?"

"I don't mind," he muttered, and Lally took Olivia by the hand to lead her upstairs while Will finished cleaning the kitchen.

"She's nice," Jake told him, a pronouncement, before he sloped off to the sitting room, no doubt to pore over more facts in his encyclopaedia of disgusting ones.

Yes, Will thought, she was nice. *Too* nice. It would be all too easy to take advantage, to ask for more, to expect it, even. It felt so good to have a clean kitchen, a nice meal, a woman he could hear humming upstairs as the water ran. He missed it all. He missed it all so very much.

He'd just finished cleaning the kitchen when Lally ran downstairs, dressed in her pyjamas, dressing gown, and smelling of strawberry shampoo. Her hair, usually in a bird's nest of damp tangles after her bath, had already been neatly brushed. He felt an ache in his heart, like a physical pain.

"Olivia's going to read me *three* stories," she said, and he glanced up from his daughter to see Olivia coming into the kitchen, ducking her head.

"If that's okay?"

"It's great, but…" He trailed off, unsure what he was trying to say. *You don't have to? Don't let my kids love you and then walk away?* Never mind *him*. The possibility, unlikely as it surely was, still jolted him. He knew he wasn't ready to love anyone other than Rachel yet, but even so…

Olivia looked so lovely, her cheeks rosy from the heat of Lally's bath, her hair escaping from her plait and curling in tendrils around her face. He felt an entirely different sort of ache.

"But…?" Olivia prompted, and he realised he'd been staring. Again.

"But you don't have to," he half mumbled, looking away, embarrassed by the nature of his own thoughts.

"I really don't mind."

And so Lally was tugging on Olivia's hand to go back upstairs, and Will listened to her light, laughing voice as he chivvied Jake into the shower and fed Piper and, realising what an absolute tip the sitting room was, did his best to clean it.

By the time Olivia came down again, Jake was already in his own bed, tucked up with his encyclopaedia, and the downstairs—thanks mostly to Olivia—was no longer in a frightful state. There was something inherently peaceful about a tidy house, Will reflected, the lighting dim, the downstairs quiet.

"Lally's ready for you to say goodnight," she said, and he murmured his thanks before heading upstairs.

"Olivia read me *four* stories," Lally told him as she sat tucked up in bed, ready for his kiss.

"Aren't you lucky." He pressed his lips to her forehead.

"Can Olivia come again?" Lally asked as she snuggled down into bed. "Can she read me stories every night?"

"I'm not sure about every night," Will murmured, before he listened to Lally say her prayers, kissed her again, and then tucked Jake in and turned out his light. By the time he headed downstairs, it was eight o'clock and Olivia was standing in the middle of the kitchen as if she didn't know where to go.

That's when it hit him. She was waiting to go *home*. Somehow, in the midst of all the family atmosphere, he'd managed to forget that she didn't live here, that she didn't have her car, that he needed to drive her back to Casterglass. He was an *idiot*.

"I'm so sorry," he managed. "I completely forgot…you need a lift home."

"Oh." Olivia looked startled. "Well…"

"I should have driven you back at five," he fretted as the enormity of the problem consumed him. He couldn't drive her back now; the kids were already in bed. "I could ask my neighbour," he offered fairly dubiously. "She lives a few miles away…" And he didn't know her that well, and she didn't seem to particularly like children.

"There's no need to go to so much trouble," Olivia said quickly. A blush had tinted her cheeks rosy pink. "That is, I don't mind staying the night. I saw you had a double bed under all those boxes upstairs. If you don't mind? Otherwise I can call a taxi."

As if he'd allow her to go home in a taxi! "I don't think taxis come all the way out here," he told her wryly. "I'm happy for you to stay if you are."

She ducked her head, blushing all the more. "I don't mind."

And neither, Will realised, did he. Yes, he was still feeling a confusing welter of emotions, but among the complicated tangle was a definite frisson of pleasure. "Well, if you're staying," he heard himself saying as if his voice was coming from outside of his body, "why don't we open a bottle of wine?"

Wait, what?

"Oh, all right," Olivia replied hesitantly. "That would be

nice."

"Especially after a day like today." He retrieved a dusty bottle of red from the pantry and a corkscrew from the drawer. Suddenly he was a sommelier, uncorking the bottle with a flourish and reaching for two wine glasses that only needed a *little* dusting. Lately he'd been more of a tumbler-of-whisky sort of man.

He led the way into the sitting room; he'd stoked the fire earlier and the room was both cheerful and cosy. Intimate, too, with the only light coming from a table lamp and the fire. Almost romantic.

No, he could *not* think that way. He shouldn't even want to.

"Here you are," he said as he poured her a glass and handed it to her. "Thank you for all your help today."

"I enjoyed it," Olivia told him. "I love being with kids."

"You're certainly a natural."

She smiled and said nothing, burying her nose in her glass, and belatedly Will wondered if that was a sore point. She was, he knew, thirty-six. Had she wanted children? Did she still?

"Anyway, Lally's head seems better?" she asked.

"Yes, it was just a bump, thank goodness." He remembered his blind panic of earlier in the day and couldn't help but wince. "Sorry for the overreaction on my part."

"Better to be safe than sorry," Olivia replied. "And anyway, it's understandable, isn't it, considering what you've already experienced?" She spoke matter-of-factly, which he found he appreciated. No pity, no tiptoeing around, just simple, stated truth. He wished more people were capable of it.

"Yes, I suppose it is," he answered. "I think that's why Jake has become rather obsessed with various illnesses—he had a first-row seat to Rachel's cancer."

In the four weeks since they'd started working together, he hadn't really talked about Rachel. In fact, he realised, he hadn't talked about her at all, and he saw that in the slight widening of Olivia's eyes.

"It must have been so hard," she said quietly. "And that's obviously an understatement. But there aren't really any words, are there?" She shook her head with a grimace of apology. "At least none that I can think of, except perhaps 'I'm so sorry'."

"Yes, you're right." He felt the need to clear his throat again, but took a sip of wine instead. "There are no words."

"Did you have anyone to help? One afternoon in and I'm appreciating how difficult it must be, being a single parent. And when Rachel was sick…"

"It was tough." Rachel had been diagnosed so soon after they'd moved that they hadn't known anyone well enough to help out. His parents had come for a little while, so he could attend her chemo appointments with her, and they'd been there at the end, when he'd brought Rachel back for home hospice care. He recalled them tiptoeing around the house, telling Jake and Lally to hush, while he'd sat next to Rachel's bed, holding her limp hand and watching the life slowly ebb from her body as her breaths came slower and slower. Not a great memory.

"And what about after?" Olivia asked gently.

Will cast his mind back to those blurry, pain-filled days after Rachel's death. All he had to hold on to were some vague impressions, an exhausted incredulity, and snapshots of painful moments—Lally, not yet four, hitting and kicking him as she sobbed she wanted her mummy. Jake standing by the window in a black suit—Rachel's mother had insisted he attend the funeral—looking stoic and withdrawn. Will himself, aching, empty, feeling lost and tired and angry, wanting to get drunk yet knowing he couldn't.

"I'm not sure I really know the answer to that," he confessed. "Rachel's family is a bit of a mess—her parents divorced when she was young. Her mother married twice more and her dad vacated the scene. So that was already quite complicated." He sighed, and Olivia nodded, encouraging him to continue. "And my family…" Where to begin with his family, with the pain he still felt? "We were always close," he said, and felt his throat tightening.

"That was why I didn't want to move up here, actually." Had he even told her that before? How he'd come up here more or less kicking and screaming? "They were in Norfolk, and so was my sister, Kerry. I loved having everyone nearby, and they were devoted grandparents." His throat was, alarmingly, getting even tighter. "But Rachel was so set on Cumbria…and I could see her point; we'd never afford a house, a proper house in Norfolk…" He sighed again, and then tugged his collar, as if that could help with his throat. It didn't.

"So I agreed, and my parents took the opportunity to move to the Algarve…something they'd always been wanting to do, apparently." Not that he'd known. "And my sister decided to emigrate to Australia. Everyone living their best lives now, everyone that is, but…" He found he couldn't go on. His vision was blurring; he took a slug of wine although alcohol was probably the last thing he needed right now.

"I'm so sorry…" Olivia said, which was surely the cue for him to stop, yet somehow he couldn't. He hadn't told anyone this stuff; he hadn't had anyone to tell it to, since moving up to bloody Cumbria.

"So there was no one to help when Rachel died, really. No one wanted to travel all the way up here… Rachel's mum insisted she be buried in Norfolk, said she would have wanted that, since she'd never even got to know anyone up here…which might have been true, I don't even know. And my parents came home for the funeral. They were good with that, very supportive while they were home, but they left after two weeks and seemed to think that was ample time… I don't know, I felt like I was barely able to breathe at that point." His voice had turned ragged, way too ragged. He drank more wine. "So we ended up coming back up here, because it felt like I had nowhere to go. I had mates back in Norfolk, but they all felt young and I'd suddenly turned old." He drew an unsteady breath. "And my family was gone, my business, such as it was, was up here...and Jake actually liked school, and Lally was in preschool... I didn't have the energy to uproot them and it felt like there was nothing to go back to..."

With a strange sort of removed horror, he realised there were tears streaking down his face. He was *crying*. He hadn't cried in front of another person since Rachel had died. Oh, he'd had a bit of a weep on his own, but it had felt self-indulgent, with the children just upstairs, and pathetic and lonely, with no one to comfort him. But even knowing that, he knew, he absolutely knew, he didn't want to cry in front of Olivia.

And yet he was.

"Oh, Will." Her voice was gentle, filled with compassion rather than pity, and somehow she was putting her arms around him and drawing him to her so his head was on her shoulder, her hand in his hair, and it felt so *good*, but it felt so wrong as well, humiliating, emasculating, ridiculous... He was *sobbing*. He could hear himself; the sounds were guttural, ugly. What was happening to him? Why couldn't he stop?

And yet he couldn't; he kept crying, and Olivia kept holding him, and there was something so cleansing about it, but, he realised after what he hoped was only a few minutes, something so utterly mortifying, as well. He had just made a complete and utter *prat* of himself, crying like a baby. How could he ever look Olivia in the eye again? And yet, he realised even as he started to ease back, dreading to look her in the face, he found he couldn't entirely regret it.

Could he?

Chapter Twelve

OLIVIA KNEW FROM the moment Will started to withdraw from her arms that he was, deeply and completely, regretting his momentary weakness. And yet she couldn't regret it, or the intimacy she'd felt when she'd held him in her arms; she had tears in her own eyes, simply from witnessing his pain, and if she could have, she would have put her arms around him yet again and drawn him towards her, but she knew from the look of stony misery on his face, the way he was already angling his body away from hers, that that was the last thing he wanted. But oh, she ached to hold him, to comfort him, *to love him.*

Down, girl. She couldn't go full bore *quite* yet, surely.

Will glugged the last of his wine, his gaze determinedly averted. "Sorry about that," he managed, trying for a jokey tone and failing. "I don't know what came over me. It's been a tough day, I guess, and I'm really tired." He tried for a laugh that came out more like a cough as he wiped his eyes. His face was blotchy; he'd been properly crying, his body shaking as Olivia had held him. She could still remember exactly how he'd felt in her arms, the solidness of his body, the woodsmoke smell of his hair.

She hesitated, wishing she knew what to say, or maybe just that she had the courage to say it. "You don't have to apologise, Will," she managed quietly. "At all."

"Well." He tugged at his collar, then dropped his hand. He still wasn't looking at her. "That was the last kind of thing you needed right now, I'm sure."

"I didn't mind." He shook his head as if to negate that sentiment, and Olivia fell silent. When it came to moments like these, to actually putting your heart on the line just a little bit, she was a complete coward and she knew it.

A silence stretched between them, the only sound the crackling of the fire. Will was staring off into the middle distance as if he couldn't bear to look at her, and now Olivia felt as if she were the one who could now cry. *Don't ruin it*, she wanted to tell him, *just because you've shown me you can be weak. It's okay to be weak—goodness knows, I am.*

But she didn't dare say any of that, because she doubted Will wanted to hear it, and anyway did she have the right, considering her own unpleasantly sordid history? Did she even have the right to be here, pretending to be all about family when less than three months ago a woman had called her a homewrecker, and she'd been right?

Now Olivia was the one looking away, and still the silence stretched on, turned uncomfortable.

"I feel like a prat," Will said suddenly, and for some reason this made Olivia let out a startled laugh.

"Well, you shouldn't," she told him, trying to smile. "Would it help if I cried, too?"

He looked at her with a seriousness she hadn't expected. "Do you need to have a good cry?"

"Well." Incredibly, or maybe not so much, she felt tears rise simply at the question. "Maybe."

"What happened in York?" Will asked, startling her further with his perception, and alarming her, too.

"How do you know something happened?"

"The way you've spoken about it...it's a bit like...like you *had* to leave."

Okay, now there was a serious danger that she might actually bawl just as he had. Bawl and confess, which she definitely did not want to do. She couldn't bear for Will to think of her badly now, or ever, really. "Well, yes, I suppose I did," Olivia admitted. Her heart turned over in an unpleasant way, and her stomach swirled sickly. She didn't want to tell him anything more.

"A broken romance?" he guessed.

She swallowed hard. "Something like that."

"I'm sorry."

She nodded, not trusting herself to speak, but then managed stiffly, "It's nothing compared to what you've had to go through, though."

"That doesn't make it any easier for you."

"No." She wouldn't tell him the details. She couldn't.

She felt a sick mixture of embarrassment and shame, and she was afraid it was visible in her face, so she looked away, praying he wouldn't ask any more questions.

"I know it's hard to talk about these things," Will said with a wobbly little laugh. He wiped his eyes again. "Jeez, I'm a mess."

Olivia turned back to him, relieved it seemed he was going to leave it at that. "You're not. You've been holding it together, raising two children—"

"Yeah, and I'm not sure I'm doing too well at that. One is a hypochondriac—"

She couldn't help but smile. "It's a phase. I was the same at his age."

"Were you really?"

"Pretty much. I used to get stomach aches. Kept me from going to school. They were real, but they were caused by anxiety."

Will frowned. "What were you anxious about?"

"Oh, just you know, school. I had a horrendously stern teacher in Year Four." She paused, and Will didn't say anything, clearly waiting for more. "And, a bit like Jake, I was prone to worry. I've always been shy—sometimes, when I was younger, I felt invisible."

"I can't imagine you ever being invisible." His voice was low, thrumming with sincerity.

"Well, I was, in a way. I wasn't sporty or extroverted or anything like that. I didn't even want to be, but you don't win popularity points hiding in the greenhouse."

"But you learn to love gardening," Will surmised with a smile. "Do you think Jake is anxious?"

"I'd be surprised if he wasn't." She gazed at him squarely. "It hasn't been that long, and you've all experienced one of the most devastating losses a person can endure. It's okay not to be okay, you know. You don't have to bounce back."

He sighed. "I'm not expecting to bounce, exactly, but a little elasticity would go a long way right about now. It's been eighteen months."

"In the grand scheme of things, that is really not that long."

He leaned his head back against the sofa, a faint smile on his lips. "You sound very wise."

Olivia let out a huff of laughter. "Me?"

Will opened his eyes, looked at her directly in a way that made her heart flip. Her insides were doing all sorts of gymnastics today. "Yes, you." Another silence, this one different than before, full of a sudden, growing expectation. Or was she imagining that? "I miss her," Will said quietly. "So much."

Okay, she'd been imagining that. Obviously. Olivia shifted in her seat, tucking her legs up under her. "Tell me about her."

He was silent for so long that she wasn't sure he was going to answer her question. "She was a ball of energy," he said finally. "Always moving, thinking, planning. She was the kind of person who would wake up, see the sun was shining, and decide to go to the beach. Twenty minutes later you'd be in the car, a picnic in the boot." He let out a soft sigh as he shook his head in memory.

"I know people like that."

"I'm not one of them."

"Me, neither."

They shared a commiserating look and then Will resumed, "And she was organised, too. It wasn't just a whirlwind—it was, as she liked to say, planned chaos. She always knew where everything was; she always had a plan, but from the outside it could look crazy."

"It sounds fun."

"It was." He was silent for a moment. "I wish I'd appreciated it a little more, though. Before she got sick...sometimes I just wanted quiet. Or the dreaded 'me time'." His mouth twisted. "Now I've got all the me time in the world."

"Except you have two small children to take care of," Olivia reminded him gently. "Hindsight is twenty-twenty, isn't it? You can't berate yourself for not wanting to be caught up in the whirlwind every second of the day."

"Maybe." He opened his mouth, then closed it, and Olivia had the sense he'd been going to say something important and then had decided not to. She wouldn't ask. "I just wish," he said after a moment, "that I'd appreciated it all a lot more at the time. I know you're right—hindsight is twenty-twenty. But when you lose someone…it really makes you think…" He stopped, his voice choking a little, and Olivia reached out to brush his hand with her own.

"I can only imagine," she said softly.

His head bowed, he twined his fingers with hers, making her heart beat faster. "You don't want to imagine."

"No." They sat there for a moment, their fingers twined, Olivia's head spinning both from the wine and Will's touch. Did he *realise* he was holding her hand? Or had he just done it unthinkingly? She was afraid to move, to breathe, because she didn't want him to stop touching her, and yet it felt wrong to think that way. He was talking about his dead wife, for heaven's sake. She could surely pick her moments a bit better.

"Sometimes I don't know how I can keep going," he confessed in a low voice. "Day after day, being the only one. I wake up in the morning and I think: *Again? Really?* And I just want to pull the duvet over my head."

"I know how that feels," Olivia whispered. "In a much smaller way."

"And then I look at Lally and Jake, and I think, I'm all they have. If I mess up, if, God forbid, I die, then they've got no one." He drew a hitched breath. "There's a bottle of whisky in the pantry. It's got a few inches left in it. I have a battle with that bottle every night, because I just want to *forget* for a little while."

"I can understand that, Will. Truly."

"Can you?"

"Maybe not the way you can—"

"You don't need to give me the usual caveats." He spoke with sudden ferocity. "Grief doesn't give you a special licence. I wish it did sometimes, because God knows I've wanted to act like a complete sod at times, but it *doesn't*. I'm just a man. Plenty of people have gone through worse. Much worse."

"But it still hurts."

"*Yes.*" His fingers squeezed hers. "Yes, it really does."

She nodded, and then she met his gaze, and he was giving her one of his intent looks that felt like a bolt of lightning straight to her soul, and right then she was electrified; she was on fire, because Will was still looking at her and then he leaned forward just a little bit, a few inches, and she did too…

Olivia's head was spinning. Her heart was beating fast, so fast. And Will was still clutching her hand. He inched forward again. So did she. Time stopped, and then jumped, and then stopped again. Was she imagining this, because she wanted it so much? And she *did* want it, want him. But could he actually feel the same way…?

A log settled in the grate, making them both jump. Olivia's heart was thundering now, loud in her ears. Her mouth was dry, and meanwhile Will's mouth moved closer. Then so did hers.

And then…then he was kissing her, in a fumbling sort of

way, a tentative yet eager press of lips that felt like primary school and the most profound thing she'd ever done all at the same time. She scrambled for purchase with one hand, and grabbed his shirt. His other hand gripped her shoulder. The kiss started to morph from a juvenile press of lips to something deeper and sweeter and, well, *exciting*.

They were grappling as they kissed and then somehow Olivia was lying back on the sofa, Will braced on top of her, and the kiss was going on and on and her head was *spinning…*

She felt his hand skim her stomach and part of her was thinking *yes* and another part was thinking *whoa* and then suddenly, before she could process either of those thoughts, Will reared back as if he'd been bitten by a snake, lurching up from the sofa with a look of what could only be called horror on his face.

Oh.

Olivia lay there on the sofa, limbs splayed out, clothes rumpled, lips feeling stung, mind horribly blank. This was not going the way she'd hoped, and she wasn't even sure what she'd been hoping for. *Not this.* Definitely not this.

"No…" Will said. He sounded stunned, as if he'd been Tasered. "No, no, I'm sorry…"

And then, before Olivia could even begin to formulate a response, not that she had any idea of what she'd actually say, he was stumbling from the room and up the stairs without so much as a backward glance. A few seconds later she heard the sound of a bedroom door shutting.

Wow. Okay.

She lay there, stunned and still, as the logs settled in the grate and from the kitchen Piper let out a sleepy groan. Minutes ticked by, and she realised she was waiting. Surely Will was going to come back down again? Explain, even if it was only a stammering apology?

I'm so sorry, but I never meant that to happen. I really like you, but. Too much wine, things got out of hand. You know how it is…

She could take any of those well-trod lines right now, Olivia thought bleakly, but not this silence. She was being completely blanked, ignored, and she wasn't even in her own home. She was in Will's, and he'd just…left.

She recalled his horrified expression as he'd stumbled from the room and she closed her eyes. This was worse, or at least almost worse, than that night with Matt. Lying in his arms, shutting her eyes and her heart to the reality of the situation, the ping of his phone.

I've got to go…

She thought then that she couldn't have fallen any lower. Now she realised she could. Slowly she sat up, moving gingerly, as if checking for injuries, broken bones. *Broken heart.* No, not that. Not yet, anyway. A shuddering breath, and then another, and she managed to anchor herself. No, she decided, this wasn't worse. Almost, but not quite.

Not knowing what else to do, Olivia tidied up. She banked the fire and corked the wine bottle—there was only the dregs left—and took their glasses into the kitchen. She washed them in the sink, watched by a baleful Piper, and as she set them upside down in the drainer to dry she realised he must want to go out, so she opened the back door to a dark, dank, moonless and freezing night. Piper rooted around for a bit while Olivia stood there shivering, trying not to feel entirely miserable and failing.

What had actually happened? Will had kissed her, right? She had a sudden, plunging terror that she'd somehow jumped him without realising. But no, he'd moved in first. Hadn't he? And never mind what had happened tonight, what about tomorrow? She couldn't stand the thought of facing Will at breakfast; talk about stomach aches caused by anxiety…! Already she felt her stomach cramp and she had to take a deep breath of clean, cold air to keep from heaving. This was so not good.

Piper trotted back inside, settling in his bed in the little boot room off the kitchen while he gazed at her in beady-eyed expectancy, and Olivia realised he must want a biscuit. She found a box of Bonios above the washing machine and gave him one, which, judging by the way he wolfed it down and then settled his head on the paws, was the right thing to do.

Then she locked the front and back doors, turned off the lights, and headed upstairs.

It wasn't until she turned on the light in the spare bedroom that she remember that it hadn't been made up for a guest; in fact the whole room was packed with plastic crates and cardboard boxes, and the mattress was bare. Great.

Was there anything more wretched than shifting boxes and hunting for sheets while feeling more heartsick and lonely than she'd felt in a long while, and exhausted besides? It was nearing midnight by the time Olivia found a motley mismatch of sheets in the airing cupboard in the hall and made the bed, boxes and crates stacked all around her. She took off her jeans but left her top, pants and socks on, because it was actually freezing now, and then she huddled under the clammy sheets and scrunched her eyes closed, trying her best to shut out the world.

She didn't do a good job of it. Even though she didn't want to, she was picturing that intent, focused look on Will's face right before he'd kissed her. The slide of his hand through her hair or, shockingly, along the bare skin of her stomach. The feel of his body on top of hers, that pleasantly heavy weight...

And then, quite suddenly, she wasn't remembering Will, but Matt. That intentionally self-deprecating smile. The "aw, shucks" way he'd hang his head, and then look up quickly, to check that she'd been watching. At the time, it had all been so heart-meltingly adorable, and she'd been so thrilled he cared enough to see how she'd react. In retrospect, it was calculated and rather corny.

And yet she'd fallen for it—hook, line, and predictable sinker. She'd believed she was special, different. She'd spoon-fed herself lie after lie about how the rules didn't apply, how exceptions had to be made, how true love simply *had* to prevail. What a chump she'd been. What a spineless, deluded, self-serving *loser*.

And even though she knew the situation was different now—Will was widowed, not married—she still felt some of the same old emotions. The desperate disappointment of believing something was real when it wasn't. The painful realisation that she was no more than the runner-up when she convinced herself she was the winner. Lying in bed alone, wondering where it had all gone wrong, feeling empty and aching inside.

And really, considering, did she deserve anything else? Anything more?

No, Olivia thought as she drew the duvet up over her shoulder and shivered under the sheets. No, she did not.

Chapter Thirteen

A GREY, PREDAWN light filtered through the curtains as Will blinked the sleep from his gritty eyes. A glance at the clock on his bedside table told him it was a little after five. The house was still, the only sound the clank of the heating coming on. For a few seconds he felt nothing but a blank grogginess—and then memory slammed into him.

Olivia. Him crying in her arms. Their kiss…and then how he'd run away, like a complete idiot. Like a *coward.* He'd stumbled upstairs, flung himself on the bed, and practically passed out, sick at heart, sick with shame. He'd woken an hour later, and everything had been quiet and dark, but even then he hadn't ventured out of his bedroom. What a coward he was. What a shameful, selfish, stupid *coward.*

With a groan he rolled up from bed. He had no idea what he was going to say when he saw Olivia, but hopefully he had a few hours to think about it. He tiptoed downstairs, determined not to wake Lally, who could be a notoriously light sleeper, and headed into the kitchen. The sight of it completely tidied, their wine glasses in the dish drainer, the bottle corked, made him groan again. He realised that he'd left the lights on, the fire going… He hadn't even let Piper out or locked the doors. Olivia must have done it all, and after he'd kissed her and then more or less run away screaming. What on earth must she think of him? What did he even think of himself?

Kissing her had been…well, it had been wonderful. Will had felt as if a part of himself that had been damped down for eighteen months had suddenly blazed back to life. He'd missed touching someone. Kissing someone. And not just someone, any old person, but *Olivia*. Someone he genuinely cared about.

Too bad he'd made a complete mess of it, then.

He boiled the kettle and made coffee, battling a sweeping tidal wave of self-recrimination the whole while. He couldn't believe what a complete cad he'd been. She probably hated him now. He hated himself, and not just for running away and leaving Olivia to it. For kissing her in the first place, for wanting to kiss her, because how could he have done that, when he'd been telling her moments before how much he missed Rachel? What kind of man could sob for his dead wife and then kiss another woman in virtually the next breath?

Will groaned aloud while Piper gazed at him inquiringly, hoping that Will coming downstairs an hour earlier than usual meant he was going to get his breakfast. Will decided he might as well, and with everything in him aching he reached for his bowl.

With Piper happily fed, he had nothing to do but sit and nurse his coffee, wondering what he was going to say to Olivia when she came downstairs, and if last night had completely scuppered any chance of them having a friendly working relationship. What if she no longer wanted him at Casterglass?

As much as Will would miss that, and he would— terribly—he realised he would miss Olivia herself more. He'd come to really enjoy their time together, their easy chats, the ready laughter, the comfortable silences. He hated the thought that he might have ruined it all, by being so *stupid.* In so many ways.

He supposed the only thing he could do was offer a completely unvarnished and total apology, no caveats, no excuses, no ifs, ands, or buts. Just sorry. *Sorry, sorry, sorry.*

A creak on the stair had him looking up, his heart practically leaping into his throat. It was only half past five. It had to be Lally.

But it wasn't. Olivia stood in the doorway, already dressed, her hair plaited. She looked pale and strained, her eyes huge in her face, shadows like bruises underneath. Guilt twisted Will's insides all over again.

"Good morning," he said, and then cleared his throat. Winced. There was nothing for it but to plunge right in, yet now that the moment had come upon him so quickly and unexpectedly, he found he was struggling to know what to say, or perhaps just how to say it. "Coffee?" he managed and she nodded.

Will got up to pour her a cup from the cafetiere, conscious of everything. The silence that stretched between them, hurting his eardrums. The whisper of Olivia's clothes as she sat down. Piper's happy, satiated sigh as he flopped down in front of the Rayburn and then lifted his head, eyebrow cocked, as if he sensed the tension radiating through the room.

"Thank you," Olivia murmured, wrapping her slender fingers around the mug Will put in front of her. Her head was bowed, her plait falling forward over one shoulder. Will sat down opposite her, reached for his mug, and then put it down again.

"Look," he said. "There's no easy way to say this. I acted like a real cad last night. A complete rotter. I told you there were no caveats for men in my position—widowed, I mean—and then I went and treated you so very badly. I'm sorry, Olivia. I…" He'd run out of steam, feeling helpless. "I shouldn't have kissed you," he said at last. "Honestly, I don't know what I was thinking. I suppose I *wasn't* thinking, and that was the problem." Although her head was still lowered he saw her cheeks start to colour, her fingers tightening on her mug. "And I definitely shouldn't have run out on you, without apologising or explaining. Or putting Piper to bed!" He shook his head. "When I came down this morning I saw you'd tidied everything up, and it made me feel worse. That isn't to say—I mean, thank you." She still hadn't spoken, hadn't lifted her head. He blew out a frustrated breath. "I feel like I'm going about this all wrong."

"No." The word was little more than a whisper. Finally she raised her head, but Will could not make out the expression on her face at all, and that worried him, because usually he could. He knew her eyes lightened like forget-me-nots when she was amused, and darkened to navy when she was focused. He knew how a wry little smile would flirt with her lips and then slip away, and how she looked down, her lashes brushing her cheeks, when she felt shy.

He'd seen all that, had documented every fleeting mood or changing emotion, but he couldn't tell anything from the carefully blank look on her face now. She reminded him of a china doll, with her big blue eyes, her pale face, and bright spots of colour high on each cheekbone. A pale, perfect doll giving nothing away.

"You've said it just right," she told him, her voice quiet and contained. "I understand perfectly."

Which somehow did not reassure him in the least. He gazed at her, wishing he was better at this, wishing he hadn't messed things up last night, as well as, it seemed, this morning. He hadn't dated anyone for over fifteen years. He was well out of the game, and he wasn't ready to jump back into it, if last night's reaction was anything to go by. Besides, these kinds of "I-like-you-but" explanations were not his strong suit. He'd never actually had to give one before; Rachel had been his first girlfriend.

"I still want us to be friends," Will said and Olivia gave a jerky little nod. "I mean I really hope I haven't messed things up between us, with the garden."

She raised her eyebrows, managed a small smile that wasn't the normal, generous curving of her lips and didn't reach her eyes. "Do you actually think I'd let something like this interfere with the garden? It's only seven weeks until opening."

"Well, that's a relief, I guess." He tried for a laugh, but it came out as something between a wheeze and a cough. Olivia took another sip of her coffee, her gaze lowered. He didn't feel this conversation had gone as well as he'd hoped somehow, and yet nothing was really wrong.

"Thank you for helping yesterday," he said after a moment, longing to get them back on their old footing even as it felt impossible. "I really appreciate it."

"I'm just glad Lally is okay." She didn't look at him as she spoke.

"I think A&E was a bit of an overreaction, all things considered."

"Well, you can't be too careful."

This chitchat felt *awful*. They were so beyond this— when they were working, they could often finish each other's sentences, even read each other's thoughts. All Will would have to say was "I was thinking about…" and Olivia would fill in: "The camelia? I think it needs to be moved, too." He felt none of that synchronicity now.

"The doctor said she's all right to go to school today..." he ventured. "I thought we could start putting those paving stones in."

For a second, as Olivia raised her head to gaze at him, she looked trapped, horrified, even, and then her expression cleared and she nodded slowly. "Yes, that would be good." She rose from the table. "Althea's actually coming to pick me up in a few minutes. I thought I'd get an early start on the day."

"What?" Will stared at her blankly. It was only just gone six in the morning. "I could have driven you over after the kids are in school—"

"You know what it's like when you've slept in your clothes?" Olivia said as she moved to the sink and washed out her mug. "You feel so ratty. I'm dying for a shower."

You could have a shower here, Will almost said, but didn't. It didn't feel right, all things considered, and yet he didn't want her to go, especially not when things still felt so unresolved between them. The trouble was, he didn't know how to resolve them.

A pair of headlights washed the front hallway in yellow. "She's here," Olivia said, and there was no disguising the relief in her voice. "I'll see you in a couple of hours, okay?"

She didn't look at him as she hurried from the room, grabbing her coat, shoving her feet into boots. Within a few seconds she was gone, the headlights washing the hallway again before plunging everything once more into predawn darkness.

"*PLEASE* DON'T SAY a word," Olivia implored as she climbed into the passenger seat of Althea's Range Rover. "Please."

Althea took one look at her, undoubtedly noting her pale face and bitten lips, and nodded. "Okay. I won't."

With a shuddery sigh of relief Olivia slammed the door shut and sank back against the seat, her eyes closed, Will's words reverberating through her tortured mind. *I shouldn't have kissed you. Honestly, I don't know what I was thinking.*

Thanks, Will. Thanks a lot.

"You look terrible," Althea stated, and Olivia managed a wobbly laugh.

"I feel terrible."

"At least you texted last night. Otherwise we might have thought you'd been left for dead at the side of the road."

"What a charming picture you paint," Olivia managed dryly, which was a feat considering how utterly leaden she felt inside, as if she could barely drag her body along.

"I've always had a way with words." Althea paused, and even though her eyes were closed Olivia could *feel* her probing glance. "Are you sure I can't ask any questions?"

"I'm sure, but in any case you're probably making it all a much bigger deal than it actually is."

"You're the one making it look like a big deal," Althea

replied, "looking like death warmed over."

"But not by the side of the road?"

"Ha ha. At least you still have your sense of humour."

Did she? Olivia felt weirdly empty inside, yet so very heavy at the same time. She'd barely slept last night, and that conversation with Will had been pure torture. The guilty look of self-recrimination on his face had eaten at any remaining shred of self-respect she'd been trying to nurture. First she'd fallen in love—or at least infatuation—with a married man; next she'd picked a widower. *At least this time the wife was dead*, she thought with gallows humour, and then felt as if she could cry. For about eight hours.

"Well, in any case," Althea said, her tone turning briskly practical, "there's enough to be worrying about. You've only been gone a night, but I feel like everything is starting to fall apart."

"What? How come?"

Althea gave a weary sigh. "The Food Standards Agency has rescheduled their visit for *July*." She gave a grimace of disgust. "So we can't open the café until after that. Good thing I hadn't put a food order in yet! And Sam has put back his flight back a week—as if we can get the glamping up and running in five weeks! We haven't even ordered the yurts, never mind the ropes course. And to top it all off, Health and Safety have to review the whole place before we can even open the doors, and they're booked up with visits until the end of June." She gave a grimace. "So forget our May bank holiday grand opening. It's not happening."

"I'm sorry, Althea," Olivia said, sincere although not surprised. The idea that they could have the castle completely ready for visitors in a few months had always seemed more than unlikely to her, despite her sister's immense determination. "Why has Sam put back his flight?" He had been due to arrive in only a few days.

"Who knows?" Althea shrugged irritably. "He just said something had come up. Sometimes I wonder if he even *wants* to come home."

Olivia thought of her Skype call with Sam a few weeks ago and had to agree with her sister's concern. Now, however, was not the time to mention that. She felt far too weary to listen to a tirade from Althea about their brother's lack of enthusiasm.

"Well, the garden will be in good shape," she told Althea as brightly as she could, which wasn't very bright at all. "The walled garden is coming along nicely, and we should have the path to the waterfall, with the bridge in place. Plus the pond and rhododendrons are already sorted." Will was intending to start work on the bridge that week. "And I had an idea for a treasure hunt that we can have in place before then, too." She paused, wanting to ask Althea again about the playground equipment she felt the castle really needed to be an attractive destination for families, but then decided that argument could wait for another day. The few times she'd mentioned it she'd got absolutely no traction at all.

"Well, that's something, I suppose," Althea said morosely. "But I wanted it to be all sorted for the May weekend, so we could have a full summer of takings."

"Rome wasn't built in a day," Olivia reminded her. "And neither was Casterglass."

"Clearly," Althea replied, just as morose. She turned into the castle's drive and Olivia felt a rush of relief at being home. Now if she could only climb into bed, pull the duvet over her head, and stay there forever.

"Darling," her mother said, pressing her cheek to hers as she came into the kitchen. She was in the middle of brewing tea, which by the smell of it was something bizarre and very herbal. "We missed you!"

"I was only gone a night," Olivia told her with an attempt at a smile as she returned the hug. Even if it had felt like a long, unfortunate lifetime. "I'm going to grab a quick shower," she told her mother and Althea. "And then head out to the garden. Will's coming over to lay the paving stones in a couple of hours."

Althea's eyebrows rose. "Will's coming over?"

Olivia saw the ripple of fascination cross her mother's face and she said quickly, trying not to sound irritable, "Yes, of course he is. It's one of his workdays. Now if you'll excuse me."

As she headed upstairs, she heard her mother's provocative murmur. "Has something happened that I know nothing about? How *interesting*."

"Something's happened," Althea replied, "but I don't know anything about it, either."

Groaning under her breath, Olivia hurried into the bathroom.

It felt comforting to step into a hot shower, even if it was little more than a trickle, thanks to Casterglass's antiquated plumbing. Olivia closed her eyes as she let the water stream down her face like tears. She wanted to cry, wished she could summon the tears that would surely feel like a catharsis, but she couldn't. That awful emptiness inside her wouldn't allow them to come.

Get over it, she told herself. *It was just a kiss, after all.*

Except it hadn't felt like just a kiss. She thought of how much Will had shared, how she'd held him in her arms. How he'd cried and then how he'd kissed her. No, it had definitely felt like a lot more than *just a kiss.*

But that's how she had to think of it, Olivia reminded herself as she stepped out of the shower and wrapped a towel around herself. Just a kiss—and one Will so clearly regretted, and he would do his best to make sure it wouldn't happen again. She should regret it, too, but she found that despite the intense heartache she couldn't. And she knew if it happened again, she wouldn't even be sorry.

I'm falling for him, she realised with a thrill of something like horror. Maybe she already had. And meanwhile, for Will, it was all just a terrible mistake.

Chapter Fourteen

OVER THE NEXT few weeks, Olivia threw herself into the garden more than ever. She was up at dawn, yanking on her garden gloves and weeding flower beds or transplanting seedlings, doing whatever she could to keep her mind off Will. She enjoyed the ache of her muscles, the blankness of her brain, due to the physical exhaustion. It was so much better than having to think.

The morning after their kiss, Will had turned up to work bang on time, Piper loping in behind him as he'd come into the garden. Olivia had been busy tying a clematis to a trellis, and so she'd only managed to toss a quick and hopefully cheery hello over her shoulder as Will came in heaving the paving stones.

"I'm busy here, but go ahead getting the path ready," she'd told him brightly, focused on the clematis. If they could stay apart for a little while, she felt it would be a lot better for the both of them. Well, for her, at least, until she could regain her equilibrium. If she could.

They'd spent the morning apart—Olivia with little jobs

in the walled garden, Will heaving stones. When they'd broken for lunch, Althea had ushered everyone inside for an impromptu, semi-emergency meeting; Olivia had half wondered if she'd planned it on purpose, for her sake, but then she decided her sister was too focused on getting the castle visitor-ready to think about something like that.

Still, it had been a relief not to even have to look at Will as Althea had gone through her weekly to-do list, checking in with everyone on how things were going, which, despite her obvious worries, seemed to be okay. Seph had the workshops pretty much up and running, and had sorted the website. Poppy had designed a visitor's brochure and had arranged to have it printed through an online service for practically pennies. Even twelve-year-old Tobias had got in on the act and was in the process of turning one of the castle's smaller drawing rooms into a games room, decked out with a vast array of board games, for visitors to play.

"It's too bad the billiards table was ruined, during that flood," their father mused as he nibbled on a cucumber.

"You mean at Christmas?" Althea asked, for that was when they'd had water cascading down the stairs.

"No, no, years ago. We didn't realise it until weeks had passed, as we never went in there. It was the smell of mildew that alerted us. By that time you could have had a few fish swimming in what had become a billiards *pond*." He chortled at the memory, while Olivia exchanged a look with Althea. Everything about that story was so typical of her father, the castle, their childhood.

"I'd forgotten we had a billiards room," Althea admitted. "So I'm not surprised it wasn't discovered for a while. In any case, it all sounds like things are progressing, even if they won't be ready for May."

"That always was a big ask, darling," their mother said with a commiserating smile. "Unless, of course, you meant May next year."

"No, I didn't, Mummy. I meant this May." Althea sighed. "I know it was a bit ambitious, but I thought we ought to try."

"Why not still open the castle itself?" their father suggested. "It's in as good working order as it will ever be, and Poppy's made such a smashing brochure. And we have the workshops, and the walled garden. It's not a complete washout, Althea, darling."

Althea made a face. "It's a bit damp squibby, though, isn't it, to just offer a few things? And to be honest, I don't think we'll have the permits in place to charge for any of it."

"Oh, permits," their mother scoffed. "In this part of the country? They won't be checking for ages. We could run the castle for years without bothering with permits, I'm sure."

"There is the small matter of insurance…" their father murmured. "Which you can't obtain without the permits."

"In any case, we want to be above board," Althea told their mother rather sternly.

"What if we had some sort of gathering?" Olivia suggested. "Maybe a cream tea on the lawn, and we invite all the locals? Just to get the excitement up? We could advertise a bit, open the gardens—you don't need a licence for that— and have some of Seph's pieces on display, along with the others. It would be a sort of taster."

A beat of silence made Olivia think the plan must be mad, but then her father beamed at her. "Darling, that's *marvellous.*"

"I don't know…" Althea began doubtfully, which Olivia thought was entirely predictable. Her sister seemed hard-wired to be dubious.

"I think it's a great idea," Will chipped in. Olivia caught sight of his warm, approving smile before her gaze skated away in near-panic. *Don't look at me like that*, she thought frantically. *Don't look at me like that and make me fall for you all over again.*

"Well, I suppose we could think about it," Althea said, which was high praise indeed, coming from her.

BACK OUTSIDE OLIVIA had fully intended to keep working in the walled garden, but Will beckoned her over towards the far gate.

"Do you want to see what I've done so far?" he asked, a look of such puppyish eagerness on his face that the cool reserve Olivia had been trying to cloak herself with started to melt.

"Sure."

Will opened the gate, Piper squeezing in behind him, and then ushered her through. Olivia held her breath as she went past so she wouldn't have to breathe in the smell of him that had become so familiar—leather and woodsmoke, a tangy hint of aftershave.

"What do you think?" Will asked as he stood beside her, and they both gazed at the path he'd started to lay out, leading down to the water.

"They look perfect," Olivia told him honestly. Large and flat, made of golden York stone, they were like a yellow brick road, leading to the river. She turned to smile at him, meeting his eyes, and then wishing she hadn't. When she looked at him properly she remembered how it had felt to have him kiss her, to kiss him back, and her heart started beating hard as if he was going to do it again right then, which of course he wasn't.

"Really great," she added, taking a step back. "You have such an eye, Will."

"Thanks." Will glanced at her with a frown, probably because she was edging away from him like he was a dangerous animal, which in a sense he was.

"I should get back. I've got another clematis calling my name." And then, even though she knew it looked weird, she turned around and hared back to safety. That was the way it had to be, at least for a little while.

AND SO SHE kept her distance and threw herself into gardening, grateful for how much there was to do, how tired she was able to become. Too tired to think. Almost too tired to feel. When there wasn't something pressing to do in the garden, she helped Althea keep the front rooms looking at their shabby best, or tackled the ever-growing pile of admin, or visited Seph in the barns that had been converted to workshops.

"Wow, this is like, for real," she said rather inanely when she ventured into Seph's inner sanctum. Seph was standing by her workbench, wearing a leather apron, her pink dreadlocks piled on top of her head.

"For real?" She raised an eyebrow. "What else would it be?"

Olivia gave a little laugh. "I just meant...well, I don't know what I meant. I'm impressed, that's all." She glanced down at the tools laid out on the bench—a little brass hammer, a hand plane, some screwdrivers and files, along with a hunk of cedarwood on the bench that was yet to be shaped.

Seph was silent, as she so often was, and not for the first time Olivia wished she knew what her sister was thinking. Seph could be such a closed book—tight-lipped, narrow-eyed, shrugging away questions and compliments both. Over the years Olivia had done her best to break through her shell and slip beneath the cracks, but she never felt as if she got very far.

"What first got you into woodworking, Seph?" she asked now. "I don't think I've ever asked."

Seph shrugged. "Dunno. There wasn't much else to do, I suppose." She picked up the hunk of cedarwood and tossed it from hand to hand, seeming restless.

"It must have been lonely," Olivia ventured, "when you were on your own." She'd left for boarding school before Seph was even born; her sister had only been a baby when Sam had gone. Basically, Seph had lived as an only child, and with parents like theirs, lonely had to be an understatement.

"It was all right." Seph's tone gave nothing away.

"I came in because I wondered if you'd be able to carve some woodland animals for a sort of treasure trail I wanted to have in the garden. I thought I'd make a map, and children could find and tick off each one, maybe get a prize at the end."

Olivia was encouraged to see a wary spark of interest in her sister's eyes. "That's a good idea," she said. "But it might take awhile, depending on how many animals you wanted me to make."

"That's not a problem at all. We can just see how we go, eh? It doesn't look like we'll be opening for the May bank holiday, anyway."

"No, but it might be nice to have them ready for your cream tea."

Seph smiled, and Olivia smiled back, heartened. She should have taken more of an interest in her sister's woodworking before this, but Seph could be so surly. When she smiled, Olivia reflected, she looked like almost an entirely different person; really, with her piercing blue eyes and smooth, pale skin, she was gorgeous—the pink dreadlocks just added to her ethereal beauty. But, Olivia had to admit, as Seph turned back to her woodworking, when she scowled she really did look fairly terrifying.

"WHEN ARE WE going to see Olivia again?" Lally demanded, kicking her legs against her chair as Will raced around the kitchen, trying to get everything ready so they could actually make it on time for school, for once. Mrs Tabbard had had to "have a chat" with him last week about tardiness.

"I understand your situation is challenging," she'd told him in a tone of utter diplomacy, "but it really is better for the children, as well as the school as a whole, if all pupils can be present before the morning bell."

Will had muttered abject apologies, feeling well and truly scolded, and today he was absolutely determined to get to school on time.

"I don't know, love," he told Lally, distracted by a note Jake had only now thrust at him, letting him know that today was a dress-down day; apparently all the pupils were meant to wear yellow in support of anti-bullying.

"Why can't she come visit?" Lally asked, while Will gazed at his two children, both dressed in clean uniforms for once, with something like despair. Did Jake even have anything yellow?

"She…she's busy." He would have liked to have Olivia visit again, but he hadn't dared suggest it. Over the last few weeks they'd regained a bit of their old camaraderie, but Will still couldn't shake the uneasy feeling that those were just roles they were playing, masks to take on and off. Olivia's smile was ready enough, but it never reached her eyes.

"Dad, I need something yellow." Jake sounded aggrieved. At least he didn't have a stomach ache today, and he wasn't complaining about potentially having a life-threatening illness. Small mercies, Will supposed, and he suspected at least in part thanks to Olivia and her understanding.

"I don't know if you have anything yellow. Or you, Lall." Her wardrobe was composed almost entirely of purple and sparkly pink.

"Mummy has yellow," Lally said. "She has loads of yellow clothes. It was her favourite colour."

Startled, Will managed a level: "So it was."

"She had a pair of long yellow socks," Jake recalled, excitement entering his voice. "And a big yellow T-shirt with emojis on it. Can I wear that?"

"And I could wear her yellow scarf," Lally chimed in. "The one with daisies."

Will was amazed his children could remember Rachel's clothes, and so specifically, after all this time. They stared at him eagerly, waiting for his response. He felt like a deer in the headlights, trapped by their childish expectation. In the now twenty months since Rachel had died, he hadn't touched her clothes. They were still hanging next to his in the wardrobe, still taking up an entire bureau. He hadn't even though about it much; there had been no pressing need to deal with them, because he had enough space for his own clothes, and no one to chivvy him into doing those mundane yet painful duties that were necessary after someone had died.

"Okay," he said at last, because what else could he say? He hadn't been intending to build a shrine, or anything like that. It had just sort of happened.

He led them upstairs to his bedroom, and Lally ran to Rachel's bureau, opening the top drawer. Will swallowed hard at the sight of scarves, a jumble of bright colours and different materials. Rachel had loved scarves—big woolly ones to wrap around her neck, colourful silk ones to tie back her wild, curly hair. He couldn't remember ever seeing her without one, really.

"Here it is!" Lally cried, and held up the yellow daisy-patterned scarf that Rachel had loved to wear; she'd worn it after she'd lost her hair to the chemo, to cover her head. "Can I wear it, Daddy?"

"Yes, love, of course." Will found he had to swallow again; the lump in his throat was growing bigger. "Let me tie it for you." Doing his best to smile although his eyes felt damp, Will tied back Lally's dark hair—so like Rachel's—

with the scarf. She twirled happily, curls flying out.

"How do I look?"

"Wonderful," Will said, and his voice choked just a little.

Jake laid a hand on his arm, giving him a serious look. "Are you okay, Dad?"

"Yes, Jake, I'm fine." He patted his son's hand. "I'm fine."

Jake was quiet for a moment while Lally continued to spin. "I miss her, too," he said finally, and that was nearly Will's undoing. He pulled Jake into a quick, tight hug.

"I know you do."

They found the yellow T-shirt and socks for Jake, and with everyone kitted out, they headed to school a mere fifteen minutes late. Mrs Tabbard would have a fit, Will thought with a sigh, but he found he couldn't care as much as he had been earlier that morning. Something had shifted in him, when he'd been going through Rachel's clothes. The sight of her dresses hanging next to his shirts—she'd always loved dresses, the funkier the better—had made an ache inside him open up, but it wasn't as bad as he once might have feared. It had felt like a scar rather than a wound.

He knew he didn't want to give away all her things—that didn't feel right—but he could box them up, save them for Lally and Jake, for when they were older. Lally might like some of Rachel's dresses, and Jake might like to see and remember what his mum had worn. But he didn't, Will realised, have to keep them in his bedroom, a living shrine, a constant memory, without him even realising that was what it was.

Which brought his thoughts round, as so often seemed to happen, to Olivia. He'd come to realise that he'd handled the morning after their kiss badly. He'd hurt her, he'd realised, with his quick dismissal of what had happened between them, insisting it was nothing more than a thoughtless mistake. He could see that now, even if he hadn't at the time. Was that the source of the unspoken tension that he still felt thrummed between them? His insensitivity, her hurt? Maybe it was finally time to address it.

OLIVIA WAS HARD at work when he arrived at Casterglass, just as she had been nearly every day since their kiss. She was like a whirling dervish, spinning from project to project, always planting, pruning, weeding, cutting, clipping. The walled garden was really starting to look amazing.

"Hey." He smiled at her as he approached her kneeling in front of a bed of newly planted hydrangeas, Piper trotting off to investigate some interesting smell. "How are you?"

"Good, thanks." She didn't look up from her weeding. "You?"

"Good. Sorry I'm late. A bit of a brouhaha with school today. I didn't realise they had to wear yellow."

"Oh?"

Before that night, she would have looked up, Will knew.

He would have seen that wry, teasing glint in her eyes; she would have put her hands on her hips, cocking her head as she looked at him. *Oh, no. And let me guess. No yellow in the house?* They would have laughed about it. She would have made him feel better, less alone. Now she kept her head bent, her hair piled on top of her head so he could see the smooth nape of her neck, browned by the sun. The end of April had been unseasonably warm and dry, which had been great for the garden.

"Olivia." His voice came out low, a little rough.

Olivia looked up, her eyes widening slightly before her expression turned guarded and she sat back on her heels. "Yes?"

Will raked a hand through his hair. Blunt was better. He'd always felt that way, except when it made him vulnerable. He took a deep breath. "Look, I don't feel like we talked about—about what happened properly."

Her eyes darkened but her gaze remained steady on his. "About what happened?"

She wasn't going to play dumb, was she? Or did she just want to make him say it? "About—you know—when we kissed."

She nodded slowly, not speaking, waiting for him to say more. And what was he going to say? He should have had something more in mind when he'd started this conversation. An actual script would have helped, or at least a general idea.

"I went through Rachel's clothes today," he blurted. "They haven't been touched since—since she died. I didn't really think about it. But the kids needed something yellow, and she loved yellow. So we took some of her stuff."

Olivia's eyes were full of compassion, the wariness gone. "I'm sorry, Will. That must have been hard."

"It was, but not as hard as I expected it to be, which was good. But it made me realise…I've got a bit stuck, without meaning to. It's hard enough keeping everything together, managing the house, the kids…"

"I can understand that."

"I haven't really thought about the future. It's all been day-to-day, just surviving. But…when I talk to you…when I look at you…" He swallowed. "I want to think about a future. I want to believe I can have one. With someone."

Colour touched her cheeks, turning them pink. "I'm not really sure what that means."

"I'm not, either," Will confessed. "I just feel like I was a bit too quick to dismiss what happened that night. I was embarrassed. I felt like I acted like a real cad, not to mention a complete softie, blubbing the way I did. And I *did* act like a real cad. But…I liked kissing you." Now he was the one blushing, and not a delicate pink. A fiery, fire-engine red. "And I'd want to…that is, if I was in a place to…" He was fumbling, unable to formulate the words, speak his heart. "If I wanted to be with anyone, it would be with you. And one day I hope that I'll feel ready to, you know…" He stopped abruptly as he realised with a frisson of horror that he'd never even asked Olivia how she'd felt about the kiss. His memory of it was exquisite but blurry—what if it had been all on him? Maybe he'd been *mauling* her, and her slight brittleness now was because she'd been so offended. She wasn't attracted to him at all; maybe she hadn't even *wanted* to kiss him. What if he'd got it all completely and utterly wrong?

But Olivia was smiling, humour lightening her eyes the way it used to. "I'd like it to be with you, too," she said quietly. "When we're both ready."

Chapter Fifteen

"OLIVIA, THIS LOOKS amazing."

"Really?" Her sister's utter, unvarnished praise had Olivia blushing and blinking in pleased disbelief. Althea did not dish out compliments all that often.

"Yes, it really does." She shook her head slowly. "So delicate and lovely. I love it."

"Wow, thanks." Olivia glanced down at the treasure map she'd made in pastel watercolours, to find the carved woodland creatures Seph was still in the process of making. It was early May, just four weeks till D-Day, and Sam was finally coming home tomorrow. Things with Will had reached a surprisingly comfortable equilibrium. Even though they'd both been practically wriggling with mortification when he'd talked about that night, Olivia had been grateful for the conversation along with the clarity. *If I wanted to be with anyone, it would be with you* wasn't exactly a heartfelt "I love you", but it made her fizz inside all the same.

It also left her with questions. When would Will be ready? When would she? And in the meantime, did they just live in limbo, waiting for a time when they'd both feel up to dating? Not that Olivia objected. It wasn't as if she had a dozen other men jostling to join the queue.

But you'll be thirty-seven in a few months. And you still want a baby.

Not exactly something she could share with Will. *Do you mind making your mind up a bit more quickly? Because I'd really like to get pregnant.*

And anyway, she wasn't *that* sure about him, was she? He was a widower, after all, with a lot of emotional baggage, not to mention two children in tow. That was a lot to take on, as anyone with sense would tell her.

Ah, but who was she kidding? She'd take them all on today, if she could. In a heartbeat. Which left her feeling strangely settled in the status quo but also anxious for change.

"It seems incredible," Althea said slowly, startling Olivia out of her thoughts, "but things are actually coming together. We've got all the permissions and health and safety things lined up for July, and Sam emailed to say he's ordered some glamping yurts." She shook her head wryly. "Apparently he knows someone and was able to get them for relatively cheap. A thousand pounds a yurt, which he tells me is a steal."

"That's wonderful."

"It is. And Poppy's designed a Casterglass logo—have you seen it?"

"Yes, the orchid and the scroll?" To highlight both her

parents' interests, which Olivia thought had been a lovely touch.

"With our coat of arms in the background. I love it." Althea let out a slightly shuddery breath, and Olivia glanced at her in concern.

"With everything going so well, why do you look a bit green around the gills?"

"Because it's nerve-racking." Althea passed a hand over her face. "We've got everything tied up in this venture. Everything. If it goes bust, I have nothing for me and the kids to live on."

"If it goes bust, we sell the castle, and you'll have your proceeds from that," Olivia said gently. "No one is going to leave you high and dry, Althea."

"*If* we can sell it. I looked on Rightmove the other day and do you know how many castles and estates like this one are for sale?" Olivia shook her head. "One hundred and *four*. And those are just the ones listed on that site. There are probably loads of others. Some of them have been for sale for years. Decades. Becoming more and more dilapidated by the day."

"But with all the work we've done—"

"And they're not even worth that much," Althea continued, her voice growing shrill. "You can get a stunning medieval fortress in Ayrshire for *six hundred thousand pounds*. You can't buy a semi in Birmingham for that! Admittedly, it's missing a roof in parts, but still."

"Well, we've just redone our roof." Olivia smiled, surprised at how peaceful she felt about this. Once upon a time she would have shared Althea's anxiety, would have worried about her life spinning out of control. Would have felt helpless, as if she couldn't be her own agent, because that's how she'd always felt growing up. How she'd felt with Matt. Working on the garden—and getting to know Will—had helped her, she realised. Helped her to believe in herself.

"There's no point worrying about the worst what-ifs," she told Althea. "All you can do is work hard and hope for the best. And you have worked hard—harder than anyone. The castle looks amazing, and we have loads to offer. And your children love it here. You've made the right choice."

Althea gave her a rather watery smile. "Have I?"

"Of course you have!" Olivia had never seen her sister so besieged by doubts. "And what about John? If you hadn't come back to Casterglass, you never would have met him."

"He asked me to marry him last night."

"What!" Olivia stared at her sister, feeling as if she'd had the breath knocked out of her. "And that made you feel wobbly?"

"Yes, because I made a complete hash of my first marriage. For twenty *years*. Do you know how...how stupid and insecure I feel, because of that?"

"You've never seemed stupid or insecure to me." Even though Althea had confided in her about her trials with Jasper, Olivia had never got the sense that her big sister's confidence had been so thoroughly knocked. Althea was always moving on, making a plan. But as Olivia knew, appearances could be deceiving. Just like hers was—dreamy, innocent Olivia, just waiting for Mr Right. Not snatching him from another woman, oh no. The familiar guilt that rushed in when she thought like that didn't this time, at least no more than a trickle. Was she actually starting to forgive herself? Olivia hadn't thought it possible. Maybe that was another change Casterglass was so slowly working in her.

"I love John," Althea said, pleating her fingers together. "Of course I do. And I do want to spend my life with him. But when he asked…I don't know. It brought back all these memories. All these fears, of losing myself, of being sucked into a marriage like it's a black hole."

A black hole? Marriage to Jasper *had* been bad. "That's understandable," Olivia told her, "but that doesn't mean you have to act on them."

"It's hard, though, when your heart is saying one thing and your head another. It drowns out whatever is in your head."

"True." Just like with her and Matt. Her head had been telling her, quite plainly and loudly, not to pursue a relationship with a married man. Her heart had been putting its metaphorical fingers in its ears and singing "la la la". It was amazing, really, how easy it was to drown out reason. To lie to yourself. *To hurt innocent people.* Ah, there was the guilt. She swallowed, did her best to push it away and focus on her sister.

"Did you give him an answer?" Olivia asked, and Althea shrugged.

"Sort of. I said I was glad he'd asked, but I needed to think about it."

"And how did he respond?"

"He said that was fine, but truthfully I think he was a bit hurt." She sighed. "We've been so happy these last few months, and I know neither of us is getting any younger. Poppy and John's daughter, Alice, are practically like sisters already. It seems so simple, obvious, and yet some part of me feels like running away screaming."

"It has only been a few months," Olivia pointed out. "No need to jump the gun, surely. You're not that old."

"No…" Althea trailed off with a sigh. "I *do* want to marry him. It's just getting over my fear of becoming a doormat again."

"John would never treat you like a doormat."

"No, but that's beside the point. I need to feel secure enough in myself first. I know that." She squared her shoulders. "Anyway, there's no sense thinking of any of that before the opening. This summer's mad already, with everything going on. I told him I couldn't possibly even consider his proposal before September."

Which sounded a lot more like Althea. "And he was okay with that?"

"He had to be, I suppose. He said he wasn't going anywhere, at least." Her eyes sparkled and her lips trembled as she pushed them up into a smile. "He really is a good man."

"He is," Olivia agreed. "The best." Although Will was, perhaps, a close second. A *very* close second.

WILL WAS SURPRISED and pleased when he, Lally, and Jake had been invited to Sam's homecoming dinner, although admittedly not by Olivia, but by her mother.

"It's about time we had a party," she said, throwing her arms wide. "And celebrate what we've achieved so far! Not that it will be a big do—just everyone associated with the renovation project." Which, Will found out, included about forty people. Besides him and Lally and Jake, there was John Braithwaite and his daughter Alice, Seph's friends who had helped with the workshops, a couple of roofers and their families, and the other artisans and their families, as well.

Jake and Lally were both practically bouncing with excitement as Will drove up to the castle a surprisingly balmy Friday evening in mid-May. The terraced lawn in front of the castle was set up for a barbecue, with tables and chairs, a large barbecue, and even a rather battered marquee. Will was glad he'd mown the grass recently, as well as trimmed the box hedges and fortified the ha-ha. Everything looked shipshape, bursting with colour and life. He felt a frisson of pride, a glow of achievement. He'd been part of this. A big part, even.

"Olivia!" Lally scrambled out of the car and ran towards Olivia, who was coming out of the kitchen with a tray of glasses and a pitcher of lemonade.

"Hello, Lally." She managed to wrap one arm around the little girl as she balanced the tray with one hand. Will stepped forward to rescue it.

"Can I help by taking this?"

"Thanks."

He took the tray from her, unable to keep his gaze from moving over her in appreciation. Her hair was in its usual plait, blond wisps framing her heart-shaped face. A spattering of freckles had come out across her nose from the recent sun, and her long, slender arms were bare and tanned. She wore a strappy, flowing sundress in a crinkly white material with a butterfly embroidered on the front. As Will looked at her, he found himself remembering exactly how her lithe curves had felt in his arms. Under his body. He forced the thoughts away as he managed a smile.

"Thanks for having us here tonight."

"Of course, it's a pleasure! We can finally celebrate." Holding Lally's hand, Olivia started walking towards the lawn where a few dozen people were already milling about, chatting and laughing. "You should meet my brother, Sam," she called over her shoulder. "He only arrived an hour ago and he's completely jet-lagged, but he's here."

Will joined the crowd on the lawn and was introduced to Sam Penryn, who shook his hand with a ready smile, although Will sensed something restless yet restrained from him. He had wavy, dirty blond hair left a little long, and like his sisters, blue eyes, although his were a piercing cerulean. He was tanned and muscular, clearly a man used to the outdoors and plenty of activity. Olivia had told Will that her brother was always doing some extreme sport or activity for charity, and he looked like it. He also looked like he'd rather not be here, bouncing on his heels, his gaze darting around as if looking for exits.

"You must be jet-lagged," Will remarked, and Sam nodded.

"Yeah…not sure what day it is, really." He let out an uncertain laugh. "It's really strange to be back, to tell you the truth." He shook his head, either in disbelief or to clear it, Will couldn't tell, but he appreciated how discombobulated Sam had to feel. On top of the jet lag, he'd returned home to a place he hadn't spent much time in for the last decade, at least according to Olivia, and in his absence it had changed significantly.

He glanced around to check on Jake and Lally, and found them with Olivia, by the marquee; they were looking up at her adoringly and she was smiling down at them, friendly and at ease. When they started jumping up and down, Will decided he should go over.

"You lot look excited," he remarked casually as Olivia met his curious gaze with a smile.

"I was just suggesting they test-run the treasure trail," she told him. "Now we've printed out the maps, and Seph has finished the carvings. They're not in place yet but if you wanted to bring them over on the weekend…" She raised her eyebrows in enquiry, while Will hesitated. Olivia cocked her head, her gaze sweeping over him. "Unless you already have plans?"

Which would be decidedly odd, because he never had plans. Except this time he did, or rather, he would have, if he ever said yes to anything.

"Dad wants to go to Norfolk," Jake confided, and Will found himself flushing.

"Jake—"

"I saw the invitation."

Olivia looked at Will, questioning. "Invitation…?"

"For a mate's fortieth birthday," Will half mumbled. "I wasn't going to go, but…" When he'd received the invitation a couple of weeks ago, he'd automatically dismissed it. There was no way he could get the childcare coverage, and there was no one he was comfortable leaving Lally and Jake with, anyway. Jake had night terrors, and Lally still sometimes wet the bed. Besides, he couldn't even remember what it was like to go to a proper party, and he hadn't seen any of his Norfolk friends since Rachel's funeral. Seven hours in the car was way too long to travel just for the weekend…

"Why weren't you going to go?" Olivia asked, and Will stumbled through his explanations, while she continued to look unconvinced.

"They could stay here," she suggested when he'd finished. "If they wanted to, and you were comfortable with that. Then they could do the treasure trail, as well." She smiled down at them as Jake and Lally started jumping again.

"Oh yes, please!" Lally turned to Will. "Can we, Daddy, please, can we?"

"I don't know…"

Olivia bit her lip. "Sorry, I shouldn't have barged in with a suggestion." She glanced at the two children. "Do you see that table there, with the drinks? Why don't you ask my sister Althea for some lemonade?" Clearly sensing the grown-ups needed to talk, Jake and Lally scampered off. Olivia turned to Will, her blue eyes nearly navy with self-recrimination.

"I'm sorry, that was thoughtless of me. I shouldn't have invited them without discussing it with you first."

"No, no," Will said, startled by her apology. "I didn't mind. It's just…I couldn't ask that of you."

"Why not?" Olivia asked, the question so simple Will was left speechless.

Why not? Because he didn't have friends like that anymore; because he'd become so used to being alone. Because after losing one person he was afraid to let anyone else in. Because his children were a lot to handle. "It just seems like a lot," he managed after a moment.

"It isn't," Olivia assured him. "I like children. A lot. And there will be plenty of people around to help—my parents can be surprisingly useful, and Tobias is always happy to play games. It'll be fun." Her narrowed gaze scanned his face. "But only if you're comfortable with it, Will. Do you even want to go to this party?"

"Sort of, yeah." He passed a hand over his face. "It's a mate of mine from work. A tree surgeon I hired on occasion, for the big jobs. I haven't seen him since…" He trailed off, but he could tell Olivia understood.

"I know it's a long way to go," she said quietly, "but I can't help feeling it would be good for you to see some of your old friends." She laid one slender hand on his arm, her fingers soft on his skin. "You don't need to be so alone."

But I feel alone. He swallowed down the words. "I know."

"So you'll think about it?"

As if on cue, Jake and Lally raced back with their glasses of lemonade. "Well, Daddy? Can we? Can we stay at Casterglass?" They looked at him with an eagerness he hadn't seen in a long time. Part of him didn't want them to get attached to the castle, to Olivia. What if it all went pear-shaped, and they ended up getting hurt? He couldn't bear for that to happen, and yet keeping them from making friends, from seeking happiness, seemed cruel. Still he hesitated. Did he even want to go to that party? What would he say to all his old friends, the ones who hadn't been in touch for over a year? They were living their best lives, going on holidays, having babies, the whole shebang. And he was…not.

"Please, Daddy," Lally said, her tone quiet and heartfelt, and Will's heart ached.

"Okay," he said, and he smiled at Olivia as Jake and Lally cheered. "Okay. It sounds like a plan."

Chapter Sixteen

"ARE YOU SURE you're just friends?" Althea asked, her tone full of scepticism as Olivia buzzed around the bedroom next to hers, making up the two twin beds for Lally and Jake. "You are watching the man's children, after all."

"I'm sure." An impish sense of possibility—something she hadn't felt in a long time—made her add, "For now, anyway."

Althea's jaw dropped and Olivia couldn't help but laugh. "Olivia, are you serious?"

"I haven't actually said anything, you know."

"You certainly haven't said anything about the night you spent at his cottage. Do you want to tell me about that now?"

Olivia hesitated and then admitted, "We kissed. Once." Althea squealed, and she wondered why she was choosing to impart this information now. Maybe because ever since she and Will had had that "when I'm ready" conversation, she'd felt light inside, almost as if she were walking on air. She wasn't waiting, she realised; she was just *being*. It felt good, to not have that anxiety cramping her insides, even as their time on the garden was surely coming to a close. What the future held, she had no idea, but she felt happy. And the more time she and Will spent together, both in and out of the garden, the more she hoped—and even believed—that they'd both be ready, maybe even someday soon.

"You kissed? And then you ran away like Cinderella?"

"Something like that. It was awkward, and it was clear he regretted it. He's still grieving for his wife."

"So what has made you change your tune? Because you were all doom and gloom before, and now you're sweetness and light."

"Well, we talked again," Olivia confided as she put fresh pillowcases on the beds' pillows. "And he said he might be ready for a relationship someday."

If she expected Althea to be as thrilled about this news as she had been, Olivia realised, she was disappointed. Her sister was giving her an "are-you-serious?" look.

"So he's asking you to wait, for, I don't know, forever?" she stated in a voice dripping with incredulous scorn.

"Not forever, and he didn't even ask. He just said. And as it happens, I'm happy to wait. I really like Will. I understand why he's not ready." Each of these simple statements filled Olivia with a quiet, contented pride; she wasn't being insecure, or needy, or clinging. She wasn't grasping for a relationship, the possibility of a relationship, anywhere she could find it because she was desperate for the married with

2.1 kids scenario that so many women had. She just *was*. And she liked it.

"That may be so," Althea said, her voice full of doubt, "but how long will it be until he's ready? And what if he's never ready? What if he's just stringing you along?"

"I think he means what he says, Althea," Olivia replied. "And anyway, you don't see any other single blokes queueing up to ask me out, do you?"

"Well, there might be, if you looked around." Althea frowned. "I just don't like the idea of a guy who keeps you dangling. I know how that feels—it was basically my whole marriage—"

"Will is not Jasper," Olivia stated firmly. "And like I told you, he hasn't asked me to wait. He's just let me know that if and when he's ready for a relationship, he'd want it to be with me."

Althea pursed her lips. "It still seems a bit manipulative to me."

Olivia let out a huff of exasperation. "Stop transferring your issues to me, Althea! I'm actually happy with the way things are. I don't want to rush into a relationship, either, as it happens."

"Because of that married guy?"

Her sister sounded so dismissive, but then she didn't know the whole story. Olivia tried to avoid the guilt that threatened to rush in; Althea believed she'd dropped Matt as soon as she'd realised he was married. That it had never got very far at all. And Olivia still didn't want to come clean on that score.

"Yes, because of him," she said.

"Olivia—"

Thankfully she was spared her sister's lecture by the sound of a car driving up the lane. Olivia peered out the window and saw Will's truck pulling in next to the kitchen door. "They're here," she announced, grateful to end the conversation. "I'd better go down and meet them."

In addition to taking care of Lally and Jake, she'd also agreed to have Piper, and so it felt like a very full house as Will brought in a bag each for the children, and another for Piper's food and dog bed. The children had already raced out to the garden as Olivia took their bags upstairs.

"Are you sure this is all right?" Will asked, following her up the stairs, his forehead knit with anxiety. "I won't be back until Sunday suppertime—"

"As if I'd back out now," Olivia returned with a laugh. "It's fine, Will. Honestly." She put the bags in their room, turning to him with a smile.

"Lally wets the bed sometimes," he said in a rush. "Not often, but I've brought a change of pyjamas."

"Okay."

"And Jake sometimes has night terrors—there's nothing you can do, just sit with him till he stops screaming." He winced. "Are you sure—"

"Yes, I'm sure." She patted his arm. "I'm right next door,

and it's only for one night. Sam used to get night terrors. I know what they're like."

For a second Will's eyes took on a glossy sheen, as if he were near tears. "You're being so kind," he said, almost as if he couldn't believe it.

"I'm happy to do it," Olivia assured him, touched by his gratitude. "I told you, I love children, and Lally and Jake are both very sweet." She put her hand on his arm. "Please don't worry yourself. Have a good time."

Will put his hand over hers, and for a second Olivia forgot to breathe. Forgot how much his touch affected her—his palm warm and dry, his fingers laced with hers for a brief, tantalising moment. Such a simple touch, nothing more than a gesture, and yet…

"Thank you," he said in a low voice, and all Olivia could do was nod. Her hand was tingling. Her whole body was tingling, every single nerve remembering how good it had felt when he'd kissed her. Aching for him to do it again.

"It's not a problem," she finally managed, her voice sounding rusty, and Will removed his hand from hers.

"Okay, then. I'd better get going."

She nodded, not trusting herself to say anything more without revealing how much that little touch had affected her. In any case, the next few minutes were a flurry of goodbyes; Will hugged both Jake and Lally and gave Piper a quick pat on his head and a fondle of his ears.

"Thank you," he said yet again as she walked him out to

the car.

"You don't need to thank me all the time, honestly. It's fine."

"I know, but…" He shrugged, smiling wryly, and then, so quickly she didn't have time to process it, he stepped forward and put his arms around her. Olivia's arms closed around him automatically, her body acutely conscious of every point of contact with his. Shoulders. Chest. Tummy. Thighs. *Help…*

He gave her a quick, tight hug and then stepped back while Olivia's senses reeled and she tried desperately not to show it.

"Bye then," he said, and then he clambered in his truck and was gone.

FORTUNATELY THE REST of the day was too busy to dwell overmuch on that hug and how it had affected her, although even so every spare second Olivia found herself recalling it— or at least, her body did.

Still, she kept busy organising the treasure hunt with Lally and Jake, and guiding them through it. She'd arranged some stickers and Haribo sweets as a prize, with which they were delighted, and, since it was still warm out, they went down to the river and splashed in its shallows while Olivia threw sticks for Piper to fetch.

"I love it here," Lally pronounced as she flung herself on

the mossy bank next to Olivia.

Olivia smiled down at the wet little girl and then glanced up at the hazy blue sky, the fronded branches of the willow tree creating a green lacy overlay. "I love it here, too," she said, surprising herself. She'd always felt fond of Casterglass, despite its dilapidation, but now she realised how deeply and truly she loved the place. It had soaked into her marrow bones, her very soul. It was part of her; her own well-being linked with that of the castle's, and in transforming the garden, she'd begun to transform herself. She felt like Sleeping Beauty, awakened not by a kiss, but by a garden. Although the kiss had helped.

Lally laid her head against Olivia's shoulder. "Can we stay here forever?" she asked, her tone serious.

Olivia gave a little laugh. "Not forever, but definitely until tomorrow night."

Lally thrust her lower lip out in the beginnings of a pout. "But I want to stay."

"Tell you what," Olivia said as she stood up and then helped Lally up from the riverbank. "You can come here whenever you want."

"Even for sleepovers?"

"Especially for sleepovers." She felt that was a promise she could make, and one she was happy to keep. "But right now we need to think about our tea. Jake? Piper?"

As the sun was starting toward the horizon, a definite chill entering the air, they walked back through the garden to the castle, its windows lit up by the late afternoon sun. A sleepy sense of contentment stole over Olivia as Lally slipped her hand into hers. This day had been wonderful, and yet it would have been absolutely perfect if Will had been here, too.

THE NEXT FEW hours were taken up with helping to make dinner while Tobias played *Candyland* with Lally no less than six times, and then several games of backgammon with Jake. After that Olivia oversaw baths for Lally and Jake, grateful that they didn't complain about the tepid trickle of water that constituted the castle's plumbing, and then, after several stories rustled up from her childhood collection, tucked them into bed.

The whole day had been so easy, so delightful, that Olivia did not have a single qualm as she tucked them both in and left the door a little bit ajar, with the hall light on. Downstairs she tidied up while Althea raised her eyebrows, clearly looking for details—or dirt.

"It's fine," Olivia told her with a laugh. "It's all been fine."

"If you don't fall in love with Will," Althea said rather darkly, "you might fall in love with his children."

"I think I already have," Olivia admitted. "They're wonderful—they've been angels today, really." That wasn't quite true; Lally had had something of a tantrum when Jake had found more woodland animals than she had, and she'd cried when Olivia had brushed her hair after her bath. Jake had point-blank refused to eat any green vegetables at teatime, and he'd bickered with Lally over which bed to take, and then taunted her that he had the comfier bed. But even so it had been nothing Olivia wasn't used to or couldn't handle— and it had opened up that well of longing in her that she'd been trying to keep under control for so long.

I want a baby. A husband. A family of my own...

Yes, she could so very easily fall in love with Will's children.

OLIVIA JERKED AWAKE, breathing hard even though she didn't know why. Her bedroom was pitch-black, the curtains drawn against a moonless night. And then she heard the screaming—one long, shrill note after another. It raised gooseflesh on her skin, the hair on the back of her neck. It sounded otherworldly. It was, she realised, Jake, screaming in the grips of a night terror.

She scrambled out of bed, fumbling for her dressing gown and slippers, because the castle got cold at night, even in May. The screaming went on and she felt her way blindly to the adjacent bedroom; someone must have turned the hall light out before going to bed, because it was utterly dark; she couldn't even see her hand in front of her face.

"Jake. *Jake.*" She held his shoulders, anchoring him rather than trying to wake him up. His eyes were open, blank and staring; his mouth, too, in that awful, endless scream. Lally had woken up as well, her thumb in her mouth, as she watched him unblinkingly, unmoved.

"He usually screams for a while," she told Olivia matter-of-factly. "Then he goes back to sleep."

"Okay. Right." She'd told Will Sam had had night terrors, but she realised she had forgotten what they'd felt like. Terrifying, which made a certain amount of sense, she supposed. "What does your daddy do when this happens?" she asked Lally, who gave a little shrug before removing her thumb from her mouth.

"Sits with him. Talks to him. Says stuff like he's there and Jake doesn't need to be scared."

She could picture Will doing just that. "Okay." Olivia put her arm around Jake's tense shoulders and began to speak softly. "It's okay, Jake. I'm here. Nothing is going to hurt you, I promise." He continued to scream, his eyes blank and staring, and she continued to talk gently, even though she longed for him to stop. The others must be awake, wondering what on earth was going on, but no one came to the door.

Then, finally, thankfully, after about five minutes but which felt like fifty, Jake subsided. It was like a tap being turned off; suddenly he was silent, and he lay back down as if he'd been felled, his eyes closed, his breathing normal. Olivia let out a shuddering breath. *Wow.* That had been intense. How often did Will have to deal with it? she wondered. Yet one more thing he had to cope with on his own.

Remembering Will's other warning, she turned to Lally. "Do you need the toilet?"

Taking her thumb out of her mouth, Lally nodded.

A few minutes later, Olivia crept back to bed, exhausted yet unable to sleep, startling at every noise, worried that Jake might wake again. This couldn't happen every night, she decided, since he hadn't woken up when she'd slept at Will's, but how many nights did he suffer this way? Once in a while? Two out of three? It made her heart ache for Will, for having to put up with so much all on his own. It also made her body ache with exhaustion, because this parenting gig, even for a temporary twenty-four hours, was a lot harder than she'd realised. Yes, she still wanted the baby, the husband, the family package, but by a groggy dawn Olivia had to admit it looked better all glowed-up from a hazy distance rather than in the fatigue-dazed reality.

Fortunately, two strong cups of coffee in the morning helped to clear her head, and Lally and Jake were both eager helpers in the garden. Olivia walked the length of the garden while the children were her "weed-spyers", pointing to anything that resembled a weed. More often than not Lally thought a flower was a weed, and yanked a whole bunch of hosta to prove it, but Olivia managed to take it in her stride.

Then, out of the blue, when Lally was chasing Piper a few metres ahead of them, Jake turned to Olivia with a startlingly direct look. "Are you going to marry my dad?"

"I—what?" Olivia blinked at him foolishly, completely wrongfooted.

"Are you going to marry my dad?" Jake repeated clearly, as if she were simply hard of hearing. "You've been spending a lot of time with him. I thought maybe us coming here for the weekend was, like, a test."

A test? "No, no, it wasn't a test, Jake," Olivia did her best to reassure him. "Not at all. Your dad had a birthday party to go to—remember?"

Jake shrugged. "He doesn't usually go to parties. I thought that was just an excuse."

"No, it wasn't," she assured him, even as she half wondered if Jake was speaking more truth than either of them realised. Had Will been setting some sort of test, to see if she could handle his kids? But, no. That was fanciful, ridiculous. They weren't even dating yet, for heaven's sake, and he did have a party to go to. Besides, she'd been the one to suggest having Lally and Jake at Casterglass, not Will. He'd been gobsmacked by the suggestion.

"Oh, well." Jake shrugged, philosophical. "I thought I'd ask."

"Your dad and I aren't even dating, you know," Olivia ventured cautiously. She felt as if she were treading on dangerously thin ice, talking about this at all, with an impressionable child. Surely Will should be having this discussion first? "I'm sure he'd tell you if he was even thinking of being in a relationship with someone, never mind marrying them."

Jake shrugged again, the logistics of adult romantic relationships clearly beyond him. "I wouldn't mind, you know," he said after a moment. "If you did."

"Oh, Jake." Olivia felt the sting of tears behind her lids. *I wouldn't, either*, she thought, but didn't say.

He gave her another one of those direct looks. "As long as you didn't argue."

Olivia gazed at him, nonplussed by another turn this whole surreal conversation had just taken. "Why would we argue?"

"Mum and Dad argued a lot," he told her, shocking her with his matter-of-fact tone. "Mum was always shouting. Dad would just grumble."

Olivia had no idea what to say. She'd never, ever got the sense from Will that he and Rachel had had a contentious marriage. Far from it. "That must have been hard," she remarked after a moment. She didn't want to pepper Jake with questions, but he was clearly waiting for a response.

A third shrug. "I didn't like the shouting."

"No, I don't like shouting, either." What else could she say? She longed to comfort this little boy, but she didn't want to pry into Will's marriage in this way—and yet she was itching to know more.

"I think my dad likes you," he told her frankly, and Olivia blushed.

"Well, I—I don't know…" she stammered, hardly able

to believe she was talking about these things with an eight-year-old.

He sighed. "Anyway, I was just saying. I wouldn't mind."

Was that his seal of approval, then? Olivia nodded, not knowing what to say, and then turned when Lally let out a triumphant shout.

"I found lots of weeds, 'Livia!" she called, and Olivia's heart sank as she saw Lally hefting a newly planted wood fern.

With an apologetic look for Jake, she hurried forward, all thoughts of marrying Will Turner temporarily forgotten.

Chapter Seventeen

WILL WAS NOT having a good time at the party. At least, not as good a time as he'd been hoping to have—reconnecting with old friends, child-free for an entire twenty-four hours. His mate Pete had given him a handshake and a hard clap on the shoulder when he'd arrived, and then disappeared into the melee of people Will barely knew. Those he did know gave him uneasy smiles or said "All right?" in a slightly nervous tone, as if they didn't really want to hear his answer.

Will wasn't surprised by the uncertain reception; people were scared of death. They acted as if it were contagious, as if having your wife die aged thirty-six was something that could be passed on by close contact, a bit of conversation. Or maybe the awkwardness was just too great; nobody ever knew what to say, and the resulting yawning silences were simply too much to bear.

In any case, Will decided to grab a beer and plonk himself on a chair in the corner, happy enough to sit out the festivities. He wouldn't know what to say, either, and as he sipped his beer and looked around, he realised he had very little in common with the people who had once been important to him.

He'd been idealising his life in Norfolk, he reflected, because Cumbria had been so hard. He'd allowed certain ideas to cement in his mind since Rachel's death—ideas with their basis in truth, but perhaps not as set in stone as he'd made them. Like him not wanting to come to Cumbria in the first place. Or how great they'd had it here in Norfolk. Or how good his friends were, or how close-knit his family, even.

As he sat and sipped, he remembered some of the difficulties they'd faced—the business he'd set up that still struggled because of all the competition, the rising house prices, his parents being doting grandparents, but only when they felt like it. More than once he or Rachel had asked for some fairly urgent childcare help only to be told they weren't available—which was fair enough, he supposed, since his parents had their own lives to live, but he realised he shouldn't have been as surprised as he'd been when they'd moved to Portugal. And Kerry had been the same—a doting aunt who whirled in and out of their lives but could never be nailed down. Half of his friends were childless, which put them completely out of sync, and the other half were as busy as he'd been. None of it had been truly amazing, but he supposed it had been comfortable enough. Familiar, at least.

If Rachel had lived, he wondered, would his feelings about Cumbria be different? They would have done up the house, made friends with the neighbours, not that they had all that many. Still, Rachel had always been good at that, far more extroverted than he was. They would have done the hikes and camping they'd been planning on, climbing all the Wainwrights, wild swimming in Coniston Water, living their best lives.

Will sighed, pushing the thoughts away. There was no point dwelling on what now could never be. Rachel *had* died, and he still had a lot of life to live…which made him think, as ever, of Olivia.

Was he ready to start dating again? It had now been twenty-one months since Rachel's death. That was a long time. Lally, he suspected, was starting to forget her mother, her memories no more than hazy snapshots rather than particular episodes or events. Jake had clearer memories, but Will could tell they seemed more distant to his son, with every passing day. And as for him? He had plenty of memories—lots good, a few bad. Not just the memories of the disease and her death, which held a horror as well as a poignancy, but the arguments they'd had in the run-up to moving, and then when they had moved, and it had constantly rained and he'd hated the house and he hadn't been able to find any work.

Rachel had been determinedly upbeat, but Will had struggled, had taken it out on her. Why had he done that? Why had he been such a jerk? She'd given as good as she got, though—he remembered their slanging matches, the way

Rachel's temper would ignite like a firework.

"All right, mate?" Pete gave him another hard clap on the shoulder as he sat down next to Will. "You're sitting in the corner here like Johnny No-Mates, but I guess it's hard to be back?"

Will shrugged. "A bit, maybe."

"How are the kiddies?"

"They're okay."

"And Cumbria? You've got used to the rain, I guess?" He let out a somewhat forced laugh.

Will managed a smile. "Yeah." He could tell that Pete wanted to move on already, but felt honour-bound to chat to his old friend.

"You could still move back, you know. There's work for you, I'm sure. Everyone's gone garden-mad lately, wanting full renovations of their outdoor spaces…"

"Mmm." He would not, Will knew, move back. Jake and Lally had barely any memory of Norfolk; life in Cumbria might be hard, but starting over would be harder.

Pete nodded in understanding. "You feel settled there?"

Again Will thought of Olivia, especially when he'd hugged her, which he hadn't been planning to do, and yet it had happened, and it had felt nice. *Really* nice. So nice he wanted to do it again. "Yeah," he told Pete, and for the first time that evening he felt happy. "I actually do."

By the time he was turning in to Casterglass on Sunday evening, Will was practically twitching in his eagerness to see Lally and Jake—and Olivia. The sun was hiding behind a bank of grey clouds, and the wind that buffeted him as he stepped out of the car was chilly, reminding him that the weather in Norfolk had definitely been better, but he didn't care. This, he realised, felt like home. Maybe even for the first time.

"Daddy!" Lally came out of the kitchen door as if fired from a cannon and catapulted into his arms. Laughing, Will swept her up into a tight hug.

"How have you been, sweetheart? Have you had a good time?"

"Yes, oh yes! We did a treasure hunt and we made flapjacks and we went swimming and we played hide-and-seek in the castle…" She ran out of breath as she flung her arms around his neck.

"My goodness, that sounds like an awful lot." He lifted his head from Lally's exuberant embrace to smile at Jake, who had slouched in behind Lally, ducking his head self-consciously, already too old to go in for a hug. "Hey, Jake. How was your weekend?"

"Okay." He hunched a shoulder. "I didn't get any stomach aches."

High praise indeed, then. Will met Olivia's gaze over Jake's head. She was dressed casually in a pair of jeans and a fleece, her hair pulled back in its usual plait, and he thought she looked wonderful.

"You survived?"

"Just about." She rested one hand on Jake's shoulder in a gesture that seemed both natural and affectionate. "It was fun."

"Not too exhausting?"

"No," she replied, but he saw a flicker through her eyes that made him think she must have been up in the night. Had Lally wet the bed, or had Jake had one of his night terrors? He wouldn't ask now, in front of them.

"Right, well, we should leave you in peace, then. I'll just get the kids' bags—"

"They're here, in the kitchen."

He followed her into the kitchen, taking the opportunity of a few seconds away from Lally and Jake to ask her in a low voice, "How was it, really?"

"I told you, it was fine." She brushed a wisp of hair from her eyes. "Jake woke up in the night, if that's what you're wondering, but he settled back down and it was all fine. Fun." Her smile deepened, reaching her eyes. "Really."

"Good." Will blew out a breath. "I'm glad."

"The more important question is, did you have fun?" Olivia asked. "Your big weekend away."

"I did, but I was actually glad to come back here." He paused and then said awkwardly, blushing a little, "It felt like coming home."

Olivia laid her hand on his arm. "I'm glad," she said with

quiet sincerity.

"Have dinner with me," Will blurted. Olivia's eyes widened. "I mean us," he clarified quickly. "Have dinner with us. As a thank you for this weekend."

Actually, he'd meant have dinner with him as a date, but he'd instinctively and instantly backtracked, because he hadn't been on a real, honest-to-goodness date in way too long. Still, this was a progress, of a sort. A meal. Together. And with the kids.

"Okay," Olivia said, her gaze scanning his face as if looking for clues. "That would be nice."

"Friday?" Will suggested. "I'll pick you up at six."

"Sounds great."

He hefted the bags as she stepped back, and moments later he was climbing into the car with Lally and Jake, Piper faithfully keeping watch in the back, tongue lolling happily.

"See you soon," he called as he waved out the window, and as he drove down Casterglass's drive he wished he didn't have to go, and judging by his children's faces, he thought they felt the same.

IT WASN'T A date, Olivia reminded herself for about the two hundredth time since Will had suggested going out for a meal last Sunday. It was Friday and after three outfit changes she was standing by the kitchen door, wearing her patchwork skirt and a simple knit top, waiting for Will to pick her up.

She'd played it casual with her family, saying it was nothing more than a thank you, but if Althea's narrowed gaze had been anything to go by, her sister wasn't fooled.

Her mother had been pleasantly puzzled—"He didn't need to do that, did he?"—and her father's eyes had twinkled rather knowingly, although he'd merely smiled. Seph had said nothing at all, and Sam, who had remained distracted and distant since his return from New Zealand, had given her a look that was only somewhat quizzical.

"Are you guys dating?" he'd asked, and Olivia had been quick enough in her reply.

"No, not—" She stopped from saying yet, not wanting to push her luck. "Not like that."

"Like what, then?" Sam asked, but he didn't seem to mind when Olivia wasn't able to reply. A few days ago she'd asked him if anything was troubling him, and he'd given her a suspicious look.

"Why are you asking that?"

"Because you seem troubled," she replied frankly. "And you'd also seemed reluctant to leave New Zealand. What's going on, Sam?"

"Nothing." He spoke too quickly. "It's just been a manic few months, that's all. And I am jet-lagged, you know." And then he'd hightailed it out to the far meadows where he was setting up the glamping site. Olivia didn't see him for the rest of the day.

Still, she wasn't going to waste her emotional energy

worrying about Sam when she had an evening with Will to look forward to—and be nervous about. He'd made it clear it wasn't a date, and yet even with Lally and Jake present, Olivia couldn't help but feel that it sort of was, at least a little bit. Another test, perhaps? Or was she being ridiculous even to hope? And what about that sly little voice that whispered inside her head whenever she fell silent, telling her she didn't deserve any of this, or even a chance at it?

Last night she'd looked at Matt's Facebook page, just to check that he and his wife, Liana, were still married. She'd kept herself from checking it before because it had felt like salt in a very open wound, but she was surprised, as she looked at his profile pic, that she didn't feel much at all at seeing that handsome face, the dark hair swept away from the high forehead, the crinkled, hazel eyes that had sparkled when he'd looked at her. He'd made her feel so special, and yet she knew now that that was how he made everyone feel—at least judging by the words his wife had spit at her.

Do you think you're special? You're not the first, you know.

Did it make it worse or better, that she'd been one in a potentially long line? Olivia had decided that overall it was better, because even if she'd been a homewrecker, she hadn't been solely responsible for Matt and Liana's marital problems. Matt himself surely bore the brunt of the responsibility, not that he would ever acknowledge it, of course.

But she really didn't want to think about Matt now. At

least from what she'd seen on Facebook, he was still with his wife. That was something, wasn't it? She wasn't responsible for a divorce. Yet.

She heard the rumble of Will's truck coming up the drive, and started forward gladly, eager to put the past behind her—and focus firmly on the present, as well as a possible future.

THE RESTAURANT WILL had chosen was the Bridge Inn, ten minutes away in the tiny village of Santon Bridge, perched directly across from a little arched stone bridge, with sweeping views of the fells in every direction, the placid surface of Wastwater glinting under the evening sunlight to the north.

The children were in a state of high excitement; a meal out was clearly an unusual occasion, and Will seemed, at turns, both jumpy and relaxed, joking and smiling, but looking, Olivia thought, twitchy and trapped in the headlights whenever she asked him a question directly. She couldn't tell if he was a good kind of nervous, because this was a date, at least sort of, or a bad kind, because he was regretting asking her along, backtracking into the whole I'm-not-ready mode.

She did her best not to worry about it and enjoy the evening—the setting was stunning, the sky a wide swathe of deep, dazzling blue, the sun lighting up the fells and making Wastwater shimmer like a mirror. For mid-May it was positively balmy, and yesterday's downpour only served to make the air fresh and everything look damp and new.

I love it here, Olivia thought suddenly. *I really do.* They were seated at their table on the sunken garden terrace with its patio heaters and festoon lighting, the fells providing a dramatic violet-hued backdrop. *I love it here, and no matter what happens with Will, I'm glad I came back to Cumbria. To Casterglass.*

"Daddy," Lally asked, "can I have fish fingers? And do I have to eat the beans?"

"No beans for Lally," Will answered. "Noted."

"Do I have to have the children's menu?" Jake asked plaintively. "I'm almost nine."

"You think you can handle the big burgers?" Will raised his eyebrows. "Go for it, bud."

Jake grinned and Olivia's heart lightened. She was glad the children were here, grateful that she knew them well enough that she could join in the light-hearted banter. Grateful, too, that Lally felt comfortable enough to ask her to help her with the simple crossword on her paper placemat, and Jake asked if he could tell her the top five most infectious diseases. Before Will could protest Olivia nodded, her arms folded on the table.

"Go ahead. Hit me."

"Tuberculosis," he said with relish. "Pneumonia. Malaria—"

"Jake." Will looked affectionately exasperated, but Olivia

wasn't fazed.

"Go on."

"Hepatitis—"

Fortunately by then their meals came, and Olivia was busy cutting up Lally's fish fingers while Jake tackled his huge burger—too engrossed to reveal what the last one was.

As she was digging into her own burger, Olivia felt someone's gaze on her. It was an older woman at the next table over, out with her husband, giving her a twinkling smile.

A bit uncertainly, Olivia smiled back.

It wasn't until the end of the meal, after they'd averted a disaster when Olivia had caught Lally's nearly full glass of fizzy lemonade before it had tipped onto the floor, and Jake had eaten an impressive two-thirds of his massive burger, that she learned what that smile had meant.

She was washing her hands in the ladies' when the older woman came in, giving her another one of those beaming smiles.

"You have such a lovely family," she said, and Olivia stiffened, startled.

"Oh—"

"You can just see the love shining out of each one of you," the woman continued. "It made me so happy to watch you. It reminded me of when our children were young, a long time ago now. My eldest is forty-four." She let out a little laugh and Olivia smiled in return. She could hardly disabuse the stranger's notion now, could she? And really, was it so far-fetched?

She could dream a little, couldn't she…?

And for a second she did, imagining that Lally and Jake were hers, Will her husband. They'd all be bundling into the truck to head home to their cosy cottage; Will would give the children a bath while she laid a fire and poured them both a glass of wine…

It seemed so real, so completely possible, that Olivia felt as if it would be a shock if it *didn't* happen. She really needed to get a grip.

She dried her hands as she gave the woman a smile of farewell.

"Thank you," she told her. "We've had a really nice evening."

And yet the fragments of that fantasy continued to tease her as they got back in the truck. Will would drop her off at Casterglass before heading back home, but Olivia could still imagine that they would all be going home together, that she and Will would curl up by the fire, that they would go upstairs together, hand in hand, to that rumpled king-sized bed…

Now she really needed to stop.

The sky was black, studded with stars, as Will pulled up to the castle, a dark hulk of stone against a darker sky. Lally had fallen asleep in the back seat, slumped against Jake, who was trying to make out his encyclopaedia of gross facts by moonlight.

"I had a really good time tonight," Will said as he turned to her.

Olivia's heart did a funny little skip. "So did I."

"I'll see you to the door."

She didn't argue that it was hardly necessary, considering the kitchen door was about ten feet away, and she wondered, with some incredulity, whether Will was going to kiss her goodnight.

They stood by the door, as awkward as a pair of teenagers, Will's hands jammed in the pockets of his trousers as he scuffed the ground with one foot. From the corner of her eye Olivia saw Jake looking up from his encyclopaedia, his narrowed gaze trained on the pair of them. No kiss, then, surely.

"I...I wanted to say..." Will began, and Olivia's heart skipped again.

"Yes?"

"I like you," he blurted, blushing. "I really like you. And I'd like to think that maybe we could...one day, at least...you know..." He trailed off and a sudden, impish smile teased Olivia's mouth.

"We could one day maybe you know?" she repeated teasingly, and Will laughed.

"Date. There, I said it. Maybe one day we could date. I mean, one day soon, not just...in the hazy future." He was both blushing and smiling, his round faced creased, and

Olivia felt a rush of warmth, of something alarmingly close to love.

"One day in the next ten years or so?" she asked. "Or one day sooner than that?" Her heart thudded from just asking that.

"Sooner," Will said. "Definitely sooner."

And then Olivia was smiling, too, and they were both grinning at each other like a pair of loons, when Jake opened his car door.

"Lally just dribbled on me," he complained. "And she's snoring. Can we please go home?"

Chapter Eighteen

T HE NEXT WEEK passed in an agony of expectation. Every time Olivia saw Will, her heart flipped and her skin felt as if it were electric, as if her whole body was buzzing. When he casually brushed her hand as they hefted a piece of lumber—they were finally building the bridge—she felt as if she'd been electrocuted, but in a good way.

Every time she looked at him she imagined kissing him, and she was starting to worry that her thoughts might be visible on her face. Surely he could tell how much she wanted him to touch her? She felt as if she were sending telepathic messages, as if her desire was radiating out from her fingertips. And unfortunately, she had no idea if Will felt the same—although she was starting to hope and even believe he did.

They were working flat out to get the garden picture-perfect ready for the bank holiday afternoon tea, as was everyone else with their various areas of responsibility. Olivia had designed posters with a border of strawberries and ivy that advertised the event; Tobias and Poppy had plastered them around Casterglass, and even in some of the villages farther afield.

Althea had arranged for a local farmer to supply vats of clotted cream and punnet after punnet of strawberries, and she was making all the scones herself. Her mother had hefted crates of old china that had been put away in the attics decades if not centuries ago, and washed them all by hand, ready for the big day. Her father had unearthed a bottle of very old and expensive champagne from the cellar, to be a raffle prize. Sam had designed a simple obstacle course for children, a preview of the ropes course he was intending to build. And the walled garden and path to the river would be open for visitors to wander, and children to complete the treasure hunt, with a pack of castle-themed stickers as a prize.

Really, they were very nearly there, and yet Olivia still felt as if she were racing around all day, remembering little details, trying to make things perfect. That wisteria needed tying back, she would think as she rushed through the walled garden. That paving stone looked uneven, and was that a weed? She fell into bed after eleven every night, exhausted yet still buzzing.

Will had started bringing the children to Casterglass after picking them up from school, and working alongside her until dinnertime. It had been easy enough for the three of them to join the Penryn family dinner, and after a single eyebrow raise Althea accepted this development in her stride, and the good-natured banter had flown around the table, along with discussion of all the developments with getting the estate visitor-ready.

And through of all this, Olivia longed for Will to turn to her, take her in his arms, and say, "Remember when I said one day soon? Well, it's now."

But he didn't, and she told herself she didn't mind, and really, despite the way her body burned, she didn't. She liked working side by side; she liked the easy conversation they shared, and the just-as-easy silences. She liked it all, and she was happy to wait. Mostly. Occasionally the old anxieties crept in, and she wondered what would happen when the castle actually opened. Would Will disappear from her life? She'd suggested, albeit somewhat hesitantly, that they keep him on one day a week, to help with maintenance, and Althea had harrumphed something close to a yes. But one day a week wasn't what she really wanted. She wanted every day, all the time, together forever...

Which was a bit much, considering.

Then, on Thursday, she received a telephone call from her friend Julie in York. After a preliminary asking of how she was, Julie got right to the point.

"You know the boxes you've been storing at mine? Well, they need to be moved."

"What?" Olivia had half forgotten that when she'd returned to Casterglass, she'd sold her furniture and moved most of her other possessions to her friend's, taking only the essentials back home. She'd been wanting to get out of York as fast as she could, and Julie had had a spare bedroom free. The decision had felt simple.

"I'm getting a lodger," Julie told her. "I didn't think it would happen so quickly, but I advertised last week and I settled on a tenant today. They're moving in next week, so I need the boxes gone by this weekend."

"This weekend…" But it was only one week before the big tea! There was no way she could take a whole day off to schlep to York and back, and for what? A bunch of junk?

Except, Olivia recalled hollowly, it wasn't actually just junk. There were all her sketchbooks, and some summer clothes she rather liked, as well as personal effects—photos, knick-knacks, mementoes she definitely wanted to keep.

"Can't you put them somewhere?" she asked Julie a bit desperately. "I'm right up against it for work—I could come the weekend after next—"

"I've had your stuff for nearly four months," Julie reminded her. "And I haven't minded, but you said you'd get it after a couple of weeks."

"I'm sorry," Olivia said wretchedly. "I completely forgot."

"Understandable. And I'm sorry I have to rush you, but they've got to go."

There was, she realised, nothing for it. The garden was in good shape, she reminded herself, and Althea had everything else under control. Mostly. She could, if pressed, spare a day. It seemed she would have to.

"What's wrong?" Will asked when she returned to the greenhouse where they'd been repotting seedlings for the veg patch she was planning for later in the season. "You look like you just received some bad news."

"Not bad news, just something inconvenient," Olivia told him. "I have to go to York for the day on Saturday, to pick up some of my stuff a friend was storing. She doesn't have room for it anymore."

"That's not too much of a problem, is it?"

"No, it's just we've been so pressed. I don't want to take a whole day off." And, she realised, she didn't really want to return to York and all of its painful memories. And, she realised on top of that, she was going to have to ask someone to come with her. Sam? Althea? They would both be so busy.

"So you'll drive there?" Will asked, and Olivia ducked her head, blushing a bit.

"Yes, although I don't actually drive. I never learned."

Will's double take was almost comical. "Really?"

"Really. I didn't need to at uni, or in York, and I just…didn't." She shrugged. "The older I became, the less confident I felt even trying to learn."

"And yet you've accomplished so much," Will said. "You could still learn, you know."

"Not before Saturday." She sighed, shaking her head. "Althea will have a fit if I ask her to drive me."

"I'll take you," Will said, and Olivia turned to him in surprise. Belatedly she realised how it might have seemed as if she'd been fishing for him to suggest just that.

"Oh, I didn't mean for you…" she began only to have Will laugh and shake his head.

"I know, but I don't mind. We can make a day of it. I've never seen York, and I think we could both take a break from the garden, to be honest."

"What about Lally and Jake? Should we bring them?"

"I'd rather not. Lally's not good on long drives—she gets car sick. I mean, *really* car sick." He grimaced. "Do you think your family would be willing to put up with them here?"

"I'm sure of it," Olivia said, her enthusiasm for the idea starting to grow. They'd all become incredibly fond of both Lally and Jake over the last few weeks, and she really didn't think anyone would mind having them around. She could get her stuff out of York, and never have to go there again— which, despite the friends she'd made, was a welcome prospect. And she'd have time alone with Will.

"So?" Will's grin turned impish, a little uncertain. "It's a date?"

Was it a real one at last? Olivia felt her smile widen, till it was practically at her ears. "It's a date," she confirmed.

IT WAS POURING rain when Will picked up Olivia to head to York, not that he cared about the weather. He was feeling buoyant, almost as if he were floating, excited to spend the whole day with her…on a *date*.

Lally and Jake raced into the castle's kitchen almost as soon as Will had parked, Piper trotting happily behind. Olivia came out, dressed for the weather in a fleece and jeans, the sort of clothes he saw her in most days, and yet somehow today she looked different. Or maybe he just felt different.

"Hey," she said, sounding shy.

And suddenly just as shy, Will managed a quiet "hey" back.

Olivia brandished a flask of coffee, and a couple of home-baked muffins. "Fortification, for the trip."

"Perfect."

He gave Lally a quick hug and Jake a pat on the arm, both of them squirming away, eager to spend the day at the castle.

Althea smiled at him as she shooed him away. "We'll be fine here. Lots of work to be done for my little helpers."

"Thanks," Will said gratefully, and then he was climbing into the truck, Olivia swinging in beside him, and they were off.

"Not a great day for travel," Olivia remarked wryly as the rain spattered the windscreen, making the wipers work overtime.

"No, but we've had a pretty good run of sunshine," Will replied, and Olivia raised her eyebrows.

"What, a whole week?"

He laughed. "I must be becoming Cumbrian, to obsess about the weather like this."

"You said it felt like home," Olivia remarked after a moment, her light tone turning serious. "Did you really mean that?"

Will considered his response. He sensed there would be a subtext to whatever he said, and perhaps to this entire conversation, and maybe to the whole day. Their date. There was a certain expectation on his side, and probably Olivia's, that made him feel both nervous and excited. "Yes, I did mean it," he told her. "Surprisingly, because I think I had idealised Norfolk in my mind—it was where I was happy, where Rachel was healthy, where my parents and friends were. And that's all true." He paused, reflecting. "But none of it was perfect. And when I went back for that party, I realised it wasn't home anymore. People have moved on. I have."

"I suppose I feel that way about York," Olivia ventured. "I'm a bit nervous about going back even just to pick up my stuff, to be honest."

He wasn't exactly surprised, but he hoped for more insight into her former life. "You are?"

She nodded, looking out the window as if she wanted to avoid his gaze. "Things didn't end very well there."

"The relationship?" he guessed. He had told her quite a bit about Rachel, although admittedly not all of it, but she'd barely said anything about her own broken heart. Should he ask? Would it be prying? Yet he wanted to know, mainly because he just wanted to know about *her*.

"Yes, although I shouldn't even call it a relationship. It wasn't, not in any real sense." She let out a little shuddery sigh, and Will wondered what to say in response. What did she mean, it wasn't a relationship? Had she been seeing this guy, whoever he was, or not? He decided silence was the best option, and after a moment Olivia spoke again, her voice low. "I really do regret the whole thing. Completely."

"I'm sorry." He had no other words, and wasn't sure there were any. Still, he wondered what she wasn't saying. Had the man been unkind, perhaps even abusive? The possibility made his gut tighten. When he'd first met her Olivia *had* seemed as if her confidence had been knocked. There had been something fragile about her, a sense of self-doubt that had, in the last few months, ebbed away the more they'd worked on the garden. She'd grown in confidence, in certainty, in joy. He was glad for that, but it did make him wonder. Just what had happened with this bloke she didn't like to talk about? What had this guy done to her?

"I think it's time for coffee," Olivia announced brightly, and reached for the flask she'd brought. They chatted about easy topics for the rest of the three-hour journey, steering clear of relationships or anything potentially fraught. It was easy enough simply to shoot the breeze, brainstorm about the garden, joke about silly, random things. He *liked* being with her, Will thought. He really did.

As they drew closer to York, he noticed how Olivia started to tense, her body stiffening, her gaze darting everywhere as if she expected to see something—or someone—she really didn't want to. The guy, Will presumed. He was starting to really think she had suffered some sort of abuse, or maybe just a really bad break-up. Something not good, anyway.

"Turn right here—it's the third on the left," she said once they'd reached the city proper; they'd stopped chatting about twenty minutes out of York, and she'd only spoken since then to give directions.

Will turned onto a row of pretty mews houses just outside of the city centre. Olivia gave him a tense, fleeting smile that seemed to have very little to do with actual happiness or good humour.

"Is it hard?" Will asked quietly. "Being back?"

"I just don't want to see anyone." She bit her lip, as if she'd revealed too much. "Let's get this over with."

Her friend Julie, at least, seemed happy to see her, giving her a big hug and welcoming Will just as warmly.

"I'm sorry to have to make you collect these," she told Olivia in a voice full of apology. "It's just my hours have been cut at work and I need the rent from a lodger."

"Don't worry." Olivia managed an understanding smile. "You've been so kind, Julie, having them at all. I'm embarrassed to admit I'd forgotten I still had all of this stuff here!" She shook her head, laughing wryly, but Will could see how hard it was for her to act light-hearted. She looked both tense and fragile, and he ached to comfort her. Protect her, even, all that caveman kind of stuff coming to the fore.

"Maybe you didn't need any of it then?" Julie suggested. "You could just bin the lot, you know!"

"Trust me, I thought about it," Olivia returned with a smile.

"I understand you not wanting to come back," Julie added more quietly, shooting Will an uncertain yet curious glance.

Olivia didn't reply and Will had the sense that he was definitely missing something as he and Olivia started to heave the boxes back to the truck. He enjoyed the brief glimpses into Olivia's life that he got, hefting those boxes—he spied a pile of sketchbooks, all delicate watercolours and charcoal drawings; some gardening books; a framed photo of her and Althea, another one of her with her parents, on her graduation from university. He didn't want to pry, so he didn't sift through any of it, but he wanted to. He wanted to know more about her.

While he was carrying the last box downstairs, he overheard a whispered conversation between Olivia and Julie in the kitchen.

"—sure you know what you're doing?"

"It's not like that, Julie."

"I just don't want you to be stupid. Or get hurt."

A sigh; he could picture her fragile smile. "Thanks for the love, but I won't. And I'm *not* being stupid, trust me."

Will hurried outside, not wanting to be caught eaves-dropping. It sounded, he realised, as if Olivia had been giving Julie the brush-off—or really, had been giving *him* the brush-off. After all the optimism and excitement he'd felt earlier—this was meant to be a date, after all—Will struggled not to feel a little chastened. A little hurt. Did she not like him? And why had Julie been so quick to warn Olivia off him? Was it because of this unknown guy who seemed to loom larger and larger on the horizon?

"Ready to go," Olivia called brightly as she gave Julie one last hug and then started towards the truck, not quite looking at Will.

Will said goodbye to Julie and then they were heading off; they'd only been there for about half an hour. All in all, it was not quite the visit he'd been expecting.

"Do you want to stop somewhere?" he asked uncertainly. When he'd told her he'd take her to York—when he'd called it a date—he'd been imagining something slightly more interesting and fun. A wander down the Shambles, a poke through the cathedral, maybe afternoon tea, complete with finger sandwiches and those pretty little cakes.

"Maybe on the way," Olivia told him. Her gaze was still averted. "Let's just get going for now."

"Okay." What else could he say? But this wasn't turning out at all as he'd expected. As he'd hoped.

They drove in silence all the way out of the city; it was only a little past one in the afternoon. They'd stop for lunch, at least, Will hoped. Do something fun. Redeem the day. The *date*.

As he drove past the York City Limits sign, a visible shudder went through Olivia, and she kept her face turned to the window.

Chapter Nineteen

THAT HAD BEEN a lot harder than she'd anticipated. It took Olivia another fifty miles away from York before she finally started to recover her equilibrium. By that point she realised Will had to have suspected something was going on, and she felt badly for going all quiet and distant on him when this day was meant to be fun, even flirty. She still wasn't ready to explain why, though.

"How about some lunch?" she finally asked with some semblance of brightness, when they'd been in the truck for nearly an hour.

Will turned to her, one eyebrow quirked. "Are you okay?"

"Yes. Yes. Sorry." She shook her head, rubbed her eyes even though she'd managed to keep herself from crying. "Bad memories, that's all. A bit of déjà vu, which I should have expected but didn't."

"That bloke did some number on you, huh?" Will kept his gaze on her for a second before he turned back to look at the road.

"I suppose, in a way." She paused and then said, with difficulty, "I'm sorry, but I'd really rather not talk about it. It's in the past, and that's where it should stay." She didn't want to seem as if she were pushing Will away, but she had a sense that was how he felt as he remained silent as he kept driving.

Finally, when the silence felt as heavy as a blanket smothering them, he nodded towards an exit off the motorway. "How about somewhere off there?"

"Okay."

More silence as he headed onto the slip road, and then a few minutes later turned into the car park of a cosy-looking pub. The rain had abated and the weather was nice enough that Will suggested they eat in the pub's garden, which had several umbrella-shaded tables with a view of the Yorkshire dales.

"We're in Postman Pat territory now," Olivia remarked jokingly, but she barely got a smile from Will. He looked terribly serious—his brow furrowed, his gaze intent. Her stomach dipped. *Uh-oh.*

"You know, Rachel and I argued a lot," he told her once they'd ordered drinks. Olivia blinked, surprised by the sudden sharing of confidences. "Generally, I mean, but also about moving to Cumbria. I didn't want to move there, or anywhere, and she did, a lot. She was frustrated with me for being such a wet blanket and I was angry with her for not seeing my side." He cleared his throat. "If I'm perfectly honest, it was pretty rocky for nearly the whole year before she was diagnosed. Six months of thinking about moving, and then another four and a half months of us actually doing it and settling in. And all the time we were arguing."

"Jake mentioned something about that, actually," Olivia admitted, and Will grimaced.

"Did he? I'm not surprised, but it still hurts. The last thing you want is your child being privy to all that, but I know he must have heard some of our arguments. Rachel had a temper, and I tended to shut down, which made her even angrier." He sighed and looked down at the table, tracing the grain of the wood with one finger. "I was even talking of moving out, right before she went to the doctor. I wasn't going to do it, not really—I think I always knew that—but we talked about it. Rachel flung it at me one night and I retaliated in kind."

She hadn't expected that, somehow. Arguing was one thing…but separating? Thinking about separating? She didn't know how it made her feel, to know Will and Rachel hadn't had the fairy tale. Maybe no one ever did. Life was real and hard and sometimes painful, even when you were in love. "I'm sorry, Will," she said quietly.

He nodded, accepting the sentiment but seeming determined to continue. "When she was diagnosed, it put a screeching halt to all of our bickering—I mean, you just can't then, can you? And it was so, so quick… She had just one round of chemo after her diagnosis before they decided it wasn't working. She'd already become too frail to stand it, and her organs were just...shutting down. She died two weeks later."

"I didn't realise it happened that fast," Olivia murmured. She'd known it had to have been fairly quick, but a matter of *weeks*... She couldn't even imagine what Will must have been going through, to have to process Rachel's cancer diagnosis, chemotherapy, and then—gone. Just like that.

"Yeah, just six weeks," he confirmed with a shake of his head. "Crazy. I think both our heads were spinning. Rachel was very practical about it, though. As soon as she was diagnosed, she started preparing for her possible death. That was something else that made me angry, but I'm glad she did. The doctors didn't pull any punches. We both knew it was serious, but I didn't want to go there in my mind and she was willing to. She recorded a bunch of story books for the kids, wrote them letters for their birthdays, and made photo albums for every year she'd had with them. She was amazing about it all." He cleared his throat again. "But I'm telling you all this to make sure you understand our marriage wasn't perfect. It was pretty crappy at times, even, and neither of us acted the way we wished we had." His blue-eyed gaze was intent and focused on her as he finished quietly, "So whatever was so terrible about this relationship you had in York—whatever happened that made you want to hightail it out of that city as fast as you could—I'd understand, Olivia. I really would."

Olivia stared at him, speechless, touched, and feeling really rather wretched. He was providing her the perfect opportunity for her to talk about Matt, was basically *begging* her to, and she…couldn't. She just couldn't.

She thought of how disapproving Julie had been, when she'd seen Olivia come in with Will, her gaze shooting to the wedding ring he still wore as her mouth had thinned. The second she'd got Olivia alone, she'd started to lecture. *What are you doing with a married man? Haven't you learned, Olivia?*

Olivia had been so stung by the assumption she hadn't been able to gather her wits enough to tell Julie that Will was widowed. In any case, Julie had quickly backtracked, saying she was worried for Olivia's sake, didn't want her to get hurt, and while Olivia knew that was true, she also knew there was more to it. All her friends had been quick to judge when she'd got involved with Matt, and why shouldn't they have been?

But it still hurt somehow to be judged by one mistake. To be completely defined by it, which was how it had felt, with everyone shaking their heads, clucking their tongues. *Really, Olivia! What were you thinking?*

It was part of the reason she'd been so desperate to leave York, but even so she hadn't shaken the feeling, the belief, that getting involved with a married man would somehow always define her, even if she was the only one who knew about it. She couldn't bear for Will to give her the same thinned-mouth look Julie had, or worse, a look of shocked disappointment, maybe even revulsion.

"Thank you for saying all that," she finally managed. "And for telling me about you and Rachel. It really means a lot to me." She hesitated, and Will leaned forward, so eager and hopeful, wanting to hear more. To help her, to grow closer to her. She could see it in her eyes.

And Olivia almost, almost told him. *I was blinded by desperation and hope and I made a really, really stupid mistake.*

But then he would want details, and she would have to give them, and then she really would be left with no excuse. If they were going to date, she knew she would have to tell him sometime—probably—but right now, when everything between them was so fragile and not quite started, she couldn't bear to have everything fall apart. To lose what they'd already shared, little as it was.

She reached over to touch Will's hand. "I will tell you about it," she promised. "Sometime. I just…can't right now. I'm sorry."

Disappointment flashed in Will's eyes but he nodded. "Okay. I understand," he said, although Olivia thought he probably didn't.

They managed to redeem the rest of the day, at least, chatting and laughing over lunch before they got back in Will's truck. The farther they travelled from York, the more Olivia was able to shake off the dark cloud being there had caused to hover over her. By the time they reached Casterglass, she was pretty much back to her normal self.

Lally and Jake raced out from the garden as soon as Will pulled up the castle drive, Piper barking and bounding joyfully after that. Olivia felt a deep-set sense of rightness, a slotting into place. Home. She was home.

"You're back, you're back!" Lally shouted while Jake looked hopefully at his father.

"Did you get me anything?"

"Get you anything?" Will exclaimed with a laugh. "I was only gone for the day."

"I got you both these." Smiling, Olivia showed them the chocolate bars she'd picked up at a rest stop when Will had filled up on petrol. "For being real troupers."

"Thanks, 'Livia!" Lally said happily, clutching the chocolate bar in one rather grubby fist.

"For after supper," Will told her.

"Why don't you stay for supper?" Olivia suggested.

"If you're sure…"

"Of course we're sure," Althea said as she came in from the kitchen. "Really, you should know by now you're practically family." This with a significant look at Olivia that made both her and Will blush.

And really, it *felt* as if Will was family as they all chipped in to help with supper and set the table. Later, as they got caught up on a day of castle news—the bunting had thankfully arrived, and Sam had made an amazing simulated version of his ropes course on a tablet that visitors could look at—it felt both surprising and completely natural for Olivia's shoulder to brush Will's as they sat next to each other at the big table, and then for him to rest his hand on hers, which did not escape the eagle-eyed Althea. Olivia was sure to be interrogated once he'd left, but for now she just enjoyed the feeling of warmth and possibility and, yes, love that sitting next to Will gave her.

With everything so perfect and so possible between them, how could she bear to risk—ruin—it all by telling him about Matt? And yet, Olivia thought disconsolately, if they were to have any sort of future together, how could she not?

THE WEEK BEFORE Casterglass's unofficial opening and afternoon tea was utterly manic. Will couldn't remember ever being so tired, even when he'd been in the darkest throes of Rachel's illness. He stayed at Casterglass until it was time to pick up the children, and then took them back to the castle and worked until they needed to go home for bed. Now that the day was actually imminent, a thousand little things had come to his attention: the lack of a handrailing on the stepping stone path to the river; the signposts that needed to be painted and stuck to direct people to the wild flower meadow, or the terraced lawn, or the beach; the lawn that needed mowing three times in one week because it had rained and it was May, the time of year when you could practically *see* the grass growing.

Olivia was just as busy, tying up vines, repotting seedlings, and always, always weeding. She was also putting finishing touches on the menus that would be handed out, with watercolours of strawberries and scones, and helping Althea with all the last-minute details of planning a party that around five hundred people were expected to come to.

"Poppy and Tobias have really outdone themselves with the marketing," she told him on Wednesday, when they were having a tea break in the summerhouse. "In addition to papering every village from here to Broughton, they've put it up on all sorts of touristy websites. Anyone who is coming to the Lake District for the half-term holiday is going to know about it."

"That's fantastic," Will said. They'd kept up their easy camaraderie all week, even though the trip to York had, at least in Will's mind, been a bit of a damp squib. He'd wanted Olivia to level with him in the same way he had with her, and yet she clearly hadn't felt able to.

Which was ironic, really, because he'd been the more emotionally distant one in his marriage, but clearly Olivia had closed-off areas of her life that she wasn't ready for him to be privy to. Which was okay, Will had to keep reminding himself, because they weren't even dating yet. Just because he was feeling ready to take that next step didn't mean Olivia was quite there yet.

And, he knew now, he *was* ready. The last few weeks had been an exquisite sort of torture, spending almost every waking moment near Olivia and yet not able to touch her. Every time they accidentally brushed hands or legs or he just breathed in the lavender scent of her, he ached with longing. And yet no moment had arisen for him to take that final step and seal the deal, as it were.

He was thirty-seven years old, and he felt like a teenager—awkward, uncertain, desperate with desire. And also afraid. Trying to date after being so long on his own, and so long being married, felt like dancing through a minefield. Did he even remember what it was like, to date someone? How he was supposed to act? And what about his children? They adored Olivia, it was true—there could be no question about that. But what if it all went pear-shaped and they got hurt? They'd already been through so much. Will couldn't bear for them to be put through any more.

And yet, *and yet*...surely Olivia, a *life* with Olivia, was worth the risk? Every time he looked at her his heart turned over. Every time she tilted her head in that way he knew so well, her eyes crinkling, her mouth pursing, he felt a rush of—well, maybe not *love*, but something amazingly and alarmingly close to it.

He wanted to take that final step. They were so nearly there already, with their conversations about being almost ready. All they needed, Will was sure, was a kiss to seal the deal. But in that manic week, he was finding it difficult to engineer the right moment.

It was Jake, surprisingly, who forced his hand.

Will was stringing fairy lights along the bridge that he'd spent the last few weeks working on. He was proud with the way it had come out—a gently arched wooden walkway with handrails. Simple, but in keeping with the surroundings, and the waterfall he'd constructed looked natural, spilling down into a deep, still pool below.

"This would be a good place to take Olivia," Jake stated matter-of-factly as Will finished stringing the lights. He glanced at his son, bemused.

"Take her?"

"If, you know, you were going to be all…" He made a face. Will stopped messing with the lights to give his son a proper look.

"Going to be all…?" he prompted.

Jake's expression of distaste deepened. "Kissy."

Will choked back a horrified laugh. "Jake, Olivia and I aren't—"

His eight-year-old son rolled his eyes, looking far too knowing. "Come on, Dad. Everyone knows something is going on between the two of you."

"Nothing is going—"

"Maybe not yet," Jake cut across him. "But you could take her here, maybe when the sun is setting? I like her. Lally does, too."

Clearly Olivia had his children's seal of approval. "So," Will ventured, still cautious, "you wouldn't mind if…"

Another eye-roll. "No, Dad, we wouldn't mind. Trust

me."

AND SO WILL orchestrated it for the Friday evening, the night before the afternoon tea. He hadn't had time before then, but at supper Jake had given him a meaningful look, which Will took to mean now or never. The marquee was set up, the kitchen was bursting with punnets of strawberries and platters of freshly baked scones, and the gardens were at their most beautiful. Tomorrow's forecast looked breezy but clear, which was better than the usual downpour for this time of year.

"Olivia," Will practically barked in his nervousness, once the dinner table had been cleared. "Would you mind if I, ah, showed you something?" Althea's head whipped around, her eyes narrowing in a way that made Will think she knew exactly what he was intending. Olivia clearly didn't, though, for she just gave him a slightly puzzled look.

"Show me something?"

"Um, yeah. At the waterfall."

Jake and Lally exchanged conspiratorial smiles and Will resisted the urge to tug at his collar. It seemed everyone was in on this plan. Everyone but Olivia.

"What's wrong with the waterfall?" Olivia asked, alarm in her voice. They'd mitigated several near-disasters in the last few weeks: a leak in one of the barn roofs, a cracked urn, a broken mower.

"Nothing, nothing. I just wanted to show you…something." He sounded, Will thought, ridiculous. Or maybe even creepy.

"All right." Olivia gave a little baffled shrug, and then followed him out through the walled garden.

"It's amazing in here, isn't it?" Will remarked as they wound their way along the brick paths through the neatly tended beds; everywhere he looked something was in bloom—the lilac bush by the greenhouse, the wisteria climbing up the wall, the strawberry plants in their raised bed, the early evening sunlight gilding everything in gold. "You've done a fantastic job."

"Well, it hasn't been just me, of course."

"The walled garden mostly has," Will replied. "And I think it's what will stick in people's minds."

"What about your waterfall?" Olivia shot back with a smile. "I couldn't have imagined it would look so, well, waterfallish."

He laughed at that, and almost took her hand, but he was feeling so nervous something stopped him. He realised he hadn't actually formulated a plan beyond getting her to the bridge. Casanova he was not.

"Careful," he murmured as he unlatched the gate and let her go through first. "I think the stones are stable, but you can never be too sure."

"They'd better be, or someone might slip and break their leg," Olivia half joked.

"And sue you," Will agreed with a small smile. "We can't be having that."

Although the sun hadn't started to set yet, in the wood it was shadowy and dark, and he reached out a hand to steady her, only to then keep her hand encased in his. Smooth.

Olivia gave him a funny little look but didn't pull away, and Will decided that was a win. Had he ever been this nervous before? He must have been, but he couldn't quite remember. Even when he'd proposed to Rachel, that hadn't been so nerve-racking; they'd been eating chips at the beach, and chatting dreamily about the future, and Rachel had teased, "So, are we getting married, then?"

And Will, startled and pleased, had answered, "I guess we are."

Not the most romantic proposal, but it had worked, although he didn't actually want to think about Rachel now. He wanted to think about Olivia.

They walked in silence through the dark, mossy wood, following the flagstones and then down the path Will had dug out and covered with woodchips, to the bridge that arced so sweetly over the river, the plash of the waterfall the only sound besides the whispery rustling through the willow fronds that bordered the riverbank, their low-lying branches brushing the surface of the water.

"This is so beautiful, Will." Olivia dropped his hand to rest her own on the railing as she looked down over the crystalline waterfall. "It's amazing." She turned to him, a small smile of querying expectation playing with her lovely mouth. "Was there something you wanted to show me?"

"Er." He was so not a smooth operator. "Well, not really, actually."

"What?" Now she just looked confused. Did she really not guess what was going on? Was she not expecting it, at least a little? There was nothing for it but for him to spell it out.

"Well, the truth is, I actually, um, brought you here to, ah, kiss you."

Olivia simply stared. Will felt a flush crawl up from his collar. Wow, what a way with words he had. Or not.

"Kiss me?" she repeated, and he couldn't tell from her tone if she was merely surprised or more alarmingly unenthused by the idea. What if he really had got it all wrong?

"Yes. I wanted to…well, I've been trying to find a time, a moment when I—when we could—"

The little smile flirting with her mouth deepened, reached her eyes, and gave him hope. Olivia took a step towards him. "Is this a good moment, then?"

It was a perfect moment. "Yes," Will said simply, and fortunately the rest was wonderfully easy. She came into his arms, or maybe he drew her—probably a bit of both. She fit there perfectly as she tilted her head up to his and Will brushed her lips with his own before he settled his mouth there more firmly, and he felt Olivia turn pliant and soft in his arms.

"Does this mean we're actually dating now?" she asked when they finally came up for air. "For real?"

"For real," Will confirmed, and then he kissed her again.

Chapter Twenty

OLIVIA DIDN'T HAVE much time to dwell on her exciting new status with Will, because the very next day the afternoon tea was upon them. After they'd kissed on the bridge, they'd walked hand in hand back up to the castle, and everything had seemed brighter and shinier to Olivia, the whole world possessing a brand-new gloss. She let out a giggle, and Will grinned at her and squeezed her hand. She pushed away any fleeting, niggling thoughts that she still hadn't told him about Matt—really, she thought, what did Matt matter? He was history, unimportant, irrelevant. *What matters*, she told herself, *is now. Us.* Their future together, shining so brightly.

To her surprise and blushing embarrassment, everyone seemed to know what had happened on the bridge because as she and Will came into the kitchen still holding hands, a spontaneous cheer arose from those seated around the table—her parents, Lally and Jake, Althea, Sam, even Seph. They were all grinning, and so was Will, and Olivia shook her head, laughing.

"Was I the only one who didn't know what was going on?"

"You do now," Althea fired back with good humour and Will kissed her cheek. Olivia felt, bizarrely, as if they'd had a proposal or even a wedding; all they'd done was kiss, but it had felt monumental. Momentous. Everything, she realised, had changed.

But the celebratory spirit was brief, because Althea had decided the tablecloths for tomorrow needed ironing— again—and Sam asked for Will's help to arrange orange cones over the far meadow, in case there was overspill parking.

"How many people do you think are coming?" Olivia asked.

Poppy replied smartly, "Hundreds and hundreds, judging by the hits and the comments we've gotten on the links we've posted on different websites. Some people are coming from as far over as Newcastle."

"Wow," Olivia said, unsure why she suddenly felt just the tiniest bit uneasy. "I hope Casterglass lives up to their expectations."

"And that we have enough scones and strawberries," Althea added. "I've ordered another dozen punnets, just in case."

"If it's a washout we can make loads of jam," Olivia suggested with a smile.

"And sell it in the gift shop!" Poppy added. She and Althea had been developing a line of Casterglass-themed products as well as local merchandise for when the shop opened, hopefully by the end of July. So far they had tea caddies, tea towels, fridge magnets, and coffee mugs.

Jake and Lally fell asleep on the sofa in the sitting room while they all worked on the finishing touches until nearly ten o'clock; it seemed every time Olivia turned around, there was something more to be done—a weed to be plucked, a corner to be dusted, a picture to straighten.

Finally her father called time on it all. "We're done, my darlings!" he cried exuberantly, his arms outflung. "They shall have to take us as they find us. I for one need my beauty sleep. Let us enjoy the sleep of the just tonight, and wake refreshed and ready in the morning."

"Couldn't have said it better myself," Will said, giving Olivia a sideways grin. Somehow they'd all ended up in the kitchen, as if a homing device had led them all to the heart of the home—and the large pot of freshly brewed tea that Violet had made, playing hostess with her usual gracious and slightly vague aplomb.

"I was thinking we could offer damson jam along with the strawberries," she told Althea. "I recall putting up dozens of jars when you were small. I'm sure we still have them somewhere in the larder…"

Althea and Poppy, architects of the menu, exchanged panicked looks. "I think we'll stick with strawberries, Mum," Althea said with as much diplomacy as she could muster.

Olivia could only imagine the horror of forty-year-old mouldy jam being served during the castle's unofficial—yet feeling very official—opening. Her mother had gone through various homegrown hippie stages during their childhood, and the culinary results had been dubious, never mind how they'd survived the decades.

"I can't believe people will actually be here tomorrow," Olivia said as she walked upstairs with Will to collect Lally and Jake. "After all the months of work and preparation…people are finally going to see the results. They'll go through the garden, they'll follow the treasure map—"

"They'll walk over the bridge." In the upstairs hallway, he tugged on her hand, a smile curving his lips before he brushed hers with a kiss that Olivia thrilled to. It felt both wonderful and strange to kiss him, almost as if it were forbidden but it wasn't. They were really together. A *couple*. She could hardly believe it, even as Will's arms came around her.

"I feel like I have to pinch myself," he murmured against her hair, and Olivia let out a giggle.

"I was thinking the exact same thing."

He leaned back, tucking a tendril of hair behind her ear, his fingers gently skimming her cheek. "I know this is coming a little late, but…you're okay with this, right?"

"This?" Olivia repeated blankly.

"Us, I mean. I know I took you by surprise on the bridge, and we never really discussed—"

Olivia couldn't keep from laughing aloud. "Will, we discussed it to death beforehand, trust me. And I'm definitely okay with this. I thought that much was pretty darn clear."

A shy, pleased grin tugged at his mouth. "Okay. I just felt I had to check. It's been a while since I've dated, you know. I don't know the protocols anymore."

"You're doing fine," Olivia assured him, and kissed him again for good measure. "Just fine."

They broke apart to go fetch Jake and Lally, pausing on the threshold of the sitting room to take in the sight of the two children asleep on the sofa, curled up together like a pair of puppies. Olivia's heart squeezed with love.

"I take Lally and you Jake?" she suggested, and Will shot her a grateful look.

"Sounds like a plan."

She crouched down to heft the little girl over her shoulder, all soft and sleep-warmed, her little arms curling trustingly around her neck, her head nestled into the curve between her chin and her shoulder. Will put Jake into a fireman's lift, the boy groaning softly before he curled into his father.

They walked carefully down the stairs, out of the castle, and into the darkness. The night had a hushed quality, the stars glimmering from behind a blanket of lavender-tinted clouds.

"I love this time of year," Will whispered. "When the sun sets so late and it feels like the day goes on forever."

"I wish this day could go on forever," Olivia whispered back. "It's been the most amazing day."

They grinned at each other over the children's heads before lowering them gently into the back of the truck; both Jake and Lally immediately curled up on the seat, once again deeply asleep.

Will turned to Olivia, and she thrilled to see the look of intent in his eyes. She was starting to *know* that look. The look that meant he was going to kiss her. Again. And she wanted him to.

"I wish you were coming home with us," he said in a low voice, and her stomach flipped.

"So do I." She could already picture it—creeping into the darkened cottage, Piper lifting his head from in front of the Rayburn, the creak of the steps as they went upstairs…

"Maybe one day," he said, brushing her cheek with his fingertips.

"Yes…"

He bent his head to kiss her, softly this time, like a whispered promise. Olivia closed her eyes, her insides fluttering and then settling—excitement, then joy.

"Goodnight, Olivia."

"Goodnight, Will."

She stayed out on the drive until he'd disappeared down the lane, and when she turned back to the castle she knew she was grinning like a fool. Althea knew it, too, because she gave her a pert look.

"Well, don't you look loved up."

"It takes one to know one, I guess," Olivia returned, and Althea laughed.

WILL WAS GRINNING as he drove away from Casterglass. He couldn't keep his mouth from stretching into a cheek-splitting smile, because he was so happy. He couldn't remember being this happy. Surely he'd been this happy with Rachel, especially before the move had started to strain things between them, but it felt hazy, a distant memory—almost, but not quite, as if it had happened to someone else.

For once the fogginess of his memories didn't fill him with either guilt or alarm. It was okay to let things blur around the edges; perhaps that was the only way you could live with your grief. The pain couldn't stay sharp and raw forever, and he didn't want it to. For once he had some-thing—someone—to look forward to. He wasn't alone anymore, struggling on his own, fighting the tidal wave of loneliness and futility that so often threatened to drown him. Just sharing a smile or a look with Olivia made his heart sing. Holding her in his arms, feeling the way she melted into him—well, that made his whole body sing. He was so darn happy, and the feeling was strange and new, a little uncomfortable, and a lot wonderful.

"Dad?" Jake's sleepy voice came from the back of the truck. "Did you kiss her at the bridge like I said?"

Will's smile widened. He hadn't expected his eight-year-old to be his advisor when it came to romantic matters, but there it was. "Yes, Jake," he told him. "I did."

"Good," Jake said, and then fell back asleep.

WILL DIDN'T HAVE much time to dwell on how happy he was because the next day was basically everyone to their battle stations. He arrived at Casterglass with Jake and Lally at nine o'clock in the morning; the first guests weren't meant to arrive until one o'clock, but by eleven cars were already pulling up.

"We might as well let them in," Althea said. "They can have a wander around."

"We should have charged an entry fee," Sam said, frowning. "Look at them all. We've been working like the dickens to make this place a tourist attraction, and now we're giving it all away for free."

Poppy rattled a tin under his nose. "Suggested donation five pounds per person," she told him. "And a request to tell your friends."

Sam gave a grudging smile. "You're a real businesswoman, aren't you, Pops?"

Will only caught glimpses of Olivia throughout the day; she was wearing a pretty blue sundress, her hair loose and wavy about her face. He saw her across the walled garden, listening attentively to an older lady with a knobbled walking stick; then she was running lightly across the terraced lawn to bring a stack of napkins to the tea table; then she was in the courtyard, blowing bubbles with Lally and Jake and a handful of visiting children.

And still the people kept coming. By one o'clock, the official opening time, there were already over a hundred people milling through the grounds. They'd given away nearly fifty of the treasure maps. Althea, Poppy, and Seph were all dishing out bowls of strawberries and cream as fast as they could. Walter and Violet were giving bespoke tours of the inside of the castle, with plenty of dramatic narration, and Sam had set up a tent with several tablets they'd requisitioned from various family and friends so people could try the ropes course simulator. Will had led several groups of people down to the bridge and waterfall, to oohs and aahs of delight. It was all, Will thought, pretty near perfect. He certainly felt proud.

As if the world agreed with him, the sun came out from behind a bank of puffy white clouds to bathe the terraced lawn in golden light during the highlight of the afternoon, when Walter Penryn, Baron of Casterglass, would pronounce the castle officially open—even though it wasn't. "Technicality," Althea had said breezily. "We're not breaking any health and safety regulations, that's the main thing."

People were standing or sitting around, on folding chairs, blankets, or some of the benches hewn from logs that he and Sam had fashioned in the last blitzkrieg week of rushing around making final additions. There were scones lathered with clotted cream and jam (not the damson), and bowls of luscious red strawberries with heaps of cream. Walter was holding aloft a bottle of champagne that rivalled the one they were giving away in the raffle as he cleared his throat and then began to welcome everyone in a surprisingly stentorian voice.

"Greetings, ladies, gentlemen, and little tykes! As the twelfth baron of Casterglass, I am so very delighted to welcome you to my home. Casterglass has been in my family for nearly seven hundred years, and by opening its doors to the community we have been a part of for a very long time, I trust it will remain so! More importantly, we can share the wonders and delights of this very special property, as well as its colourful history, with all of you. Although the castle is not officially open today..." He gave a little ahem while good-natured titters ran around the gathered group. "It is open to all who are here as our guests. It is my dearest wish that you come to visit again and again."

"And pay for the pleasure," Olivia whispered as she sidled next to Will. He reached for her hand, just because. "At least, let's hope so."

"But for now," Walter continued, "please enjoy yourselves. There are plenty of strawberries, scones, and cream, and of course champagne!" He brandished the bottle, to a chorus of cheers. "But before I pour the libations, I need to make special mention of my wonderful family, who have all worked together to make you being here today a reality. First and foremost, my wife and helpmeet, Violet."

Will saw Olivia smother a smile as Violet looked up from the scone she'd been scoffing with a vague "who, me?" expression. Everyone clapped, which made her look only more baffled, before her expression cleared and she blew Walter a kiss.

"And secondly, although just as importantly, I need to thank my children. Althea, who was the initial vision behind this project, as well as the overseer and dare I say it, much-needed slave driver." He gestured to Althea, who was standing behind the table of food, blushing and looking pleased as well as a bit weepy. John slid an arm around her waist while Poppy, Tobias, and Ben—who had arrived from university only this morning—all cheered for her.

"Next, my daughter Olivia, who masterminded the garden."

"Oh—" Olivia whispered, surprised even though Will knew she shouldn't be. "I didn't really," she murmured, and he pulled her towards him.

"Yes, you did."

More cheers and applause, while Olivia looked both embarrassed and happy, and then Walter continued, "And Sam, who came all the way from New Zealand to head up the glamping and assault course, and gave up a life of adventure abroad to make one here!" Walter gestured to Sam, who was by the tent with the tablet, his arms folded as he ducked his head in a quick nod.

"And last but certainly not least Persephone, who is a magnificent woodcarver and loves this castle with a ferocity that is perhaps greater than my own." He gestured to Seph, who was standing with her friend Doug, looking as if she wasn't sure she should scowl or smile. Will suspected she didn't like the attention, but at least she gave a little wave.

"And now," Walter declared, "enjoy!" He uncorked the champagne bottle with a satisfyingly loud pop, and began to pour plastic flutes of fizz while everyone cheered.

"A very good speech," Will pronounced. "This has all been a massive success. How many people are here, do you think?"

"Oh, I don't know…" Leaning into him, Olivia scanned the crowds. "Two, three hundred maybe? Maybe more? There are still cars coming up the drive." She smiled as she looked around at everyone talking and laughing, and then suddenly she froze, her body turning completely rigid beneath Will's arm.

"Olivia…?" he asked in concern.

"No…" she whispered, sounding both panicked and strangely resigned, and Will frowned, trying to figure out what was going on. Olivia's body was now practically vibrating with tension, her expression transfixed, even horrified.

"Olivia…" he said again, more urgently this time, before he saw a thirtyish woman striding towards them, a furious look on her face.

"You have some nerve," she practically snarled, while Olivia shrank into Will.

He stiffened, ready to fight for the woman he loved—yes, *loved*. "Pardon?" he said, his voice both quiet and icy, but the woman shot him a single, scathing glance before she turned back to Olivia.

"Haven't lost your taste for married men, have you?" she spat.

Chapter Twenty-One

OLIVIA STARED AT Liana's furious face with a numb kind of horror. *How* could she be here? How could this be happening? She felt almost as if she were existing outside of her body, hovering somewhere above the suddenly silenced crowd, as Liana's voice cut across their collective shock.

"It wasn't enough for you to wreck one marriage, was it?" she demanded in a high, carrying voice. "Leaving two children without their father? You had to go ahead and wreck another." She turned to Will, nodding towards his hand, and presumably the wedding ring he still wore. "She likes them married, you know? Goes after them specially. *Stalks* them."

Olivia opened her mouth and then closed it. This was so patently unfair; if anything, Matt had gone after her. *But you went willingly enough.* There was nothing, Olivia knew, that she could say to mitigate this disaster. Liana was the right-eous woman who had been scorned; she was the guilty party, the painted harlot.

"I think you should leave," Althea said firmly. She'd come around from behind the food table and was staring Liana down. "This is a family event, and what you're saying is not appropriate—"

"What *I'm* saying?" Liana's voice turned shrill, sneering. She pointed a shaking finger at Olivia. "How about what she *did*? She seduced my husband!"

"Surely your husband had some say in the matter," Althea returned levelly, remarkably unfazed by the accusation Liana had hurled at Olivia. "But perhaps you don't want to consider that. As I said, not appropriate. We're going to have to ask you to leave."

"I brought my *children* here," Liana said, and Olivia watched as Althea's gaze moved to the two pale-faced children, a boy and a girl, standing on the edge of the crowd, looking understandably apprehensive.

"Then perhaps you should have considered that before launching this diatribe," Althea replied, unmoved, although she did manage a sympathetic smile for the children.

"And what about her?" Liana demanded, jerking her head towards Olivia.

"Well, you see, she lives here," Althea replied with a small, cool smile. "So I'm certainly not going to ask her to leave."

A few nervous titters broke out, and Olivia could bear no more. Liana might be behaving unreasonably, shrewishly, but she was acting out of anger and hurt. She didn't deserve to be mocked or laughed at by anyone. Olivia could not let her sister paint her as the victim in this situation, because no matter how rude Liana was, she *wasn't*. She wasn't at all. Liana was.

"Stop, please," she told Althea, who looked startled at being told to stand down from defending her. Olivia turned to Liana. "I'm sorry, and I will always be sorry, for—for what happened." She took a deep breath, afraid to look at Will, who had been standing next to her during this whole awful interlude, silent and transfixed. "For what I did," she clarified. "I never should have become involved with…" she forced herself to say the words "…your husband. I will regret my part in the whole—affair—" it hurt, to say that "—for as long as I live. I hope you believe that."

For a second Liana looked as if she might soften, but then her features twisted into an ugly sneer. "Is that supposed to make me feel better? Or my children better? Matt left us, you know. He *left* us." Her voice rang out, throbbing with hurt.

Briefly Olivia closed her eyes, as if she could blank it all out. If only that were possible.

"I'm so sorry," she whispered.

"Are you still seeing him?" Liana demanded.

Olivia's eyes flew open. *"What?"*

"Are you still seeing my husband?" the other woman stated clearly. "Are you still screw—"

"That's enough," Althea cut her off, her voice like iron.

"There are children present, including your own."

"No," Olivia whispered, stricken. Tears started in her eyes. "No, *no*, it ended ages ago—after the first time you…" She trailed off as Liana's lip curled. She could feel everyone's eyes on her like a thousand daggers. Someone muttered something, and someone else tutted. And Will still hadn't said anything at all.

"I'm so sorry," she said again, to Liana, to Will, to her family, to everyone. Then she whirled around and sprinted from the lawn, heedless of where she was going, just knowing she had to escape.

Tears blurred her vision as she ran, zigzagging around a few startled people still heading towards the lawn, and then hurtling through the door to the walled garden, the sanctuary she'd fashioned with her own two hands, yet it didn't feel like that now. There was no sanctuary, no way to escape the truth of what had happened, what everyone knew, the stain on her past that would never, ever go away.

A sob broke past her lips and she pressed her fist to her mouth as she kept running, through the garden and then down the path Will had made with the paving stones from Cartmel, along the river, the bridge and its promises mocking her now. She made her way through the narrow path that led to the beach and the sea, only stopping when she couldn't go any farther, for the waves were lapping the shore.

If only she could go farther, wade into the sea, let the cold, salty water wash over her like tears, slip over her head, so she could finally forget it all.

For one horrifying second she was actually tempted. She could picture herself diving into the water, then stretching her arms wide and letting the waves carry her out, out, and then down. Blissful blankness, where this one terrible mistake wouldn't dog her every step, loom over her like an awful shadow, ruin *everything*, again and again.

She let out a shaky sob, her hand pressed over her mouth, as she backed away from the sea as if it were a dangerous animal, a present threat. What on earth had she been thinking, even for a second or two? It couldn't be that bad, it simply couldn't.

And yet…everyone had been looking at her in censure, in judgement, and why shouldn't they? And Will…Will, who had made her so happy, for so brief a time. She hadn't been able to summon the courage to look him full in the face, but she'd seen the rigidity of his body, had felt his shock. He would never be able to look at her the same way again, and she couldn't bear that. She'd rather never see him again at all than have him look at her in disappointment and judgement, and yet that was surely the coward's way out.

Olivia took a deep breath and then picked her way over the damp sand to the flat rock she'd loved to sit on as a child; it jutted out from the mouth the river, towards the sea. Sometimes, when she'd sat on it, she'd felt as if she were on the prow of a ship. Once or twice, rather embarrassingly, she'd pretended to be Kate Winslet in *Titanic*.

Now she hauled herself onto the flat, hard surface and hugged her knees to her chest. The breeze buffeted the surface of the sea into white ruffled waves, and a few seagulls cawed plaintively, wheeling in graceful arcs above as clouds scudded across the sky, blotting out the sun.

Olivia closed her eyes, her chin on her knees, as she recalled the whole mortifying, shameful episode. Liana's icy rage. Her sister's good intentions. Will's terrible silence...

Now he knew. She'd been reluctant to tell him, and now he knew why. He knew everything, or close enough. She'd had a relationship with a married man. She'd known he was married, and she'd still carried on seeing him. Made excuses every step of the way.

And not only did Will know, but so did everybody else. Her siblings. Her parents. Basically every resident of Casterglass. Olivia pressed her hands to her hot cheeks. She'd left York because she hadn't been able to bear the judgement of her friends and colleagues there. Now she would face even worse judgement from her family, from Will? All the people she cared about the most.

She'd have to leave, Olivia thought dismally. She'd have to find somewhere else to go, somewhere no one knew her...and yet, how could she leave? Her life was in Casterglass. The castle, the garden, her family, *Will.*

Except Will probably didn't even want to look at her now.

"There you are."

Stiffening in shock, Olivia turned slowly around and saw Will standing by their bridge, looking out to the sea. His expression was grave, too grave. Her stomach clenched. Was he angry with her? Had he found her so he could lecture her, or was he just going to tell her it was all over?

Of course it was all over. She bowed her head, ready to accept his judgement.

WILL WATCHED AS different emotions chased across Olivia's face—surprise, fear, hurt, guilt, resignation. She bowed her head, a tendril of hair falling across her cheek.

"She's gone," Will said as he walked slowly towards her. He wasn't sure what to say, how to handle this moment. He'd been so shocked by the whole awful scene up on the lawn—the woman's accusations, Olivia's wretched apologies—that he hadn't been able to say a word. He hadn't been able to think, beyond the realisation that this was what she'd been hiding. A relationship—an affair—with a married man. No wonder she hadn't wanted to tell him.

"Althea chased her away, I suppose," Olivia said, her voice so soft Will strained to hear it. Her head was still bowed, her arms wrapped around her knees. "I feel sorry for her. She wasn't the bad guy in that scenario, you know. Not at all."

"And you were?"

Olivia hunched her shoulders, then dropped them.

"Don't you think so?" She didn't look at him as she asked him the question.

"No, I don't think that." Will was silent for a moment. He wished he had more emotional wisdom to handle this moment, but he felt at a loss. He hadn't even started chasing Olivia till she'd disappeared through the walled garden. Althea had given him a stern look, and jerked her head towards the garden, and he'd started running. Althea would take care of Lally and Jake, he knew. Right then he'd realised Olivia needed him. But what was he meant to do? Say? How could he make this better? He was feeling his way through the dark, the first test of their fledgling relationship a massive one. He really didn't want to blow it.

Slowly he picked his way across the sand towards her, and then heaved himself onto the rock. Olivia still wasn't looking at him.

"Why don't you tell me what happened," he suggested quietly. "That is, if you want to."

She let out a ragged sound, something Will suspected was meant to be a laugh, but wasn't. "Now you know why I didn't before."

"Yes." He couldn't deny that.

She sighed, the sound sorrowful, coming from the depths of her being. "His name was—is—Matt. He came into the garden centre where I worked one day and chatted me up. I was flattered, from the first. He was so charming, self-deprecating—looking back, I think he knew it. It was an act for him, but to me it felt real." She drew a hiccuppy breath before continuing, "I didn't know he was married, not at first. He asked me out the first time he came in, started flirting right away. Maybe that should have been a warning sign, but I was just so flattered." She sighed, the sound heavy. "He didn't wear a wedding ring, but looking back I can see there had always been something cagey about him. The way he talked around things, was dismissive about details. 'I want to hear about *you*.'" She made a face. "I wondered why he always angled his phone so I couldn't see his screen. Little things that should have had the alarm bells ringing, but the truth is I didn't want them to so I just ignored them all. I didn't quite admit to myself that was what I was doing, but it was."

"That's easy to do," Will said quietly.

"Yes, but it was cowardly, too, and it was wrong. If someone had put a gun to my head and asked me, 'Do you think Matt is married?' I would have said yes. I know that now." She sighed and looked at him with weary resignation. "But no one ever actually puts a gun to your head, do they?"

"No," Will agreed with quiet wryness. "Generally speaking, they don't." How many times had he deceived himself over the years? He'd dug his heels in about Cumbria because he hadn't let himself believe Rachel was really serious about it. He'd ignored the warning signs of her cancer, and then refused to accept a terminal diagnosis, because he hadn't wanted to face the terrible truth. Deceiving yourself, Will knew, was all too easy.

"So we carried on, a few dates," Olivia continued, "enough that I started thinking it could become serious. And then..." She paused, her throat working. "He came in with his daughter. I'd told him I wasn't working that day, and then I'd ended up switching shifts. When he saw me he looked...gobsmacked. Horrified, really. And as soon as I caught sight of the pair of them, he started babbling about how she was his goddaughter. And then she turned around and called him Daddy."

Will couldn't help but wince at that. "Ouch."

"I know, right?" Olivia managed a small, humourless smile. "That right there should have been the end of it, but it wasn't, and for that I feel so ashamed. I didn't even ask him about her. I didn't want to know. He probably would have just said something about how he was separated or getting divorced...I don't know, but I didn't even *ask*. I just...I just wanted to put my fingers in my ears and sing 'la la la' and keep going. I know how stupid that sounds, how pathetic, but the truth is, I wanted the happily-ever-after, and I knew right then I was guaranteed not to get it, but I was beyond all reason. I was so stupid."

His heart ached to hear the bitter self-recrimination in her voice. "We're all stupid sometimes, Olivia."

"Yes, but my stupidity hurt other people. His wife confronted me in the garden centre, about a week after I saw him with his daughter. It was pretty much the same kind of showdown it was today, in front of about fifty customers, my boss, my colleagues. It was horrible, and humiliating, but today was worse." She gave a soft shudder. "Everyone knowing…judging. And I don't blame them. I don't blame them at all." She looked up at him, her eyes wide and damp, the colour of violets. "The worst part is, after she came in, after I was completely revealed and humiliated and all the rest, I still didn't give up on him."

She shook her head, the tears falling now, slipping silently down her pale cheeks. "I told Althea the rest of it, but I couldn't bear to tell her this. But the truth is, he called me, after he realised his wife had confronted me. He was full of apologies, full of regret, begged me to listen so he could explain his side of the story. And I did. We met at a pub—very cosy, all open fires and squashy sofas. And he told me how he didn't love her, their marriage was a sham, she was clinging on but he was finished. He loved me, he said. He was sure of it. And I believed him. I wanted to believe him."

"That's understandable…" Will said, thinking that this Matt was a complete and utter cad.

Olivia shook her head slowly. "Looking back, it was as if I was in some kind of fog. I didn't let myself think, not even for a moment. He said he'd booked a room upstairs—" at this Will had trouble to keep from wincing even more "—and I followed him up there, as if I was in a dream. He was about to take me in his arms and then his phone rang, and when he went to silence the call, I realised it was her. And I saw the photo on his home screen—it was of his children, a little girl and boy, just like Lally and Jake." A sob burst from her as she shook her head. "And it was as if—as if a bomb had gone off in the room. In my head. I woke up. I realised I had no right to be in that room, with him. I scrambled off the bed— I ran out without a word. I wish I'd skewered him with some home truths, but I didn't have the head space."

"But you left," Will stated quietly. He was filled with relief that she hadn't been hurt more.

"Yes, but she told me today that he left her, anyway. And that's my fault."

"That is not your fault, Olivia," Will told her firmly. "I have to say this guy sounds like a class-A arse. If it hadn't been with you, it would have been with someone else, or probably a dozen different someone elses. You didn't break up their marriage. That is *not* on you."

"I feel like I did," Olivia said softly. "And I think a lot of other people do, too. When I came back to work after Christmas, I pretty much got the cold shoulder from almost everyone. Even my friend Julie judges me—when you came to York, she assumed I was having it on with a married man. Again." She shook her head. "I feel like the scarlet woman, like I can never be anything else, and I can't even blame anyone, not really."

"No one should jump to conclusions," Will said. "Or judgements. 'He who is without sin, cast the first stone,'" he quoted self-consciously. "That's my Sunday school upbringing kicking in, right there."

Olivia smiled faintly before her expression grew serious. "And now everyone knows. I'm going to be judged all over again."

"I don't think anyone is judging you." She raised an eyebrow in scepticism and he amended, "Well, perhaps a few random people are, but not your family or your friends. Not me."

Her eyes widened as she kept her gaze fixed on him. "I feel as if you should judge me most of all."

"Me?" Will exclaimed in genuine surprise. "Why?"

"Because you've been married. Because you trusted me. Because I should have told you from the first."

"I understand why you didn't."

She shook her head, a tear spilling down her cheek. "I really am so sorry. I know it won't make a difference—"

"Won't make a difference to what?"

"To—to us."

"No, of course it won't," Will said fiercely. He saw the light die in Olivia's eyes as she gulped and nodded, trying to hold back tears. "Wait…do you mean it won't make a difference because we won't—we *won't* be together?" he exclaimed in disbelief. "Because of this?"

"Well…yes." She eyed him uncertainly, and he took her hands in his.

"Olivia, I love you." His voice throbbed with the intensity of his emotion. "I know I haven't actually said those words before now, but I do really mean them. Finding out you made a mistake in a past relationship—that's not a deal-breaker for me. Not even close. Especially when I see how much you regret it, how much you've learned and grown. And trust me, I've made quite a few mistakes of my own, within my marriage and out of it. Life isn't easy. We don't always get it right the first time, or even the second or third. And a relationship doesn't falter at the first hurdle. Life is messy. We both know that. I want to wade through the mess with you, not—not pretend to be pristine."

"But…" She shook her head, still refusing to believe she could be forgiven.

He squeezed her hands. "I had some part to play in this particular episode, anyway." Drawing his hands from hers, he glanced down at his wedding ring. "I should have taken this off when I started to fall in love with you."

"Will—"

"It might have saved you some trouble." He twisted the ring around his finger, and then, with a quick tug, managed to take it off. Olivia watched, wide-eyed, as he slipped it carefully into his pocket. "I loved Rachel," he said steadily. "And taking this ring off doesn't change that. But I'm ready to move on…with you. We both need to let go of the past." He reached for her hands again. "I love you. I want to be with you. My children want to be with you. Please believe me. This is not the end. It's only the beginning, I promise." He'd never felt more certain of anything in his life.

She looked at him with tremulous hope. "Even with everyone knowing…?"

"What I want people to know," Will said as he drew her into his arms, "is how much I love you."

"And I love you," she whispered. "So much."

He held her tightly to him, grateful that she was there, that she was his. They'd managed to overcome this first obstacle; he knew there would be others. Life was full of challenges, of difficulties, of mistakes and tragedies and hurt. And yet it was also filled with joy, and hope, and laughter and possibility and life. He wanted to experience it all with Olivia by his side. The two of them facing the world, together, whatever came their way.

"Come on," he said as he gently helped her from the rock. "There's a garden waiting for us."

"And a lot of confused people," Olivia added with a wobbly laugh. He could see from the fear in her eyes that she was afraid to face everyone again.

"And two children who will be delighted to see you," he said firmly. "Who are in love with you almost as much I am." He put his arm around her as they began to walk up the path, back towards the castle. "Come on, my love. Let's go home."

Epilogue

Two months later

"WOW, THAT'S CERTAINLY some sparkler!"

Olivia eyed the engagement ring on Althea's finger with both admiration and just a touch of envy. Although she and Will had only been dating for two months, she knew if he proposed she'd say yes in a heartbeat. But, she reminded herself, she was content to wait, because life was so good. She loved getting to know Jake and Lally better, and to know Will more, too. Most evenings if he wasn't at Casterglass, she was at their cottage. She'd even started helping with the DIY; they'd painted the kitchen and sitting room so far.

"It is, isn't it?" Althea said ruefully as she looked down at her ring; John had proposed yesterday, and she'd accepted. "I told him I didn't need a big ring, but he went ahead, anyway."

"It's lovely. And just in time to show it off for the grand opening!"

Casterglass Castle was officially opening tomorrow; the

café and gift shop, the craft shops and glamping site were all good to go. Althea had even come round to Olivia's idea of a playground, and with the judicious sale of a few more of the castle's antiques, they'd managed to put an order in for an adventure playground that Jake and Lally couldn't wait to try. It was being installed next week.

It was all really happening, and Olivia couldn't be happier. Having her secret out had been hard at first, but it had been a healing sort of pain, like lancing a wound. Everyone had been understanding, sympathetic, without judgement. Well, almost everybody. There had been a few sniffs and tuts from passing strangers in the village who had been there on the day, but Olivia could handle that. The people she loved knew the truth; they knew who she really was. And more importantly, *she* knew who she really was. It had taken a long time.

The sound of the heavy knocker on the front door reverberated through the castle, causing Olivia and Althea to give each other a startled look. No one used that door, at least no one who knew the castle, knew them.

"Maybe it's a delivery?" Althea suggested dubiously, and went around to the castle's grand entrance hall. With some sixth sense, a cross between curiosity and foreboding, Olivia followed.

When Althea had finally wrested the ancient, heavy door open, they saw a woman standing on the front step. She was young, early twenties or so, with long, red-gold hair worn loose. She was beautiful, in an offbeat, ethereal way, her batik print maxi dress skimming sandalled feet. More noticeably, she was resting one hand on a small, neat bump. Althea and Olivia exchanged another look.

"May I help you?" Althea asked politely.

"Yes," the woman replied, her voice firm even though her eyes were filled with uncertainty. She seemed very young. "I'm looking for Sam Penryn," she told them. "I believe he lives here?" In the startled silence that followed she added, almost defiantly, "He won't be expecting me."

The End

Discover Sam and Rose's story in the next book in Keeping Up with the Penryns, *The Casterglass Heir*!

Join Tule Publishing's newsletter for more great reads and weekly deals!

If you enjoyed *A Casterglass Garden,*
you'll love the next book in the…

Keeping Up with the Penryns series

Book 1: *A Casterglass Christmas*

Book 2: *A Casterglass Garden*

Book 3: *The Casterglass Heir*
Coming May 2022

Available now at your favorite online retailer!

More books by Kate Hewitt

The Return to Willoughby Close series

Book 1: *Cupcakes for Christmas*

Book 2: *Welcome Me to Willoughby Close*

Book 3: *Christmas at Willoughby Close*

Book 4: *Remember Me at Willoughby Close*

The Willoughby Close series

Book 1: *A Cotswold Christmas*

Book 2: *Meet Me at Willoughby Close*

Book 3: *Find Me at Willoughby Close*

Book 4: *Kiss Me at Willoughby Close*

Book 5: *Marry Me at Willoughby Close*

The Holley Sisters of Thornthwaite series

Book 1: *A Vicarage Christmas*

Book 2: *A Vicarage Reunion*

Book 3: *A Vicarage Wedding*

Book 4: *A Vicarage Homecoming*

Available now at your favorite online retailer!

About the Author

After spending three years as a diehard New Yorker, **Kate Hewitt** now lives in the Lake District in England with her husband, their five children, and a Golden Retriever. She enjoys such novel things as long country walks and chatting with people in the street, and her children love the freedom of village life—although she often has to ring four or five people to figure out where they've gone off to.

She writes women's fiction as well as contemporary romance under the name Kate Hewitt, and whatever the genre she enjoys delivering a compelling and intensely emotional story.

Thank you for reading

A Casterglass Garden

If you enjoyed this book, you can find more from all our great authors at TulePublishing.com, or from your favorite online retailer.

TULE
PUBLISHING

Printed in Great Britain
by Amazon